"So sweet," he whispered . . .

With one roughened palm, he cradled her cheek and tilted her face until their gazes met and held. She heard his uneven breathing. Beneath the hand she had rested on his chest, she felt the rapid, steady pounding of his heart.

She had long ago accepted the fact that she would live out the remaining days of her life alone. She hadn't realized how much she missed the scent, sight, sounds, and touch created by another person. She thought she had effectively warded off loneliness.

Now, she knew it had only been in hiding, gathering strength, waiting until her defenses were down to attack.

Austin's gaze drifted to her lips, the blue of his eyes darkening until she felt the warmth of a fire, burning hot and bright, creating even as it consumed. He lowered his head slightly and her lips parted.

"So sweet," he whispered, and she wondered if within the words, she heard an apology.

Then his mouth was pressed against hers, warm, soft, moist, and she had her first taste of a man.

By Lorraine Heath

TEXAS SPLENDOR

LORRAINE HEATH

AVONBOOKS

An Imprint of HarperCollinsPublishers

Texas Splendor was originally published in the United States in 1999 by the Penguin Group.

TEXAS SPLENDOR. Copyright © 1999 by Jan Nowasky. All rights reserved. Printed in the United States of America. No part of this book may be used or reproduced in any manner whatsoever without written permission except in the case of brief quotations embodied in critical articles and reviews. For information, address Harper-Collins Publishers, 195 Broadway, New York, NY 10007.

First Avon Books mass market printing: November 2018

Print Edition ISBN: 978-0-06-285234-2
Digital Edition ISBN: 978-0-06-204662-8

Cover illustration by Victor Gadino
Cover photography by Image 1st LLC

For my dear niece Terri

The roads we travel in our youth are seldom smooth.
You traveled a difficult road.
When you could have turned back,
you forged ahead with courage.

May all your future journeys lead you
down roads paved with gold.

A Letter from Lorraine Heath

My Dear Reader:

Texas Splendor is Austin Leigh's story, and while he is the last brother, he is the one who served as the impetus for this series.

One day, I envisioned a scene of a man sitting down to dinner with his family, hunching over his plate, and shoveling food in his mouth. Feeling the stares, he looks around guiltily. "Don't reckon you'll steal my food." I knew he'd just gotten out of prison for a murder he didn't commit—but that was all I knew. Still, he intrigued me.

Then I began to see him as a younger man, before he went to prison, and I wanted readers to experience his change from a carefree teen to a man hardened by life. I'd never written a trilogy before or stories with connected characters, but I thought Austin's growth from boy to man needed to be shown in a leisurely fashion. So I decided to give him two brothers, and I waited for their stories to come to me. Shortly thereafter, Dallas and Houston obliged.

In *Texas Destiny*, Austin is sixteen, open and innocent, providing some comic relief as his older brothers strive to teach him how to behave around a woman. In *Texas Glory*, he's twenty-one, a little less innocent, a tad more mature, and in love. But by the time his story comes along, he's spent five years in prison and has forgotten how to dream.

I'm often asked which of my stories is my favorite and I can never choose, because each was my favorite at the time I wrote it. The hero and heroine become my favorite couple and even as I'm tearing their world apart, I'm rooting for them to win in the end, to find the love and happiness they deserve.

It's been a little over twenty years since I wrote these stories, but as we were preparing them to once again be available in paperback, I had the opportunity to re-read them. At the heart of this trilogy is the story of family, the story of three brothers who circumstances shaped into very different men and the women who made them each whole. I hope you've enjoyed visiting with them as much as I have. Thank you for taking the journey through their lives with me.

Warmest wishes,
Lorraine

Chapter One

April 1887

Moments stolen . . . never to be regained. Memories not worth remembering lingering at the edge of his awareness, unwilling to be forgotten.

Five years of slowly dying.

Austin Leigh stared at the gates of Huntsville Prison, knowing that the remainder of his life waited on the other side, just as he'd left it five years earlier when twelve men he had trusted found him guilty of murder.

After surviving one thousand eight hundred and twenty-five days as a "slave of the state," he once again wore his own clothes. The blue cambric shirt hung loosely from his wide shoulders, and his denim britches threatened to slip past his narrow hips. But they were his, clothes he'd worn at twenty-one when he'd been filled with the vibrancy of youth, when he had foolishly believed that a person had only to reach for a dream in order to obtain it.

In the passing years, no one had laundered the clothes, and when he closed his eyes, he imagined that he smelled a woman's fading vanilla fragrance, felt her slender fingers clutch his shirt one last time, tasted her tears as his lips brushed over hers during an agonizing farewell.

Becky. Sweet Becky Oliver. Within his heart, the distant memories waltzed and he saw her clearly—smiling at him, laughing with him, loving him beneath the stars on a moon-shadowed night. A night when they had given so much to each other, not knowing that another's actions would snatch everything away.

Clanging chains jarred him from his reverie. With loathing, he glared at the guard unlocking the iron cuffs that circled his wrists. The shackles fell away and Austin rubbed the pink scars that had formed over the years.

"Now, then, boy," the guard began, "don't do anything out there that will land you back in here. I might not be so understanding next time."

"Just open the goddamn gate," Austin snarled through clenched teeth.

The guard narrowed his eyes as though contemplating the consequences of striking a man on the verge of regaining his freedom. Then he shoved open the gate. Its creaking hinges echoed in the stillness of dawn.

Austin latched his gaze onto the brightening sky that lay beyond the walls. It appeared untouched by the filth and degradation that existed within the prison. With long strides, he walked into freedom, relishing his first breath of unfetid air. His heart tightened when he caught sight of his two brothers standing in front of three horses.

"You look like hell," Dallas said, his voice strangled with emotions.

Austin wondered when the silver had streaked through Dallas's black hair. The furrows in his brow had deepened and bits of white peppered his thick mustache. "I feel like hell," he said, forcing his mouth to shape a grin.

Dallas jerked him against his chest. "Damn you, boy, what in the hell did you think you were doing?"

Austin worked his way out of his brother's strong grip. The last time he had seen Dallas, his older brother had been fighting for his life. Austin had dreaded the moment when he'd have to face Dallas's uncompromising brown gaze and explain his actions. "What I thought was best."

Turning, he found it easier to meet Houston's gaze. His middle brother had sat behind him during his trial. The war had ravaged Houston's face, but the passing years had treated him more kindly. Or perhaps it was simply that the black leather eye patch remained unchanged so it seemed all else had stayed the same.

Austin had intended to give Houston nothing more than a handshake, but as soon as their roughened palms met, he found himself pulled into a fierce hug. Houston had always been a man of few words, and right now Austin was grateful for his brother's silence. "See you brought Black Thunder."

He freed himself from Houston's hold and mounted the ebony stallion in one lithe, smooth movement, relishing the feel of a horse beneath him. Certain his brothers would follow, he set his heels to Black Thunder's flanks, sending him into a hard gallop.

The road opened up before him, but he feared no matter how fast or far he rode, he'd never truly escape the walls that had surrounded him . . . not until he'd seen Becky. Touched her. Held her. Made her his wife.

AUSTIN'S HEART SWELLED as he caught sight of the massive adobe house. He carried the dust of several days' travel, but at this moment, it seemed unimportant.

He was home.

As they neared Dallas's house, Austin saw a girl jump up from the veranda steps and run inside. He drew his horse to a halt and dismounted, his brothers doing the same.

The girl bounded back outside, her blond curls bouncing around her tiny shoulders, her arms flung open wide. "Uncle Austin! You're back!"

She leapt for him, and he swung her up into his arms.

"I'm so glad!" she cried. "I missed you so much!" Her soft rounded cheek brushed against his bristly one, her arms tightly wound around his neck.

He tipped back his head, taking joy in the green

glint of her eyes. Houston's oldest daughter had been three years old when he'd left. "Maggie May, when did you grow up?"

"A long time ago. Me and Rawley go to school now."

"Is that so?" He looked past her to the tall boy leaning against the veranda beam, his black hair neatly trimmed, his clothes showing little wear.

"Uh-huh," she assured him.

He set her down and slowly approached Rawley Cooper. It hadn't surprised Austin when Dallas had written to inform him that he and Dee had adopted the boy. "Hear tell that I'm your uncle now."

"You don't gotta be, on account we ain't got the same blood. Only if you wanna be."

Austin pulled the boy close. "Oh, I wanna be."

Why hadn't he realized these children would continue to grow without him around, leaving him to miss out on so much?

He heard the rapid patter of tiny feet as four small girls stampeded through the doorway, their high-pitched voices reminding him of chirping birds. "Pa! Pa! Pa!"

Kneeling, Houston cradled three blond girls against his chest. Amelia had given birth to Laurel the Christmas before Austin went to prison. Amanda and A. J. had been little more than words scrawled in a letter until this moment. The same as Faith, the dark-haired beauty Dallas lifted into his arms.

"You're home!" Dee cried.

Tall and slender, she was a sight for sore eyes

as she gracefully glided across the veranda, her smile bright enough to blind a man.

"You've gotten skinny," she said as she embraced Austin and thumped his back.

"They don't cook like you do."

She laughed. Lord, he'd forgotten how true uninhibited laughter washed over a man and filled him with unrestrained joy.

"I don't cook," she reminded him. "Amelia cooks."

She stepped aside. Before he caught his breath, Amelia wrapped her arms around him, hugging him closely. The first woman to come into their lives. God, he loved her . . . almost as much as he loved Becky.

When Amelia moved away, Austin smiled. "I know one of those girls has to be Laurel Joy. She couldn't even crawl when I left. The others weren't even here."

"You'll have plenty of opportunity to get to know them and catch up," Amelia assured him. "Right now, we've got supper waiting."

"Sounds like heaven. I haven't had a decent meal . . . in years."

Amelia and Dee slipped their arms through his and led him into the house. Like a man lost in the wilderness, Austin searched for recognizable sights to guide him toward the welcome haven of familiarity, but he found none. A portrait of Dallas and his family hung on the wall. A new rug ran the length of the hallway.

The girls rushed past him as they entered the dining room. The old oak table was gone, replaced by a longer one that could accommodate the growing family. Dallas and Houston lowered the girls onto tall chairs before taking their places. Maggie patted the empty chair between her and Rawley. "Sit by us, Uncle Austin."

Unexpectedly feeling awkward and out of place, he dropped into the chair. The bowl set before him brimmed with stew, steam spiraling upward. His mouth watered. He hadn't realized how hungry he was. He picked up the spoon, bent forward, and placed his elbows on the table, allowing his arms to circle the bowl, forming a protective barrier around his dinner. He'd slurped two spoonfuls before the hairs on the back of his neck prickled and he realized everyone was staring at him.

He shifted his gaze to Maggie. With wide green eyes, she watched him as though he were a stranger.

"Don't reckon you'll steal my food, will you?" he asked, his voice low, afraid he'd failed miserably at making light of his strange behavior.

She pressed her lips together, her brow creasing as she slowly moved her head from side to side.

Austin straightened and glanced around the table, wondering why he felt so isolated when surrounded by family. "My apologies. I seem to have forgotten how to eat around decent folk."

"No need to apologize," Amelia said. "We're family, for God's sake. You should have eaten at this table for the past five years anyway."

He shifted his gaze to Dallas. They had journeyed to the ranch much as they had traveled through life before Amelia—asking no questions, sharing no sorrows. "Reckon you'll want to talk about that."

Dallas shook his head. "It was your life, your decision. But you should know I hired a detective to find Boyd's killer. Unfortunately he hasn't had any luck."

"He still looking?"

"He's not devoting himself to it any longer, but he keeps an ear to the ground. Whoever killed Boyd knew what he was doing. He didn't leave any evidence."

"Why don't we discuss this after dinner?" Dee suggested.

Reaching out, Dallas covered Dee's hand. "Sorry. Sometimes, it's difficult to remember that Boyd was your brother."

Dallas could not have spoken truer words. Boyd McQueen had possessed a temperament that hinted the devil had spawned him, while Dee had the disposition of an angel.

"I have marble cake waiting in the kitchen," Amelia announced. "We need to eat up so we can enjoy it while it's still warm."

Warm cake and stew, the constant smiles and innocent ways of children. Austin had taken them for granted in his youth, but he was determined to appreciate them from this moment on.

Night had fallen by the time Austin stood on the veranda and watched the wagon filled with Houston's family lumber north. A crescent moon smiled in the black sky, stars winking on either side of it. "I can't believe Houston has a whole passel of girls," Austin said.

Turning his gaze in the direction of the retreating wagon, Dallas leaned against the beam. "I think another one might be on the way. Amelia didn't eat much tonight."

"What about you and Dee? You gonna have any more?"

Dallas slowly shook his head. "Nope. Faith was a miracle we weren't expecting. Reckon a man should consider himself the luckiest of men if he has one miracle in his life."

Austin understood miracles. He had one of his own waiting for him. "Think I'm gonna ride into town."

A silence permeated the air, thick, hovering, as though something needed to be said. Permission, Austin decided. He was waiting for Dallas to give him permission to leave only he didn't require his brother's consent any longer. He was a grown man, free to come and go as he chose. He stepped off the veranda.

"Becky's married," Dallas said quietly.

Austin felt as though someone had plowed a tightly balled fist into his gut. Unable to draw air into his lungs, he feared his knees might buckle. He wrapped his arm around the beam to keep from stumbling down the remaining steps. Swallowing hard, he forced the words past the painful knot that had formed in his throat. "Becky Oliver?"

Dallas faced him squarely. "Yeah."

"Who'd she marry?"

"Cameron."

Cameron McQueen? Dee's brother? Austin swallowed the burning bile that had risen in his throat. "When?"

"About two years ago."

Austin glared at his brother. "Why in the hell didn't you mention that little bit of news in your letters?"

"I didn't figure prison was the best place for you to learn about it."

"You could have told me at any time during the past few days."

"Didn't see any reason to ruin your homecoming."

His homecoming? Without Becky he had no homecoming. He leapt off the porch and hit the ground with a purpose to his stride.

"Where are you going?" Dallas called after him.

"Wherever I damn well want to go," Austin threw over his shoulder as he stalked toward the barn.

He'd never saddled a horse more quickly nor ridden as hard as he rode now. Black Thunder's pounding hooves ate up the distance between Austin . . . and Becky.

As the dim lantern lights of Leighton came into view, burning into the night, Austin jerked back on the reins. The stallion protested the rough treatment and reared up, his neigh echoing over the vast plains. Austin regained control and patted the horse's sweating neck. "Sorry, old man."

He shifted his gaze toward the town. He could make out the silhouette of Dee's Grand Hotel. And the train depot. The railroad tracks had reached the town while he'd been in prison.

He saw the outline of buildings he didn't recognize, streets, houses, a town . . . a town he'd once known . . . a town that was now achingly unfamiliar.

And somewhere within that town, beneath the shadows of the night, Becky was lying within the arms of another man.

The pain slashed through him, intense, overpowering.

And the tears he'd held at bay for five long, torturous years finally broke free. Bowing his head, he dug his fingers into his thighs as the sobs wrenched his body.

Becky had deserted him when he had needed her the most . . . and he hadn't even known it.

MEMORIES DREW AUSTIN to the general store. Businesses had sprung up on either side of the false-fronted building where Becky Oliver had worked with her father. He resented every structure that smelled of new wood, resented that little had remained the same.

He halted his horse and glared at the sign that still read OLIVER'S GENERAL STORE. Becky had lived in the rooms above. Pale light spilled through the upstairs windows so Austin figured she still lived there—with Cameron.

He dismounted, tethered his horse to the railing, and walked along the alley between the two buildings. He spotted the landing where he'd kissed Becky for the first time. Had Cameron kissed her there? His gut clenched with the thought.

He heard the bump of a crate hitting the ground.

As he rounded the corner, within the light cast by the lantern hanging on the back wall of the store, he saw Cameron McQueen heft a wooden crate from the wagon, stack it next to the back door, and reach for another one. If he and Cameron were still friends, he would have given him a hard time about the starched white apron he wore over his crisp white shirt.

Cameron reached for another box, then stilled as though sensing another's presence. He glanced over his shoulder, his blond hair falling across his brow. With his gaze wary, he approached slowly. "Austin, it's good to see you."

"I'll just bet." Austin slammed his knotted fist into Cameron's face. Cameron staggered back and hit the ground with a sickening thud that sounded like a crate of tomatoes bursting open.

"Get up, you sorry son of a bitch!"

Working his jaw back and forth, Cameron rolled over. "I'm not gonna fight you."

"You don't have to fight me, but at least give me the satisfaction of pounding you into the ground."

Cameron pushed himself to his knees, close enough to standing as far as Austin was concerned. He hit him again and sent him sprawling back to the ground. "You were my best friend, damn you! I trusted you!"

Cameron squinted at him, blood trailing along his cheek. "Honest to God, I tried not to love her."

"Not good enough. Stand up."

Cameron struggled to his feet and stood, his arms dangling at his sides like the useless broken blades on a windmill.

"At least put your hands up, give me some satisfaction," Austin commanded.

Cameron shook his head. "You wanna beat the crap out of me, go ahead. I won't stop you."

Impotent rage surged through Austin. He'd beat the crap out of him, all right—and then some. He brought his arm back—

"Cameron!" the sweetest voice called.

Austin snapped his head around. The light from the lantern illuminated Becky as she stood in the doorway, holding a tow-headed boy close against her breast.

She was the prettiest thing he'd ever set eyes on. The stolen years began melting away, just as he'd known they would.

"Pa!" the boy cried, squirming in his mother's arms.

The years came crashing back with a vengeance. She wasn't Becky Oliver, his girl. She was Becky McQueen, his best friend's wife.

"Cameron, aren't you finished yet?" she asked softly.

Austin realized then that the shadows hid him, that the lantern light wasn't touching him. From where she stood, Becky couldn't see him or the blood trailing down Cameron's face.

"I'll be there in a minute," Cameron said quietly, keeping his profile to her.

"Well, don't take too long. Supper's getting cold." She disappeared into the store, and Austin knew she was probably climbing the indoor stairs that led to the second floor, to the home she shared with Cameron.

"Honest to God, Austin, I didn't mean for things to turn out this way," Cameron said, his voice low.

Austin took a menacing step toward him. Cameron flinched but didn't back away. "Think on this," Austin said, his voice seething with the pain of betrayal. "She loved me first."

"Believe me, that thought haunts me night and day."

Austin wished he'd just hit Cameron again and kept his mouth shut. He'd wanted to hurt the man, and he knew by the despair that had plunged into Cameron's blue eyes that he had succeeded. He didn't know why that knowledge brought him no satisfaction but only served to increase his anger over a situation that he was unable to change.

He nodded briskly. "Well, I'm glad to hear it." Abruptly, he spun on his heel and strode through the alley until he reached the boardwalk. He'd never felt more lost in his life.

Although the family had welcomed him home with open arms, he no longer felt a part of them. His brothers had wives, children, and successful businesses. And what did Austin have? Nothing but a tarnished reputation that he should have never possessed.

Stalking down the boardwalk, he was surprised his feet didn't split the boards with the weight of his anger as he headed toward the far end of town where the saloon beckoned.

Smoke thickened the air as he stormed through the swinging doors of the saloon. A huge gilded mirror hanging on the wall behind the bar reflected the patrons who occupied the chairs or stood against the walls.

He felt gazes boring into him, and even in the din of male voices and raucous laughter, he thought he heard people harshly whispering his name. He ambled toward the crowded bar and hooked the heel of his boot on the brass railing that ran the length of the bar. The men closest to him sidled away like he had festering sores covering him. He slapped a coin on the counter. "Whiskey."

The bartender picked up a glass and poured the amber brew, his gaze never leaving Austin. It had always amazed Austin that Beau could serve drinks and never once look to see what he was doing.

"Heard you'd be home soon," Beau said as he eyed Austin warily.

"Well, you heard right." Austin crossed his arms on the bar and leaned forward slightly.

Beau set the full glass in front of him. "I don't want no trouble in here."

"I don't plan to start any," Austin assured him.

With a brusque nod, Beau ambled to the far end of the counter, wiping the shining wood as he went. An icy shiver skittered along Austin's spine. He despised the sensation of being watched and judged. In prison, guards had glared at him, dogs had followed his every movement, other prisoners had scrutinized him and measured him against their own low standards.

He jerked his head around and locked his blue glare onto Lester Henderson. The portly banker stood at the bar, his dark eyes set in a face that greatly resembled bread dough. Averting his gaze, Lester downed the remainder of his beer. He wiped a pudgy hand across his mouth, straightened his shoulders, and approached Austin.

"I had no choice but to vote guilty," Henderson said, his voice hitching. "The evidence—"

"I know what the evidence was. I was at the goddamn trial."

"Can't give a loan to a man fresh out of prison—"

"Did I ask for a loan?"

"No, but I just wanted to save you from asking." Henderson scurried away like a squirrel that had spotted the last pecan on the ground.

Austin wrapped his fingers around the glass of whiskey and studied the contents. As soon as he finished the whiskey, he'd set about clearing his name. He didn't anticipate that it would take long. He had always known that Duncan McQueen had pinned the blame on him.

He brought the glass to his lips, tipped his head back, and caught the reflection of a raised knife in the mirror.

He moved swiftly, but not quickly enough. Agonizing pain tore through his back. He darted to the side, spun around, and plowed his fist into Duncan McQueen's face before the man could strike again. As Duncan staggered back, Austin grabbed the hand holding the knife and slammed it hard against the wooden counter. The knife clattered to the floor.

Austin caught an unexpected fist just below his jaw. Pain ricocheted through his head as his knees buckled. He hit the floor hard, blackness encroaching on his vision. He scrambled to his knees, struggling to get to his feet, the bitter taste of blood filling his mouth.

"You bastard!" Duncan roared before lunging for Austin.

Austin reversed his efforts, dropped to his side, and kicked Duncan in the knee. Grunting, Duncan fell to the floor and grabbed the knife. Hatred burned brightly within his dark eyes as he jumped to his feet. "Five years! That's all they gave you for murdering my brother because Dallas owns this part of the state. They should have hanged you!" He brandished the bloodied knife in the air. "I reckon it's up to me to deliver the justice you deserve."

"Not in my saloon!" Beau said as he rounded the corner of the bar, gun in hand. He shoved Duncan on the shoulder. "Back up."

His head pounding, his back throbbing, Austin struggled to his feet and glared at Duncan. "What the hell are you ranting about, Duncan? You killed Boyd and made it look like I did it."

"Don't see how that could be," Beau said in a slow drawl. "Duncan showed up here in the late afternoon and sat in that corner right over there until dawn, getting drunk."

"Why would I kill my brother?" Duncan asked, loathing laced through his voice.

That was the one answer Austin didn't have.

"Everyone knows you murdered him," Duncan snarled.

Austin scrutinized the men who had gathered around the bar. The knowledge in their eyes spoke louder than Duncan's words. He saw no doubts. Not one questioning look. He saw nothing but absolute certainty staring back at him. They all thought he had murdered Boyd McQueen.

"Why the hell else would my brother have written your name in the dirt before he died?" Duncan demanded.

WHY INDEED?

Austin sat on the back steps of Dallas's house and stared at the moon. He rolled his shoulders, grimacing at the pain caused by the movement. After leaving the saloon, he had stopped at the doctor's house, but the man hadn't been there. By the time Austin had arrived home, the bleeding had stopped so he'd simply changed shirts. No need to alarm his family. They'd had enough worry the past five years. Besides, he'd survived worse in prison.

He heard the door open and the echo of soft footfalls. Looking over his shoulder, he watched Dee sit beside him on the step.

"You were right. You told me five years was an eternity when a person has no freedom," he said into the stillness of the evening.

Using her fingers, she brushed the dark strands of hair off his brow. "Not all prisons come with walls. Dallas was the key that unlocked mine."

Austin shifted his gaze to the canopy of stars, allowing a companionable silence to ease in around them.

"What's their son's name?"

"Andrew. We call him Drew," Dee said quietly.

"I hit his father this evening."

"I'm not altogether certain Cameron didn't deserve that." She placed her hand over his. "But I know how much he loves Becky. I think he may have loved her before you went to prison."

"That doesn't make what he did right."

She sighed. "I know this is difficult for you, but Dallas forgave Houston for taking Amelia from him. Maybe in time, you can forgive Cameron—"

"My situation is completely different from Dallas's. All he gave Amelia was a train ticket. I gave Becky my heart and five years of my life."

"Becky offered to testify that she was with you the night Boyd was killed, but you wouldn't allow it. You can't blame her now for the years you spent in prison. That's not fair."

"Life *is never* fair, Dee. Having Houston and Dallas for brothers should have taught me that a long time ago, but I had to learn it on my own." He looked toward the distance. "So much has changed. Everything is different from what I expected it to be."

"Not everything. Your violin is the same. I kept it for you just like you asked. I was hoping you'd play something for me tonight."

He glanced at the silhouette of the instrument resting in her lap. "I don't hear the music anymore, Dee. While I was in prison, it just shriveled up and died."

He shoved himself to his feet and walked to the barn. He needed to ride, to feel the wind rushing against his face. He had finished saddling Black Thunder when he heard a thump and grunt come from the back of the barn. He strode to the back room and peered inside. Rawley struggled to move a box. "Shouldn't you be in bed?" Austin asked.

Rawley spun around, his face burning bright red. "I wanted to get this room cleaned first. Gotta earn my keep."

Austin leaned against the door frame. "Rawley, you always worked harder than I ever did, and Dallas never kicked me out."

"You're blood, I ain't." Rawley walked to the worktable and began to put away tools someone else had left out.

"That doesn't matter to Dallas—"

"Matters to me."

Austin studied the boy as he straightened the room. "Is that why you didn't take Dallas's name when he adopted you?"

Rawley stilled. "I just figured it was best is all." He peered at Austin. "I've always wondered . . . what did you do to get a town named after you?"

Austin smiled. "I don't have a town named after me."

"Sure you do. I went through a town named Austin once."

"The capital? It's the other way around. I'm named after it. Our pa named us after towns—" Austin's mind reeled with possibilities. "Sweet Lord."

"What?" Rawley asked.

"I gotta go." Austin raced through the barn, mounted Black Thunder, and galloped into the night.

An hour later, he pounded on the door of the second floor landing over the general store. When it opened, his voice lodged in his throat. Why hadn't he considered that he might see Becky if he came here? Why did the pain have to slice through his heart, ripping open the fresh wound?

God Almighty, he wished he could hate her. He wanted to shake her. He wanted to yell at her. But most of all, he wanted to hold her, her body flush against his, her warmth thawing the chill that permeated his soul.

"I need to talk to Cameron," he croaked.

The shock reflected in her blue eyes quickly gave way to anger. Becky planted her hands firmly on his chest and shoved hard, causing him to stumble backward. "Well, he doesn't need to talk to you. How dare you hit—"

"Becky!"

She pivoted around. Cameron stood in the doorway, one eye discolored and swollen. "Drew's calling you. I'll take care of this."

Austin watched her jaw tighten before she gave him a scathing glare and shouldered her way past Cameron to go inside.

"Did you want to come in?" Cameron asked.

Austin shook his head, wondering why he'd come to the man who had betrayed him. He walked to the railing and stared at the town, light from the lanterns fighting the darkness. Cameron's quiet, hesitant footsteps as he came to stand beside Austin brought back memories of confidences shared.

"All these years I thought Duncan had shot

Boyd and arranged the evidence to put the blame on me." He glanced sideways at the friend from his youth, suddenly realizing that losing Cameron's friendship hurt almost as much as losing Becky's love. "But our paths crossed this evening and I realized I was wrong. Rawley said something, though, that got me to thinking. What if Boyd didn't write my name in the dirt—"

"He did. Sheriff Larkin took me to the place where he found Boyd. He'd written your name in the dirt as plain as day."

"What if he didn't mean me, but meant the town? What if he didn't know the name of the man who killed him, but he knew that he came from Austin?"

"That's grasping at straws, isn't it?"

"That's all I've got," Austin said. "People avoid me like I have tick fever or something worse. I knew the men on the jury had voted guilty because of the evidence, but I never thought they actually believed deep down that I murdered Boyd. I've got to prove I'm innocent, and I can only do that if I figure out who killed him. Did he have any business in Austin?"

"Boyd never confided in me. Sometimes he'd leave for a few days, but he never divulged where he went."

Austin took a few steps back. "Reckon it won't hurt to ride into Austin and see if I can find out anything."

"Guess I'd do the same if I were in your boots, but watch your back. If the man who killed Boyd *is* in Austin, I don't imagine he's going to welcome the prospect of being found."

Austin turned for the stairs, halted, and glanced over his shoulder. "If I ever hear that Becky isn't happy, I'll finish what I started out back this evening."

Cameron held his gaze. "Fair enough."

Austin hurried down the remaining steps. Some bastard had stolen five years of his life. Austin intended to make damn sure he paid dearly for every moment.

Chapter Two

❦

$\mathcal{S}$wearing viciously, Austin glared at the jagged cut on the underside of Black Thunder's hoof. He released the horse's foreleg, unfolded his aching body, and jerked his dusty black Stetson from his head. Exhausted, resenting the dirt working its way into every crease of his body, he stood beneath the April sun feeling as though he'd stepped into the middle of August.

Using the sleeve of his cambric shirt, he wiped the sweat beading his brow, grimacing as pain erupted across his back—from the middle of his left shoulder to just below his ribs. He had expected the gash he'd received during the brawl with Duncan to have healed by now, but he supposed riding all day, late into the night, and sleeping on the ground hadn't been the best treatment for the wound. When he had ridden out of Leighton several days before, he hadn't considered that he'd have no way to clean or tend the injury. Only one thought had preyed on his mind: The city of Austin might hold the key that would lead him to Boyd's killer, the man whose guilt would prove Austin's innocence.

Slipping his fingers into the pocket of his vest, he pulled out the map Dallas had given him. Wearily he studied the lines that marked the start of his journey and his final destination. He stuffed the wrinkled paper back into his pocket. He wouldn't reach the town tonight.

Settling his hat low over his brow, he sighed heavily. He was in no mood to walk, but the stallion's injury left him no choice. Gazing toward the distance, he saw smoke spiraling up through the trees. He threaded the reins through his fingers and trudged into the woods. Shafts of sunlight and lengthening shadows wove through the branches, offering him some respite from the damnable heat. With a sense of loss, he remembered a time when he would have appreciated the simple beauty surrounding him. Now he just wanted to get to where he was going.

He heard an occasional thwack as though someone were splitting wood. With the abundance of trees and bushes, he didn't imagine anyone had to depend on cow chips for a fire.

A wide clearing opened up before him. Lacy white curtains billowed through the open windows of a small white clapboard house. The weathered door stood ajar. Near the house, a scrawny boy wearing a battered hat, threadbare jacket, and worn britches struggled to chop the wood. A large dog napped beneath the shade of a nearby tree. The varying hues of his brown and white fur reminded Austin of a patchwork quilt. As Austin cautiously approached, the dog snapped open its eyes, snarled, and rose slowly to its full height, curling back its lips and deepening its growl.

Moving quickly, the boy dipped down, swung around, and pointed a rifle at Austin. Austin threw his hands in the air. "Whoa! I'm not looking for trouble."

"What are you lookin' for?"

"Austin. How far is it from here?"

"Half a day's ride on a good horse." The boy angled his head, the rumpled brim of his hat casting shadows over his face. "Your horse looks to be favoring his right leg."

The boy's insight caught Austin off-guard, although he certainly admired it. "Yep. He cut his hoof on a rock. Your folks around?"

The boy gave a brisk nod. "And my brother. I'd feel a sight better if you'd take off the gun."

Austin untied the strip of leather at his thigh and slowly unbuckled the gunbelt. Cautiously removing the holster, he laid the weapon on the ground, his gaze circling the area. He wondered where the rest of the family was working. He saw no fields that needed tending or cattle that needed watching. The aroma of fresh baked bread and simmering meat wafted through the open door of the house. "Something sure smells good."

"Son-of-a-gun stew."

"Think you could sneak me a bowl if I finish chopping that wood for you?"

The boy shifted his gaze to the wood scattered around an old tree stump, then looked back at Austin. "What's your business in Austin?"

"Looking for someone."

"You a lawman?"

"Nope. My horse is hurt. I've been walking longer than I care to think about. I'm tired, hot, and hungry. I can chop that wood twice as fast as you can, and I'm willing to do it for one bowl of stew. Then I'll be on my way."

Slowly, the boy relaxed his fingers and lowered the rifle. "Sounds like a fair trade."

Rolling his sleeves past his elbows, Austin strode to the tree stump. Ignoring the snarling dog that lumbered in for a closer inspection of his boots, Austin picked up the ax, hefted a log onto the stump, and slammed the ax into the dry wood. He stifled a moan as fiery pain burst across his back. When he reached his destination, his first order of business would be to find a doctor.

"I'm gonna take your gun," the boy said hesitantly. "And your rifle."

"Fine. There's a Bowie knife in the saddlebags." He didn't begrudge the boy his cautions, but he longed for the absolute trust he'd once taken for granted. Hearing the boy's bare feet fall softly over the ground as he walked to the house, Austin glanced over his shoulder. The boy had grabbed his saddlebags as well.

Austin glared at the dog. "Your master ain't too trusting, is he?"

The dog barked. Austin glanced to his left and spotted a hen house and a three-sided wooden structure that offered protection to a milk cow. He found that odd since the property had a huge barn.

He heaved the ax down into the wood, wondering if he was wasting his time traveling to the capital city. If he had any sense, he'd head home and try to rebuild a life that never should have been torn down. But stubborn pride wouldn't allow him the luxury of turning back. His family believed he was innocent. Becky knew he was innocent. But the doubts would forever linger in everyone else's minds.

When he had split and stacked enough wood to last the family a week, he ambled to the house, dropped to the porch, and leaned against the beam that supported the eve running the width of the house. The dog strolled over, stretched, yawned, and worked its way to the ground near Austin's feet.

"Changed your mind about me, did you?"

Lifting its head, the dog released a small whine before settling back into place. Austin was sorely tempted to curl up beside the dog and sleep. Instead, he looked toward the horizon where the sun was gradually sinking behind the trees. While serving his time, he'd hated to see the sun go down. He had despised the night. Loneliness had always accompanied the darkness.

"Here's your meal," the boy said from behind him.

Austin glanced over his shoulder, his outstretched hand stopping halfway to its destination. The air backing up in his lungs, he slowly brought himself to his feet. The britches and bare feet were the same, but everything else had changed. The crumpled hat and shabby jacket were gone. So was the boy.

"What are you staring at?" an indignant voice asked.

Austin could have named a hundred things. The long, thick braid of pale blond hair draped over the narrow shoulder. The starched white apron that cinched the tiniest waist he'd ever seen. Or her eyes. Without the shadow of the hat, they glittered a tawny gold.

He tore his Stetson from his head and backed up a step. "My apologies, ma'am. I thought you were a boy."

A tentative smile played across her lips. "It's easier to get the work done when I'm wearing my brother's britches. Besides, no one's usually around to notice."

"What about your family?"

A wealth of sadness plunged into the golden depths of her eyes. "Buried out back."

So they were *around* as she'd told him, but not in a position to help her. She extended the bowl toward him.

"Here. Take it."

He reached for the offering, his roughened fingers touching hers. They both jerked away, then scrambled to recapture the bowl, their heads knocking together. Cursing as pain ricocheted through his head, Austin snaked out his hand and snatched the bowl, effectively halting its descent. The stew sloshed over the sides, burning the inside of his thumb.

"Damn!" He shifted the bowl to his other hand and pressed his thumb against his mouth. He peered at the woman. Her eyes had grown wide, and she was wiping her hands on her apron. He remembered the many times Houston had scolded him for swearing in front of Amelia, and he felt the heat suffuse his face. "My apologies for the swearing," he offered.

She shook her head. "I should have warned you that the stew is hot. I'll get a cool cloth."

Before he could stop her, she'd disappeared into the house. Austin dropped onto the porch, wondering if he had a fever. How could he have possibly mistaken that tiny slip of a woman for a boy?

He thought if he pressed her flush against him, the top of her head would fit against the center of his chest. Incredibly delicate, she reminded him of the fine china Dee now set on her table. One careless thump would shatter it into a thousand fragments.

He saw a flash of dung colored britches just before the woman knelt in front of him. She took his hand without asking and pressed a damp cloth to the red area. "I put a little oil on the cloth. That should draw out the pain."

Her voice was as soft as a cloud floating in the sky, and again he wondered how he had mistaken her for a boy. Lightly, her hand held his, but he still felt the calluses across her palm. Her fingernails were short, chipped in a place or two, but clean. And her touch was the sweetest thing he'd known in five years.

She peered beneath the cloth. "I don't think it's gonna blister." She touched her finger to the pink scar that circled his wrist. "What happened here?"

Austin stiffened, his throat knotting, and he wished he'd taken the time to roll down his sleeves after he'd finished chopping the wood. He considered lying, but he'd learned long ago the foolishness of lies. "Shackles."

She lifted her gaze to his, her delicate brow furrowing, anxiety darkening her eyes, imploring him to answer a question she seemed hesitant to voice aloud.

He swallowed hard. "I spent some time in prison."

"For what?" she whispered.

"Murder."

He had expected horror to sweep across her face, would not have blamed her if she had run into the house to fetch her rifle. Instead, she continued to hold his gaze, silently studying him as though she sought some secret long buried. He considered telling her that he hadn't killed anyone, but he'd learned that the voices of twelve men spoke louder than one. Unfortunately, until he proved someone else had killed Boyd McQueen, he was the man who had.

"How long were you in prison?" she finally asked.

"Five years."

"That's not very long for murder."

"It's long enough."

Releasing his hand and his gaze, she eased away from him. "You should eat. You earned it."

He gave a brusque nod before delving into the

stew. She sat on the bottom step of the porch and put one foot on top of the other. She had the cutest toes he'd ever seen. The second toe was crooked and pointed away from the big toe like a broken sign giving directions to a town.

She hit her thigh. "Come here, Digger."

The dog trotted over and nestled his head in her lap. With doleful eyes, he looked at Austin.

"Digger?" Austin asked.

She buried her fingers in the animal's thick brown and white fur. "Yeah, he's always digging things up. Do you have a name?"

"Austin Leigh."

"I thought that's where you were headed."

"It is. I was born near here. My parents named me after the town."

"Must get confusing."

"Not really. Haven't been back in over twenty years." He returned his attention to the stew, remembering a time when talking had come easy, when smiling at women had brought such pleasures.

"I'm Loree Grant."

"I appreciate the hospitality, Miss Grant." He scraped the last of the stew from his bowl.

"Do you want more stew?" she asked.

"If you've got some to spare."

She rose, took his bowl, and walked into the house. The dog released a little whimper. Austin reached out to stroke the animal. A wave of dizziness assaulted him. He grabbed the edge of the porch and breathed deeply.

"Are you all right?"

He glanced over his shoulder. Loree stood uncertainly on the porch, the bowl of fresh stew in her hand. He brought himself to his feet, afraid what he'd already eaten wasn't going to stay put. "Reckon one bowl was plenty. Sorry to have troubled you for the second. I was wondering . . . with night closing in . . . if you'd mind if I bedded down in your barn."

Wariness flitted through her golden eyes, but she gave him a jerky nod.

"'Preciate it. You can hold on to the saddlebags and guns until morning if it'll help ease your fears about my staying. Before I head out, let me know what chores I can do as payment for the roof over my head."

He strode toward Black Thunder, hoping he could get the horse settled before he collapsed from exhaustion.

HE DIDN'T HAVE the eyes of a killer. Loree repeated that thought like a comforting litany as she sat cross-legged on her bed, the loaded rifle resting across her lap, her gaze trained on the door.

Five years ago, she'd looked into the eyes of a killer. She knew them to be ruthless and cold. Austin Leigh's eyes were neither. She shifted her attention to the fire burning in the hearth. In the center, where the heat burned the hottest, the writhing blue flames reflected the color of his eyes. Eyes that mirrored sorrow and pain. She wondered if any of the creases that fanned out from the corners of his eyes had been carved by laughter.

Hearing thunder rumble in the distance, she

hoped the storm would hold off until he'd left, but she thought it unlikely. The clock on the mantel had only just struck midnight.

The barn roof had more holes than the night sky had stars. Still, it would offer him more protection than the trees. And he probably had a slicker. All cowboys did, and he certainly looked to be a cowboy. Tall and rangy with a loose-jointed walk that spoke of no hurry to be anywhere.

The rain began to pelt the roof with a steady staccato beat. She cringed. The nights were still cool, but he hadn't asked for additional blankets or a pillow, and he couldn't build a fire inside the barn. She cursed under her breath. He wasn't her worry. He was a murderer, for God's sake.

If only he had the eyes of a murderer. Then she could stop worrying about him and worry more about herself. If only his eyes hadn't held a bleakness as he'd spoken of prison. She wondered whom he had killed. If he'd had good reason to murder someone.

She tightened her fingers around the rifle. Did any reason justify murder? She had asked herself that question countless times since the night the killer had swooped down on them. The answer always eluded her. Or perhaps only the answer she wanted eluded her.

She slid off the bed and walked to her hope chest. She knelt before it and set the rifle on the floor. She ran her hand over the cedar that her father had sanded and varnished to a shine for her fourteenth birthday. For three years she had carefully folded and placed her dreams inside . . . until the night when the killer had dragged her to the barn. Her dreams had died that night, along with her mother, father, and brother.

The rain pounded harder. The wind scraped the tree branches across the windows. The thunder roared.

She lifted the lid on the chest for the first time since that fateful night. Forgotten dreams beckoned her. She trailed her fingers over the soft flannel of a nightgown. She had wanted to feel delicate on her wedding night so she had embroidered flowers down the front and around the cuffs. She had tatted the edges of her linens and sewn a birthing gown for a child she now knew would never be.

The killer had charged into her life with the force of a tornado. He had stolen everything, and when she'd tried to regain a measure of what he'd taken—he had delivered his final vengeance. With one laugh, one hideous laugh that had echoed through the night, he had shattered her soul.

She slammed down the lid and dug her fingers into her thighs. She had no future because the past kept a tight hold on her present.

She rose to her feet, walked to the hearth, and grabbed the lantern off the mantel. Using the flame from the lamp, she lit the lantern. She jerked her slicker off the wall and slipped into it, calling herself a fool. Then she walked to the corner and pulled two quilts from the stack of linens. Digger struggled to his feet, his body quivering from his shoulders to his tail.

"Stay!" she ordered. His whine tore at her heart.

The dog got his feelings hurt more easily than the town spinster. Loree softened her voice. "If you get wet and muddy, I won't be able to let you back in. I won't be long." She stepped outside. Lightning streaked across the obsidian sky. Rain pelted the earth. The barn was as black as a tomb. She couldn't remember if a lantern still hung in the barn. She shivered as memories assailed her.

Satan had risen from the bowels of Hell and made their barn his domain. It had been raining that night as well, and the water had washed their blood into the earth.

She pressed her back against the door. She hadn't gone into the barn since. Her mouth grew dry, her flesh cold. So cold. As cold as the death that had almost claimed her.

Austin Leigh wasn't her worry, but the words rang hollow. Her mother would have invited him into the house and provided him with shelter and warmth. Her mother's innocent words flowed through her. "There are no strangers in this world, Loree. Only friends we haven't yet met."

Reaching deep down, she gathered her courage. Clutching the quilts, with the lantern swinging at her side, Loree darted to the barn, hopping over puddles, landing in others. She stumbled to a stop in the doorway of the barn. "Mr. Leigh?"

She raised the lantern. The shadows retreated slightly, hovering just beyond the lantern's pale glow. With all the holes in the roof, the barn resembled a cavern filled with waterfalls. Bracing herself against the memories, she took a step. "Mr. Leigh?"

She had sold all her animals except for one cow and a few chickens. She heard his horse snort and saw it standing in the distant stall. Using the lantern to light her way, she peered in the stalls she passed until she reached the stallion, secured in the driest area of the barn. How could a man who placed his horse above himself be a murderer?

Holding the lantern higher, she gazed inside the stall. The horse nudged her shoulder. "Where is your owner?"

The animal shook his head.

"You're a big help." She turned at the sound of a low moan. The glow from the lantern fanned out to the opposite stall, revealing a man curled against the corner, lying on his side, knees drawn up, arms pressed in close against his body. She eased toward the stall. "Mr. Leigh, I brought you some quilts."

His only response was a groan. Stepping inside the stall, she noticed that his clothes were soaked and he was visibly trembling. Hugging the quilts, she knelt beside him. Tiny rivulets of water ran down his face. He had removed the vest that he'd been wearing earlier and tucked it beneath his head. His drenched shirt hugged his body, outlined the curve of his spine, the narrowness of his back. "Mr. Leigh?"

Slowly he opened his eyes. "Miss Grant, I wouldn't hurt you."

"I realize that."

"Do you?" He released a short laugh. "You don't trust me because I've been in prison. A man makes choices in his life, and he's gotta learn to live with them. But he doesn't always know what those choices are gonna cost. It'd help if we knew the price before we made the decision."

The anguish reflected on his face, limned by the lantern light, made her want to draw him within her arms, to comfort him as she had her brother when he was a boy. It had never occurred to her that he would be offended if she took his weapons. She wished she could have overlooked them, but he had worn the gun so easily. "I'm sorry."

His lips curled into a sardonic smile. "You didn't send me to prison. Did that to myself." He raised up on an elbow and leaned toward her, the smile easing into oblivion. "You know the worst part? The loneliness. You ever get lonely, Miss Grant?"

"All the time," she whispered as she set the lantern aside, shook out a quilt, and draped it over his back. Shaking as he was, the warmth of his body surprised her. She pressed her hand against his forehead. "My God, you're hot. Are you ill?"

"A man didn't think my five years in prison was a just punishment. He thought I should pay with my life. He cut me across my back. I think it might be festering."

"We need to get you into the house so I can look at it."

"Wouldn't be . . . proper."

Curiosity sparked within her, making her wonder at the circumstances that had caused a man who worried about her respectability to commit murder. People appeared to kill with little provocation: a card skimmed from the bottom of the deck instead of the top, a small half-truth that blossomed into an ugly lie.

"I thank you for your concern over my reputation, but no one's around to notice." Grabbing his arms, she struggled to get him to his feet. Groaning, he staggered forward before catching his balance. She picked up the lantern. "Lean on me," she ordered.

"I'll crush you."

"I'm stronger than I look."

He slung an arm over her shoulders, and she locked her knees into place.

"I'm heavier than I look," he said, his voice low, but she almost thought she heard a smile hidden within it.

She slipped her arm around his waist. "Come on."

The quilt fell from his shoulders, wedged between their bodies, and trailed in the mud as they trudged toward the house. The wind howled, slinging the stinging rain sideways. The porch eaves couldn't protect them from the merciless storm. She let go of the man and released the latch on the door. The wind shoved the door open, nearly taking her arm with it. She pulled on Austin Leigh. "Get inside!"

He stumbled into the house. She followed him, slammed the door, and jammed the bolt into place, imagining she heard the wind howl its protest. Digger lifted his head, released a small whine, and settled back down to sleep.

Loree stared at the man standing in her house, wondering what in the world she thought she was going to do with him now. He looked ready to collapse at any moment. She set the lantern on the table and pulled out a chair. "Sit down."

He obeyed, hunching his shoulders and wrapping his arms around himself. She stepped behind him and cringed when she saw the brown stain on the back of his shirt. She might have noticed it earlier if he hadn't been wearing a vest.

"Let's get your shirt off." With trembling fingers, she unbuttoned his shirt, pulled the ends free of his trousers, and worked the clinging shirt off his body. Then she studied the long, jagged, pus-filled gash. Red irritated flesh surrounded it, and she wondered briefly how he had managed to chop her wood. "I'm going to have to lance it. Let's get you into bed."

She helped him to his feet. He followed without complaint as she led him into her bedroom. "Can you finish undressing yourself?" He stood, enfolded in silence. She cradled his roughened bristled cheeks between her hands. Images of doing the same thing to her father just before she had kissed him good night as a child swamped her. "Listen to me. You have to get out of these wet clothes and into bed. Can you do that?"

He gave a short nod as though even that was too much effort.

"Good." She hurried to the closet, pulled out a towel, and tossed it on the bed. "You can use that to dry off. I'm going to prepare some hot salt water to draw out the infection after I've lanced it. I'll be back in a few minutes." She slipped out of the room, clicking the door closed.

Austin dropped onto the edge of the bed and tugged off his boots, grimacing as the pain assaulted him. He should have realized his back him through the night, wiping the beading sweat from his brow, keeping the blankets tucked around him, wondering what sort of man would go to prison for murder . . . then weep because a woman hadn't waited for his return.

Chapter Three

—⊱◈⊰—

$\mathcal{L}$oree hadn't meant to pry. She'd retrieved Austin Leigh's saddlebags with the intent of discovering if he had other clothes to wear. Her search stopped the moment she found his treasured keepsake. Sitting cross-legged on the floor beside the tub of steaming water, she stroked the locks of auburn hair he had bound together with a white velveteen ribbon. She had little doubt the silken strands had once belonged to his beloved Becky. When she held them up to the early morning sunlight filtering through the window, they turned a warm shade of red, unlike her own hair, which held no color at all.

She reasoned that he had possessed the precious memento before he went to prison. She could not envision him requesting the hair of a woman who had married another. When she brought the hair beneath her nose, she smelled the fading fragrance of vanilla mingling with a scent that she recognized as belonging to the man lying in her bed. After tending him through the night,

A name that might have cost him her love.

Using the hard lye soap, he scrubbed unmercifully at his face and body and washed his hair. The pain still throbbed through his back, but not nearly as much as it had the day before. He'd been a fool to leave home without seeing that it was properly tended by a physician, but then he seemed to have gained a knack for being a fool.

He brought himself to his feet and dried off. Wrapping the towel around his waist, he walked to the bed and removed his shaving equipment from his saddlebag. He ambled to the woman's dresser and studied his reflection in the mirror. He hadn't really taken the time to look at himself since he'd left prison. He was suddenly hit with the hard realization that he had aged more than either of his brothers. Deep crevices fanned out from the corners of his eyes. The wind, rain, and sun had worked together to wear away, shape, and mold the face of a boy into the hardened visage of a man. He hardly recognized himself and he missed the laughing blue eyes that had always looked back at him.

He dropped his chin to his chest and released a heavy sigh. Of all the things that had changed, he hated most of all that he had changed—inside and out. He was as much a stranger to himself as he was to the woman preparing him breakfast.

Moving her hairbrush, comb, and hand mirror aside, he set his shaving box on the dresser. Using the warm water she'd left in the bowl, he stirred up some lather for his face, his gaze lighting upon all the little gewgaws scattered over her dresser.

He stopped stirring and trailed his fingers over a smooth wooden box. Embedded in the wood was a silhouette of a violin. He shifted his gaze to the door. She'd pried into his belongings . . .

Gingerly he touched the lid of the box and slowly lifted it. Music tinkled out. He slammed the lid closed. A music box.

Shaking his head, Austin set about shaving several days growth of beard from his face. Then he pulled fresh clothes from his saddlebags, stepped into his trousers, and pulled on his boots. Grabbing his shirt and a towel, he walked to the door and quietly opened it.

The aromas of freshly baked biscuits and brewed coffee wafted toward him. He leaned against the doorjamb and watched Loree stir something in a pot on the cast iron stove. She wore a dress the shade of daisies and the same white apron she'd worn the day before cinched at her waist. Her narrow hips swayed in a circular motion as though following the path of the spoon. The lilt of her soft voice filled the room with a song.

"What are you singing?"

She spun around, her eyes wide, her hand pressed just below her throat. "Oh, you startled me."

"I'm sorry."

She shook her head. "That's all right. I'm just not used to having company. I was singing 'Lorena.' My pa told me that they sang it around the campfires during the war. It made him so homesick that one night he just got up and started walking home." She turned back to the stove. "I didn't mean to disturb you with my caterwauling."

"I'd hardly call it caterwauling."

She glanced over her shoulder. "Did you find everything you needed?"

"Yes, ma'am." He held up the towel. "I was wondering if you'd make sure my back was dry."

"Oh, yes." She wiped her hands on her apron before pulling a chair out from the table and turning it. "Why don't you sit down?"

Austin crossed the short distance separating them, handed her the towel, straddled the chair, and folded his arms over its straight back. She pressed the towel against his wound. He closed his eyes, relishing her touch, as gentle as the first breath of spring. He'd been too long without a woman, without the peacefulness a woman's presence offered a man. It was more than the actual touch. It was the lilt of her voice, her flowery fragrance. The smile she was hesitant to give. The gold of her eyes.

Lightly, she pressed her fingers around the wound. "I don't see any signs of infection brewing, but it's still red and angry-looking. I wonder if I should sew it."

"Is it bleeding?"

"No."

"Then just leave it. I've been enough trouble."

"It's going to leave an ugly scar."

"Won't be the first."

Reaching around him, she picked up a brown bottle that had been set near some cloths. He suspected that she'd anticipated he would need further care this morning. It galled him to need her help. Why couldn't Duncan have cut him someplace that he could have reached and treated himself?

He supposed he should just be grateful that he'd moved soon enough to avoid giving Duncan the opportunity to slice any deeper.

"I thought I'd put some tincture of iodine on it this morning," she offered.

"Fine."

She pulled the stopper and the acrid odor assailed his nostrils. She drenched the cloth with the reddish-brown liquid. Dallas had always had a fondness for the medication, pouring it on every cut and scrape Austin had ever had. He supposed it was because his brother had seen too many men die from infection during the war. He probably wouldn't be sitting here now if he'd told Dallas about the cut.

"This is going to sting," she said quietly.

Austin gritted his teeth and dug his fingers into the back of the chair. When she touched the saturated cloth to his back, he sucked in air with a harsh hiss.

"I'm sorry, so sorry," she whispered, and he thought he heard tears in her voice.

He focused his attention on the man he hoped to find in Austin. Each day, the man owed him more. He wouldn't be sitting here fighting back the pain if the man hadn't run off after killing Boyd.

She removed the cloth, and Austin released a long slow breath. He eased away from the chair as she wrapped a bandage around his chest and across his back.

"You'll want to keep it clean and have a doctor look at it when you get to Austin."

"Yes, ma'am."

Her fingers strayed to an old wound on his shoulder.

"Someone shot you," she said quietly.

"Yes, ma'am. A little over six years ago."

She jerked her hand back as though he'd bitten her. She placed the bottle of iodine on a shelf, scrubbed her hands at the sink, and wiped them on her apron, over and over, until he thought she might remove her skin.

"Is something wrong?" he asked as he stood and shrugged into his shirt.

"I just didn't expect you to clean up so nice."

Her blush pleased him more than her words. "I . . . I've got some porridge going here if you'd like some."

He swung the chair around and dropped onto the seat. "Just some coffee."

She slapped the porridge into a bowl and set it in front of her place at the table before pouring the coffee into a cup and handing it to him. "I've got milk and—"

"Just black."

He wrapped his hands around the cup, absorbing its warmth, waiting as she poured herself some coffee and took her seat. While she dumped six heaping spoons of sugar into her coffee, he watched with amusement. He hadn't been amused in a long time. She was incredibly innocent. Living out here alone, away from town, away from the influence of people, how could she be otherwise?

Maybe not completely innocent. Even as she offered him food and shelter, a wariness remained in her eyes, a caution as though at any moment she feared he might turn on her like a rabid dog.

She glanced up and blushed again. "I like a little coffee with my sugar."

"Is that why you're so sweet?"

Her blush deepened as she lowered her gaze. Austin cursed himself and wondered what the hell he thought he was doing. He had no business flirting with a woman, especially one as innocent as she was. "I appreciate all that you did for me last night."

"You should never let a wound go unattended so long."

"I had other things on my mind." He brought the cup to his lips and peered over the rim at the woman sitting across from him. She was sprinkling sugar over her porridge. A corner of his mouth curved up. He thought she might save time if she simply poured the porridge into the sugar bowl.

Having known so few women in his life, he'd developed an appreciation for them, an appreciation that even Becky's betrayal couldn't diminish. He had no memory of his mother. Houston's wife—Amelia—was the first woman to whom he'd ever really spoken. He'd always liked the way she listened, as though she truly thought he had something of importance to share. He'd even played his violin for her when he'd never dared to play it for anyone else. Then Becky Oliver had moved to town, and Austin had thought she was an angel—his angel. As much as he wanted to hate her, he only seemed capable of missing her.

"Other than building you a new barn, what can I do to repay your kindness?" he asked abruptly, more harshly than he'd intended, memories of Becky tainting his mood.

Her head shot up, her delicate brows drawn together over eyes mired with confusion. "I think you ought to spend the day resting and gathering your strength."

"I need to see to my horse."

"I fed and brushed him this morning."

"And washed my clothes and polished my boots. Good Lord, don't you ever stop doing?"

She dropped her gaze to the remaining porridge. "I like to keep busy." She rose to her feet, picked up the bowl and cup, and carried them to the sink.

"My apologies, Miss Grant. I had no cause to take out my frustration on you."

"It doesn't matter."

But it did matter, more so because she thought it didn't. Austin scraped his chair back and stood. She spun around, the wariness back in her eyes.

"I don't doubt you took good care of my horse, but I want to check on him anyway." He walked out of the house. The dog bounded across the yard and leapt up on Austin's chest, his huge paws wet and muddy. Austin scratched him behind the ears. "If you're her protector, you need to do a better job of protecting her from me."

The dog fell to all fours and gazed up at him as though measuring his worth. Then he barked and scampered away to chase a butterfly.

Austin strode into the barn. Sunlight streamed

through the holes. Black Thunder knickered. He rubbed the stallion's nose. "So she's taking good care of you, too, is she?"

He glanced around the run-down structure. Severed and ragged at the end, a rope hung from a beam. He wondered what kept a lone woman living here. Why didn't she pack up and move into town? He had been teasing her when he'd mentioned repairing the barn, but he wasn't certain he could chop enough wood to repay his debt.

He retrieved a rope halter that was hanging on the wall and slipped it onto Black Thunder before leading the stallion into the sunshine. At the corral, he bent and brought the horse's foreleg up between his knees. He studied the festering wound and wondered if his back had looked this nasty when Miss Grant had tended it.

Releasing the foreleg, he knew he wouldn't be traveling today. He looked toward the house. The dog had either captured the butterfly or given up because he was stretched out beneath the shade of a distant tree. A weakness settled in Austin's legs. It galled him to have to admit Loree may have been right—he wasn't quite recovered.

He ambled to the tree. Always watchful, the dog opened an eye and closed it. A flash of yellow caught Austin's attention and he shifted his gaze. He leaned against the rough tree trunk. A strange sense of contentment stole over him as he watched Loree stand in the middle of a vegetable garden with a fawn nibbling something out of her cupped palm. Three other deer tore up the growing foliage. A family, he mused, and discontentment edged the peacefulness aside.

"I could string up some barbed wire for you," he said.

The deer bounded into the thick grove of trees. Loree turned, her lightly golden brows drawn tightly together. "Why would I need barbed wire?"

"To protect your garden. Keep the pesky critters away."

She looked toward the trees where the deer had disappeared. "They aren't pesky, and I always grow more than I need." She walked toward him, eyeing him suspiciously. "How are you feeling?"

Like he'd fallen from his horse, caught his foot in the stirrup, and been dragged across the state.

"A little tired. Do you have any kerosene? My horse's hoof is festering. I need to tend it."

"I'm sorry. I didn't even think to check his hoof."

"You shouldn't have to be concerned with my horse at all."

Or with me. He'd shown her far more of himself than he wanted her to see. She was a stranger, but he had disconcerting memories of telling her things . . .

He followed her into the house and retrieved his knife from his saddlebag while she found the kerosene. By the time he returned outside, she was waiting beside Black Thunder, stroking the horse's mane.

Stepping away from the stallion, she dropped her gaze to the knife Austin held. "Do you want me to hold his head?"

"It's not necessary. He's trained." Giving the horse his backside, he brought the hoof up between his knees and dug the knife into the wound. He heard a whinny just before the sharp pain ricocheted through his butt. He dropped the hoof and jumped away from the horse. "Son of a—! Damn!"

He rubbed his backside while glaring at the horse that tossed its head like a woman might tilt her nose with indignation. Then he heard the laughter.

Light and airy, like a star drifting down from the heavens. He turned his attention to the woman. She had pressed her fingers against her lips, but he saw the corners of her mouth tilting up, carrying her smile to her eyes, shining like a golden coin. "You think it's funny, Miss Grant?"

She shook her head vigorously. "No, Mr. Leigh. It's just not what I would have *trained* him to do."

A bubble of laughter escaped from between her lips and it touched a chord of warmth deep within his chest. "Believe me, he picked that trick up while I was gone."

She dropped her hand, and he watched as she fought to contain her smile. "You just don't seem to have any luck."

"Oh, I have luck, Miss Grant. Unfortunately, it's all bad."

Her smile withered. "I'm sorry."

"You aren't the cause of it." He jerked his thumb toward the horse. "I'll hold his head if you'll rub the kerosene into his hoof."

He grabbed the halter on either side of Black Thunder's head. When Loree bent to grab the hoof, Austin almost thanked the horse for nipping him. Her skirt lifted to reveal her bare ankles and pulled taut across her backside. How in the hell had he mistaken her for a boy the day before? His fever must have addled his brain.

Loree Grant was a tiny bundle of delicate femininity. Just as she had at the stove, she swayed her hips slightly with the motion of her hand, rubbing the kerosene into the horse's hoof. Sweet Lord, it was pure torture to watch, to imagine that backside pressed against him, circling—

She dropped the hoof, straightened, and faced him. "Is there anything else I need to do for the horse?"

He swallowed hard and unclenched his fingers from around the halter. "Nope."

She lowered her gaze and drew a wiggly line in the dirt with her big toe. "I should probably"— she glanced up quickly, then down—"check your backside, make sure he didn't break the skin." She lifted her gaze. "You don't want to get an infection"—she waved her hand limply in the air—"back there."

He smiled warmly. "No, ma'am, I surely don't. I swear, Miss Grant, when I stopped here yesterday, I had no intention of putting you to all this trouble."

"It's no trouble, Mr. Leigh. Besides, I'll put the tincture of iodine on it to begin with so it shouldn't fester at all."

He watched her hurry to the house and decided it was a good thing that the medication burned hotter than hell. Otherwise, he didn't know how he'd endure her gentle fingers touching his backside without his body reacting and making a fool of him.

LOREE PUMPED THE water into the sink, then set about scrubbing her trembling hands. What in the world had possessed her to offer to look at Austin Leigh's backside? She wondered if the tincture of iodine would be as effective if she simply poured it into a pan and told him to sit in it and soak his wound. If there was even a wound to soak.

She heard his boots hit the porch. She inhaled deeply, grabbed a towel, and dried her hands. She glanced over her shoulder. He stood in the room, looking as uncomfortable as she felt.

She'd drawn the curtains aside allowing the late morning sun to pour inside. She pointed to a chair opposite the one he'd used that morning. "I can probably use the sun best if you stand there."

He gave her a long slow nod, but she thought she saw worry reflected in his blue eyes.

"I'll be gentle," she assured him.

"That's not what concerns me," he grumbled as he moved to stand behind the chair.

She grabbed the bottle of iodine and a cloth. She hurried to the table, but once she arrived she wished she'd walked more slowly. She pulled the stopper and soaked the cloth. She only wanted to do this once, really didn't want to do it at all. She glanced up. He was staring hard at something on the far wall.

"I . . . I guess you need to lower . . . your britches," she said hesitantly.

She saw a muscle in his cheek jerk.

"Why don't you get behind me?" he suggested.

She stepped around him and tried not to think about the buttons his fingers were releasing. Her breath came in short little gasps. She watched as he grabbed the back of his britches and struggled to lower one side while keeping the other raised. He bent over slightly.

"Can you lift your shirt?" she asked.

She stared in amazement as his skin came into view. So incredibly white that it reminded her of clouds on a summer day, but just above his hip, his skin turned as brown as soil. He must have often worked without a shirt, and she realized with sudden uneasiness that she was about to touch a part of him that the sun had never seen.

"Is the skin broken?"

She flinched at the harshness in his voice and dropped her gaze to the area where he had halted his britches' downward journey. Torn flesh and blood marred his otherwise smooth backside. "Yes."

Gingerly she touched his britches, the tip of her finger skimming over him. He jumped as though she'd pressed a red-hot brand to his flesh.

"I'm sorry. I just . . . I just need to lower these a little more." She brought them down as far as she dared, grateful the horse had nipped him high on the cheek.

She pressed the iodine to the wound, heard his sharp intake of breath, and saw his fingers tighten around his shirt. "I'm so sorry."

"Trust me. The more it stings, the better."

She heard the strain in his voice and worked

as fast as she could, pressing the cloth to the wound—

"Good God Almighty! What are you doing, Loree?"

Loree spun around at the unexpected voice, lost her balance, and toppled into Austin as he was turning, struggling to pull up his britches. He reached out to steady her, swore harshly, and released her to grab his britches before they slipped any lower.

Loree would have laughed if it weren't for the young man standing in her doorway, glaring at her. Her heart was pounding so hard that it sounded like a herd of horses stampeding between her ears. "Dewayne, what are you doing here?"

Dewayne Thomas removed his hat, his blond hair glinting in the sunlight, his brown eyes narrowing as he scrutinized Austin. "Come to check on you after last night's storm. Heard there were tornadoes about. Wanted to make sure you were all right." He jutted out his chin. "Who's this?"

"Mr. Leigh. He was traveling to Austin, but his horse came up lame—"

"So how come he's taking off his clothes in your house?"

"He wasn't taking off his clothes. He was treating his horse and it nipped his backside." She held up the stained cloth as evidence. "I was just applying some tincture of iodine to his wound so he wouldn't get an infection."

"Good God, Loree, I'd think you'd have more sense than to let a stranger into your house after that man murdered your family."

"But what if some fella stops by who ain't a gentleman?"

"I have my rifle and Digger. Remember how he attacked you the first time you showed up after I'd found him?"

Dewayne laughed. "I still got the scars on my calf. You sure it was the man's horse and not Digger that bit him?"

Loree tilted her head in thought. "Oddly enough, he only growled at Mr. Leigh. He didn't attack him."

"Maybe Digger is getting to be like you. Too trusting."

Smiling, she shook her head. "No, he chased away a man in a medicine show wagon last week. I think Digger would attack anyone he thought would harm me."

"Well, if the storm didn't do any damage here, then I reckon I'll head home. If that fella's still around tonight, you bolt the door."

Simply to appease him, she said, "I will."

She walked outside with him, hugged him as she always did—the way she had hugged her brother—and watched him mount his horse and ride away. Then she strolled over to the man who was brushing his stallion near the corral.

"Dewayne meant no offense," she said quietly.

"None taken." He stopped brushing his horse and met her gaze. "Why didn't you tell me someone had murdered your family?"

"Why didn't you tell me you'd lied?"

"It's not the same."

"How is it different?"

"It just is." He walked around his horse and began brushing the other side as though he needed to put distance between them. "I told you I served time in prison for murder." His hand stilled, his blue gaze capturing hers. "I'm not a murderer."

Her throat tightened. She knew he spoke the truth. He wasn't a cold-blooded murderer. Remembering the puckered flesh on his shoulder—a scar similar to the one she possessed—the kind of scar a healing bullet wound left behind, she imagined he had killed in self-defense, shooting the man who had shot him. "I know that. You don't have the eyes of a murderer."

He seemed to relax as though she'd lifted a burden from his shoulders. "Who did he hang?" he asked, his voice low.

Loree stumbled back, her heart racing. "What?"

"There's a rope dangling from the rafters in the barn."

She had to give Austin Leigh credit. He didn't miss much. Dewayne had cut her brother down. Until last night, she'd never found the courage to return to the barn, much less remove the rope that had taken her brother's life. "My brother. He dragged us to the barn, tied us up, and hanged my brother before shooting the rest of us."

Horror delved into the depths of his eyes. "He shot you?"

Oddly enough, his reaction told her more about him than anything else. He wasn't a man who would hurt a woman.

"Yes, but he didn't check to make certain I was

dead. I guess since I'm so small, he assumed one bullet would be sufficient."

"Did the law find him?"

"No."

He laughed derisively. "Ain't that the way of it. They send me to prison, and they let a man who murdered three people go free. You gotta wonder about the justice system sometimes."

She had wondered about justice a lot in the passing years, wondered if it even existed.

"Is that why you let the barn go to ruin?"

Once again, his insight surprised her. She nodded. "I can't stand to go inside."

"You went inside last night, looking for me."

She felt the warmth suffuse her cheeks. "Because I was worried about you. My mother always got after me because I worry more about others than I do about myself. She said it would get me into trouble someday. I've thought about burning the barn, but I'm afraid I'd set the whole hillside ablaze."

"Imagine your brother's friend would have helped you with that."

"Dewayne is sweet and he means well, but sometimes he does or says things without thinking of the consequences."

"He seems to care for you."

"He was the one who found us. I'd probably be dead if not for him." She turned away, the bitter memories bringing forth images of soul-searing pain. A warm, gentle hand came to rest on her shoulder.

"I'm sorry."

She looked into blue eyes that reflected not only a pain equal to hers, but an absence of dreams. Each had suffered as the result of a killing, and she couldn't help but believe that he was as much a victim as she was. Neither had escaped unscathed. "It wasn't your doing."

"No, it wasn't, but making you remember was." He removed his hand from her shoulder and heaved a sigh. "So now I owe you more than I did before. There's gotta be something around here that I can do for you."

"Actually I do need something done."

"Tell me what it is and I'll do it. I pay my debts."

He paid his debts. Loree wondered if that was the reason he didn't seem overly bitter that he'd spent time in prison. He had killed someone. He'd given up a portion of his life. He'd paid his debt.

Now he wanted to repay her. She didn't think his pride would accept that his company was payment enough. No, he needed a chore. Smiling, she began to walk away, trusting him to follow. She knew the perfect chore for those beautiful long fingers of his.

Chapter Four

$\mathcal{F}$ollowing the woman as she walked past the house, Austin admired more than the gentle sway of her hips. He admired the courage that had allowed her to put her fears and ugly memories aside to come to his aid last night.

More than that, she had overlooked what she knew of his past. He hadn't received so fine a gift in a good while. Little wonder he had wept in her bed. She possessed a heart that was as pure as the gold of her eyes.

Hell, once he found the man who had stolen five years of his life, maybe he'd search for the man who had killed her family and see him brought to justice.

She came to a halt and flung her arm toward the garden. "Your chore."

The chore turned out to be no chore at all: plucking red ripe strawberries from her garden and placing them gently in the bucket so they wouldn't bruise. She had told him that she couldn't abide the fruit when it was bruised. Based on the fact that she had devoted over half her garden to growing strawberries, Austin figured she had a fondness for them.

Near dusk, she set a quilt beneath a tree and brought out two large bowls. One was filled with washed strawberries. The other with sugar.

She plopped onto the quilt, took a strawberry out of the bowl, rolled it around in the sugar, and popped it into her mouth. She closed her eyes and released a low throaty moan that made Austin want to groan.

Against his better judgment, he stretched out on the quilt beside her and raised up on an elbow. She opened her eyes and smiled at him. "There is nothing finer than the first strawberry in spring."

He disagreed. He could have named a hundred things: her smile, her sun-kissed cheeks, the strands of her hair that had escaped her braid and framed her face like the petals of a dandelion. As a boy, he'd often taken a deep breath before blasting the dandelion petals onto the breeze. Right now, he wanted to blow softly, gently, his breath as quiet as a whisper while it fanned across the nape of her neck.

Digger barreled around the corner of the house. Loree grabbed a strawberry and tossed it into the air. The dog leapt up, his jaws clamping around the ripe fruit. The animal hit the ground and rolled over. Loree laughed joyfully, reminding Austin of the first time he had placed a bow on the strings of a violin. The music had sounded just as sweet because it had been unexpected: something he had created. He found himself wishing he'd been the one to make Loree laugh. Not the stupid dog.

"Help yourself to the strawberries," she said as she tossed another one to the dog before taking one for herself.

Austin brought a strawberry to his lips and bit into the succulent fruit. The sweetness filled his mouth. It didn't need sugar. It amused him to watch Loree carefully coat each strawberry with sugar before she ate it. He grew warm as her tongue darted out to slowly, meticulously capture each errant grain of sugar that clung to her lips. He imagined her kiss would taste of strawberries and sugar.

He'd been too long without a woman, and he was having one hell of a time taming his thoughts. Watching the wind whip strands of her hair around her face, he wanted to play with it as well. He wanted to touch her rounded cheeks with his fingers and the upturned tip of her nose with his lips. He'd known too few women in his life, and even though one had torn out his heart and shredded it to pieces, he couldn't bring himself to hate women.

He figured women were like men. Some good. Some bad. Some fickle. He'd latched onto a fickle one the first time and it had cost him dearly. But in spite of the steep price he'd paid, he couldn't see himself spending his remaining days without the comfort of a woman. Once he'd cleared his name, he'd take a wife. He wanted what his older brothers had. Neither had gained their wives without paying a price.

The comforting silence eased in around them as the shadows lengthened. The dog loped to the edge of the clearing, barked, and raced back to catch another strawberry. Austin was beginning to doubt the dog's ability to protect Loree. Other than last evening when the dog had growled at him, he had seen no signs of aggressiveness. The dog reminded him of an overgrown puppy.

"Why are you out here, Miss Grant?"

She jerked her head around to stare at him. "I like watching the sunset, I enjoy eating straw-berries—"

"No. I mean why do you live out here alone? Why not move into town? I can't see that this is a working farm. What keeps you here?"

"Memories. We were happy here. I guess I feel that if I left, I'd be abandoning my family."

In the distance, he saw a white picket fence surrounding three granite headstones. "How old were you?"

"Seventeen. How old were you when you went to prison?"

"Twenty-one."

"That sounds so young."

"Not as young as seventeen."

She dug another strawberry into the sugar. "You mentioned a brother . . ."

He nodded. "Houston."

Her eyes widened as she bit into the strawberry. She laughed as the red juice dribbled down her chin. He clenched his hands to stop his fingers from gathering the juice and carrying it back to her lips, or better yet to his own. She wiped her face with her apron. "Another town?"

"Yep. My parents lived there for a while."

"Have you been to Houston?"

"Nah, they lived there before I was born."

She sighed wistfully and gazed toward the trees. "I used to dream of traveling the world and looking at the stars from different cities." She shifted her gaze to him. "Do you think the stars look different on the other side of the world?"

"I don't know. Never thought about it. Never dreamed that big."

"What did you dream of?"

Marrying Becky. Raising a family. But before that . . . a distant memory flickered at the back of his mind of standing at the edge of a gorge, yelling out his dream . . . and listening as the echo carried it back to him. Then the memory died like a flame snuffed out because there wasn't enough air to keep it burning. "I don't recall."

"My father used to tell me that I had to put my heart into my dream if I wanted it to come true. How do you put your heart into something?"

Austin hadn't a clue. He'd watched his brothers pour their hearts into the women they loved, thought he'd done the same with Becky, but if he had, she would have waited for him. He was convinced of that. Whatever their love had been, it hadn't been strong enough to endure separation, and he couldn't help but wonder what else it might not have endured.

The dog came charging back from the edge of

twilight, dropped low to the ground, and growled, baring his teeth. Worry etched over her face, Loree rose to her knees. "Digger, what is it?"

The dog barked and bounded back for the trees, disappearing in the brush. A high-pitched shriek rented the air.

"Bobcat!" Loree cried as she jumped to her feet. "Digger!"

The dog barked and the ear-splitting feline cry came again, followed by a yelp echoing pain.

"No!" Loree yelled as she began running toward the trees.

Austin surged to his feet, ran after her, and grabbed her arm, halting her frantic race to the trees. "Where's my rifle?"

"In the corner of the front room, by the hearth."

"Come with me while I get it."

She shook her head vigorously. "I'll wait here but hurry."

He didn't trust her to stay, but he heard the dog's wounded cry, the cat's victorious screech, and knew he had no time to argue. With his heart thundering, he raced inside the house. He grabbed his rifle, loaded it, and shoved a handful of bullets into his pocket. Then he tore back outside, rounded the corner, and staggered to a stop in the clearing.

The woman was gone!

"Loree!" Fear for her edged any rational thoughts aside. He stalked toward the trees where the dog had disappeared. "Loree!"

He no longer heard the thrashing of battle. An eerie silence settled over the woods. He tread carefully between the trees, his heart hammering. When he found the woman he planned to shake her every way but loose for scaring the holy hell out of him. How dare she risk her life for a stupid dog.

He found her kneeling between two mighty oak trees, rocking back and forth, silent tears streaming down her cheeks, her arms wrapped around her dog. Austin knelt beside her. "Loree?"

She opened her eyes, the golden depths revealing her ravaged grief. "He was all I had left," she whispered hoarsely. "He was just a dog, but I loved him."

"I know," he said quietly. "You take the rifle and I'll carry him to the house."

"Let me hold him for just a minute . . . while he's still warm."

She buried her face in Digger's thick fur. Austin scanned the trees, his ears alert. He didn't like the thought of Loree living out here alone with wild animals. The deer he didn't mind, but a bobcat was another story.

Gently, he touched Loree's shoulder. "We need to get back before it's too dark."

She lifted her head, sniffed, and nodded. Blood had stained the front of her dress and panic surged through him. "You're hurt."

She glanced down before lifting a vacant gaze to his. "No, it's Digger's blood. The cat was gone by the time I got here."

"You should have stayed by the house like I told you."

"I was worried about Digger. He never backs— backed—away from a fight."

"Christ, your mother was right. You put a dog before yourself—"

"I'd put anyone, anything I loved before myself. I don't see that as a fault."

He didn't mean to sound harsh, didn't want to lecture her, but the thought that she might have been the cat's next victim had him shaking clear down to his boots. "Take the rifle."

She grabbed it, and he slipped his arms beneath the dog. He ignored the pain shooting through his back as he strained to lift the heavy beast. With the darkness closing in around them, they walked in silence to the house, his boots breaking dried twigs, her feet scattering the fragile leaves that had died last autumn.

"Will you bury him near the garden? That's where he liked to dig," she said quietly as they neared the house.

"Sure will. You got a shovel?"

"In the barn."

"I'll get it. Why don't you go inside and wash up?"

Nodding, she leaned over and pressed a kiss to the top of the dog's head. "Bye, Digger."

Austin watched her run to the front of the house, leaving him feeling useless. Giving comfort had never been his strong suit, was something he hadn't even known existed until Amelia had come into their lives.

He laid the dog on the ground. He walked to the quilt where he had shared a few peaceful moments with Loree. In her rush to get to the dog, she'd knocked over the bowl, spilling sugar

She had long ago accepted the fact that she would live out the remaining days of her life alone. She hadn't realized how much she missed the scent, sight, sounds, and touch created by another person. She thought she had effectively warded off the loneliness.

Now, she knew it had only been in hiding, gathering strength, waiting until her defenses were down to attack. All the days of silence and nights alone suddenly loomed before her. A lifetime's worth. And she hated them. She hated every one of them and the man whose actions had condemned her to the loneliness.

She suddenly felt plain and poor, longing for things she would never know: a husband's smile, the laughter of children.

Austin's gaze drifted to her lips, the blue of his eyes darkening until she felt the warmth of a fire, burning hot and bright, creating even as it consumed. He lowered his head slightly and her lips parted.

"So sweet," he whispered, and she wondered if within the words, she heard an apology.

Then his mouth was pressed against hers, warm, soft, moist, and she had her first taste of a man. Deep inside, she smiled. He tasted of strawberries.

Then he deepened the kiss, and when his tongue sought hers, she raised up onto the tips of her toes, wrapped her arms around his neck, and gave to him all that he asked.

He groaned deep within his throat and she felt the rumble of his chest against her breasts.

His arm snaked around her, pressing her closer against his body.

She had never been wanton, but then the loneliness had never been this great, this consuming. Nor had the need to be held, to be loved been so strong. She did not delude herself. He did not love her. In his eyes, she had seen the stark loneliness that mirrored hers. They were kindred hearts with a haunting past that had stolen dreams. Still, he would leave and never look back.

And with that thought, she found comfort. She could accept what he offered, knowing that he would never discover the secrets that the killer had forced her to lock away. Austin Leigh would never look upon her with revulsion. Years from now, when she brought forth the memories of this man, she would only see the desire that deepened the blue of his eyes.

His mouth trailed along her throat, pressed kisses against the sensitive flesh below her ear. "So sweet," he repeated in a ragged breath, like a litany that stirred his actions.

He guided her to the bed, skimming her remaining clothes from her body before laying her down. Holding her gaze, he slowly unbuttoned his trousers as though giving her time to tell him that what he was offering wasn't what she wanted.

But she did want, more than she had ever wanted, to be without the loneliness. When he stretched his tall lean body alongside hers, she'd never felt so tiny, so delicate. He cupped her breast, his hand shaping and molding her flesh as his mouth teased and taunted. Desire spiraled through her, strong enough to send the loneliness into oblivion. For one night, she would have what she might never have again: a man's touch, a man's whispered words, a man's strength and ability to hold the loneliness at bay.

His mouth came down on hers, hard, devouring, but his hands remained gentle, as though she were shaped from hand-blown glass. She trailed her hands over the firm muscles of his shoulders, digging her fingers into his back, careful to avoid the wound that had forged a bond between them.

When his hand skimmed along her stomach, she shivered. When he touched her intimately, she gasped as his fingers made promises she knew his body would keep.

He moved until his hips were nestled between her thighs. Then slowly, cautiously, he joined his body to hers. The pain was fleeting, the fullness of him satisfying. As he rocked against her, the past blurred into insignificance, the future that awaited her lost its importance. All that mattered was this moment, this joining. Sensations she'd never known existed wove themselves around her, through her, creating beauty where she'd only known ugliness. She reveled in the sound of his throaty groans, the feel of his sure, swift thrusts.

And then she cried out, arching beneath him as everything spilled over into ecstasy.

As he shuddered above her, she heard a name whisper raggedly past his lips. Suddenly all that had passed before meant nothing . . . and the loneliness increased tenfold.

AUSTIN STILLED, HIS breathing labored, sweat glistening over his trembling body, self-loathing and guilt increasing as he felt Loree stiffen beneath him.

Ironically, he'd held no thoughts of Becky until her name escaped his lips, but he didn't think it would soothe Loree's hurt if he told her that. As a matter of fact, he could think of nothing to say, nothing to do that would ease the pain he'd caused her—and hurting her was the last thing he'd intended.

He eased off her. She rolled to her side, presenting him with her back, drawing her knees toward her chest. Reaching down, he pulled up a blanket and covered her.

He got out of the bed, snatched up his britches, jerked them on, and headed outside. He stormed to the corral and slammed the palm of his hand against the post. The sound of vibrating wood echoed around him. He hit the post again and again. He would have kicked it if he'd thought to pull on his boots. He dug his fingers into the top railing of the corral, squeezed his eyes shut, and bowed his head.

He could argue that he'd been too long without a woman, but the argument would have been rift with lies because he knew that if he had lain with a woman that afternoon, he still would have wanted Loree tonight.

She was so incredibly sweet, pure, and innocent . . . all the delightful aspects of youth that a man lost as he grew older. When he had kissed her, felt the tentative touch of her tongue, he was the man he had been before prison. A man who believed in goodness. She had touched the tender part of himself that he'd locked away in solitary confinement in order to survive within prison walls. With her arms circling his neck, she had sent his good intentions to perdition and unleashed desires and needs that he'd kept tightly reined.

And for those few moments of splendor, when he had held her close, the loneliness that always ate at his soul had ceased to feast.

Until he had carelessly whispered another's name.

Then the loneliness had consumed him once again and invited guilt to the banquet.

He slammed his palm against the post. Why in the hell had Becky's name escaped his lips? She hadn't been in his thoughts. Hell, he hadn't been thinking at all. He'd just been feeling, feeling with an intensity he hadn't experienced in years. Maybe that was the reason he'd spoken her name. He'd always associated deeply held emotion with Becky.

And that sure as hell hadn't been fair to Loree.

He might have been able to forgive himself if he had something to offer her—but he had nothing. What woman would want to marry a man fresh out of prison? A man who couldn't prove his innocence?

He had no job, no prospects.

Within his mind, he saw her golden eyes filled with trust. She had wanted the comfort he had to offer, and in taking it, she had given it back.

He'd never wanted to taste anything as much as he'd wanted to taste her, to touch as much as he'd wanted to touch her, to know . . . He found it impossible to believe so little time had passed since he'd first set eyes on her.

Again, he slammed his palm against the post. A delicate hand covered his as it gripped the pillar.

"You're gonna bust your hand if you're not careful," she said quietly.

Austin's heart thundered so loudly that he barely heard the crickets chirping. Loree stood in the pale moonlight, her gaze watchful. She'd slipped into a nightgown and draped a blanket over her shoulders.

"Can't see that it would be any great loss."

She took his hand, turned it, and pressed a kiss to his palm. "I disagree."

"Loree—"

"It's all right. I was thinking of someone else as well."

Her words sliced across his heart like a well-honed knife cutting deeply, the pain taking him off guard. He knew he deserved them, knew she had every right to say them, but he didn't like hearing them. "Who were you thinking of?"

She angled her chin defiantly. "Jake."

He heard the slightest hesitation in her voice and knew beyond any doubt that she was lying. Whether she was hoping to hurt him or salvage her pride, it didn't matter. He'd give her back what he could.

"Then he's a damn lucky man," he said, surprised by the roughness in his voice.

She dropped her gaze to her bare feet. "Anyway, there's no reason for you to sleep out here. The barn is probably still damp."

Even now, after he'd hurt her, she was still more worried about him than herself. "Sleep doesn't come easy for me."

"For me either."

He tilted up her face, and with his thumb, he wiped a glistening tear from the corner of her eye. "We're a fine pair, aren't we?"

She gave him a hesitant smile and nodded. He cupped her cheek and lowered his mouth to hers, imparting with his kiss the apology she wouldn't accept in words. She swayed toward him and wrapped her arms around his neck.

He trailed his lips along her throat until he reached the curve of her shoulder. "Loree, know that I never meant to hurt you."

"I know."

He slipped his arm beneath her knees and lifted her into his arms. Cradling her close, he carried her into the house. With his foot, he closed the door behind him and walked into the bedroom.

Carefully, he laid her on the bed. She curled on her side, and he draped the blanket over her. He walked to the other side of the bed. Without removing his trousers, he lay on top of the covers and wrapped his arm around her. She stiffened. He pressed his lips to the top of her head. "I'm just going to hold you, Loree. Believe it or not, that's all I'd intended to do when I came into the house looking for you earlier."

He heard her muffled sob and tightened his

arms around her. Another sob came. Gingerly, he turned her toward him. "Come here, Sugar."

She rolled into the circle of his arms and pressed her face against his chest. Her warm tears dampened his flesh.

"I'm sorry, Loree. I'm so sorry."

Her sobs grew louder, her tears flowed more freely, and he could do little more than hold her closely, knowing he was the cause of her heartache.

sugar bowl she'd left outside the night before. She remembered knocking it over, spilling its contents on the quilt. She traced her finger around its rim. Now it was full.

What sort of man was Austin Leigh to go to the trouble to retrieve her bowl and fill it with sugar?

She heard his booted feet hit her front porch and step through her doorway. "Your coffee's ready," she told him, averting her gaze, turning to the stove to slap her porridge into a bowl. She listened as he pulled out his chair and took his seat, a gesture that seemed more intimate after all they'd shared last night.

She sat at the table and, with trembling fingers, lifted the spoon and sprinkled sugar over her porridge. She felt his gaze boring into her, but couldn't bring herself to look at him.

"Loree, about last night—"

"I'd rather not discuss it." She lost count of the number of spoonfuls of sugar and decided it didn't matter. She'd just pour on sugar until she no longer saw the oats.

"I've got nothing to offer you, Loree."

She snapped her gaze up to his. He'd removed his hat and put on a shirt. His black hair curled over his collar. She ached to run her fingers through it. "I don't recall asking for anything."

His eyes were somber. "You didn't, but you deserve everything—everything a man would give a woman if he could."

"You didn't force me. I knew where the trail was leading, and I was willing to follow it."

"I told you sometimes a man makes choices not knowing the cost. Did you know the cost?"

She lowered her gaze to the porridge. "No," she admitted quietly. "But I'd pay it again." Looking at him, she forced a tremulous smile. "Although I don't know how I'm going to look Dewayne in the eye the next time he comes over after what he said yesterday."

"You can't look at a woman and know whether or not she's shared herself with a man."

Shared herself. She felt as though she'd given nothing and taken everything. "Sometimes you say things in such a way that I wonder if you're a poet."

He shook his head. "I have no gift with words. Last night served as evidence of that. I appreciate the coffee. I'd best get back to the barn."

Watching him walk from the house, she wondered how soon it would be before he walked out, never to return. She shoved her bowl of porridge aside, discontent rearing its ugly head. Suddenly greedy for memories that she could hoard away and bring out on the loneliest of nights, she scrambled from her chair and dashed outside, hurrying to the corral. His horse grazed nearby. A beautiful beast that belonged to a beautiful man.

She turned her attention to the barn. With a wistfulness she knew she had no business feeling, she watched Austin work. Last night she had received a sampling of what she *would* never have. She had not expected to yearn so intensely for that which she *could* not have.

"Get the kerosene!"

Loree snapped back to the present as Austin climbed lithely down from her barn.

"Fetch some old blankets, too," he told her. "I'll get some buckets of water."

"That's not very much to burn," she said, studying the meager pile of ragged lumber.

"Thought it best to start small until we figure out what we can control."

She fetched the kerosene and blankets as he'd instructed, returning to see him put the last bucket of water in place. He took the kerosene from her and doused the wood. Sweat glistened over his bronzed back, and she worried about his wound. It didn't look nearly as angry as it had the day before, but it was certain to leave him with a jagged scar.

When he finished, he held up a match. "You want the honors?"

She nodded jerkily. He lifted his foot, struck the match on the bottom of his boot, and handed it to her. She got as close as she dared and tossed the match onto the kerosene drenched wood. She watched the flame grow and spread across the pyre. The wood crackled and blackened. Smoke rose toward the clouds. She crossed her arms beneath her breasts, feeling as though she was finally doing something to put the nightmare to rest.

The barn had been a cavernous reminder of how those she loved had died. She hated the rope most of all, but she'd never been able to bring herself to touch it.

"I want to burn the rope, too," she whispered hoarsely never taking her gaze from the fiery red blaze.

He wrapped his arms around her, bringing her back against his chest. She welcomed the sturdiness of his embrace. He brushed his lips lightly across her temple. "It's already burning."

His words didn't surprise her. Somehow, he seemed capable of anticipating her needs before she knew she had them. "My brother was so young. I wish he'd hanged me instead."

Austin's arms tightened around her. "Is that why you live here alone—to punish yourself for living when they died?"

She held her silence because he had the uncanny ability to understand far more than anyone else ever had.

Gently, he turned her within his arms, tucked his knuckle beneath her chin, and tilted her head back. "Loree, I've listened to you talking about your family. I know you loved them. For you to love them as much as you do, they had to love you in return. They wouldn't want you living here alone."

Gazing into his earnest eyes, she desperately wanted to explain everything—the fear, the fury, the hatred. Surely a man who had lived his life would understand, but if he didn't understand, something far worse than living a life alone awaited her.

"I'm here because I want to be. I'm . . . content." Or at least she had been until last night.

His gaze told her that he didn't believe her. "I spent five years surrounded by men, but I was alone because there was no one I cared about, no one I trusted. You don't have to live like that, Loree.

Pack up your belongings and I'll move you to Austin—"

She jerked away from him. "I can't."

"Why?"

"Because that night still lives inside me! You don't know what I did!"

"You survived."

Tears burned her eyes. "If only it was that simple. I'm here because I deserve to be. Call it a punishment. Call it a life sentence. Call it whatever you want. I made my decision and I'm not leaving." The tears rolled over onto her cheeks. "Despite what you thought, I knew *exactly* what you meant when you said a person makes decisions not knowing the cost—but regardless, once you act on the decision, you still have to pay the price." Five years ago, the price had been her dreams.

"Even if it costs you your life? Loree, your friend Dewayne was right. You didn't know anything about me when you accepted my offer to chop your wood for a bowl of stew. I could have been intent on hurting you."

"I took your weapons."

He released a mirthless laugh. "You think that would have stopped me?"

"Digger would have stopped you."

"You don't have Digger anymore."

She flinched at the reminder. He cursed harshly and reached for her. "Come here."

She tried to resist, but he was insistent, drawing her into his arms and pressing her face against his chest. "I'm sorry. I shouldn't have said that, but I'm worried about you, Sugar. I don't like the idea of you living out here alone."

"I'll be all right," she assured him, even though she knew it wasn't the absolute truth. After he left, she'd be lonelier than she'd ever been in her life.

He held her, his hands gliding up and down her back, comforting and strong, the silence broken only by the snap and crackle of the fire. It seemed an eternity passed before he finally spoke, and when he did, it was as though their argument had never taken place.

"I think we'll be all right if we keep the fire small like this. I could go back to tearing down the barn, tossing the planks down, and you can feed them to the fire."

Releasing her, he met her gaze. "Holler if things get out of hand."

She nodded mutely, knowing that by working with him, she would hasten his departure. Knowing that every time she gazed into the deepest depths of a fire, she would see the blue of his eyes.

By NIGHTFALL LOREE was exhausted, but she felt a measure of peace. Over half the barn was smoldering ashes.

She lay in her bed, curled beneath the covers, listening as Austin moved around in the front room. After supper, he'd dragged in the bathtub and helped her fill it with hot water. While he had tended to his horse and drenched the ashes once more, she had enjoyed the luxurious warmth of the water and pampered herself by using some French soap she'd hoarded away in her hope chest.

When she had dried off and thrown on a clean nightgown, she had opened the door to discover him sitting on the steps.

"Would you mind if I took a bath?" he'd asked quietly, and she could no more ignore that plea in his eyes imploring her to trust him than she could ignore the sun rising over the horizon.

So now he was bathing, and all she could think about was the water gliding over a chest that she had touched. She imagined him shaving, combing his hair, and slipping on his britches.

She wondered where he would bed down tonight, and continually asked herself where she wanted him to sleep. She heard several bumps followed by a scrape and knew that he was emptying the tub and taking it outside. She held her breath, waiting, listening, wondering.

The house grew silent. Rolling over, she pressed her face to the pillow in an effort to hide her disappointment. He had left her alone.

AUSTIN WALKED AROUND the house numerous times, searching for the ever elusive sleep. He knew from experience that it would be long after midnight before he'd find it.

Besides he needed to air out. Loree had used some fancy smelling bath salts, and although they smelled sweet on her, they reeked to high heaven on him. Lord, if his brothers caught a whiff of him now, he'd never hear the end of it.

That thought had him turning northwest, staring at a part of Texas that rested beyond his vision. He wondered what his brothers were doing. No doubt, whatever it was, they were doing it with their wives. He didn't begrudge them the love they had in their lives, but he did envy that they had the joy of sleeping with a woman every night—simply sleeping with her.

He'd never slept with a woman through the night until last night. He'd found it incredibly comforting to listen to Loree's soft even breathing once her tears had subsided.

He wished he'd never caused the tears. He looked at the silhouette of the remaining barn. At least he could repay her by taking away some of her painful memories—memories he wished she had never possessed.

With a deep sigh, he headed for the porch where he'd stored his gear earlier before he'd begun tearing down the barn. He thought about laying his pallet out beneath the stars, but prison had taught him to appreciate fine moments when they came along. And it had been a long time since he'd known anything finer than Loree Grant.

LOREE HEARD THE door open and held her breath. She'd long ago given up on Austin joining her and had extinguished the flame in the lamp. Now only pale moonlight spilled into the room. She listened to the soft tread of his bare feet growing nearer. She felt the bed dip beneath his weight.

He lay on top of the covers as he had last night. His arm came around her, firm and heavy. She felt his bare chest warming her back through her nightgown. He pressed his cheek against the top of her head. She heard what she thought was

and dropped the stirrup. He slung the saddlebags over the horse's rump.

"Promise me you'll have a doctor look at your back."

He stilled. "I'm not worth your worry, Loree."

"Promise me," she repeated obstinately.

He glanced over his shoulder and smiled, the first genuine smile she'd seen cross his face, and it very nearly stole her breath away. She wished he'd given it to her at noon instead of in the fading twilight where it would be nothing but a shadowed memory.

"I promise," he said.

"You keep your promises, don't you?"

"Every one I've ever made."

"Then promise me that you'll take care of yourself as well."

"Only if you promise to do the same."

She nodded, her throat constricting with all that remained unsaid. How could she have been intimate with a man and not know how to tell him everything that she wanted him to know?

"Think about moving to town," he said quietly.

"I can't."

"A woman like you deserves more than memories in her life—"

"You need to get going before it gets much darker," she whispered, the tears stinging the backs of her eyes.

"When I'm finished with my business in Austin, I could stop back by here—"

"No." She shook her head emphatically. "It'd be best if you didn't."

"I'm going to worry about you, Sugar," he said in a low voice as though he wasn't comfortable admitting his concern.

"I'll be fine," she assured him.

He gave a brusque nod and, with one lithe movement, swung up into his saddle. "If you need to get in touch with me—for any reason—I'll be staying at the Driskill Hotel."

"That's a fancy hotel."

"So I hear."

He touched the tip of his finger to the brim of his hat. "Miss Grant, you are without a doubt, the sweetest woman I've ever known."

He sent his black stallion into a gallop.

Loree watched until he disappeared in the fading twilight. Then she dropped to her knees and wept. He was wrong. A woman like her didn't deserve more than memories in her life.

She deserved to hang.

AUSTIN WALKED THE streets of the state capital wondering just what in the hell he thought he was doing. His tracking experience was limited to finding cow dung over the plains of West Texas. Dallas had taught him to use a rifle, gun, and knife but even those skills were useless here. He'd left his gun in his saddlebag in his room at the hotel.

He'd arrived near midnight, anxious to register for a room and bed down for the night. He'd been bone weary and had expected to fall asleep as soon as his head hit the pillow.

But the pillow didn't smell like the one that

graced Loree's bed. As comfortable as the bed was, it didn't have the one thing he wanted: a tiny lady who had somehow managed to slip beneath the gates that surrounded his heart.

It was ludicrous to care for her as much as he did after knowing her such a short time, but he couldn't get her out of his mind. Every time he heard soft laughter, he turned to see if it was hers. When he passed women on the street, he compared them to the woman who had tended his wound—and he found them all lacking. None carried her guileless smile. None walked without pretense. He couldn't see bare toes, smudged cheeks, or golden eyes filled with tears.

And he wanted what he couldn't have: to see those eyes filled with happiness. But even the thought of going to her had no place in his heart when he had nothing to offer her. He'd only bring her more pain until he cleared his name. If he took her to Leighton, she'd have to endure the suspicious stares that followed his every step. The shadow of his past would touch her, and he couldn't stand the thought. With that realization, his determination to find Boyd McQueen's killer increased.

He walked through the doors of a saloon and began to feel more in his element. Saloons didn't differ that much from town to town.

Wiping a glass, the bartender raised a dark brow. "What can I do for you?"

Austin tilted his head toward the sign above the bar that boasted BARTON SPRINGS HIGH GRADE WHISKIES.

"I'll take a whiskey."

The bartender smiled. "Good choice."

He poured the amber brew into a glass and set it in front of Austin. Austin leaned forward, placed his elbows on the counter, and wrapped his hands around the glass. "You get a lot of business in here?"

The bartender nodded. "At night mostly. Not that much during the day."

"Could you get word out that I'm paying fifty dollars to anyone who knows anything about a man named Boyd McQueen?"

The bartender sucked one end of his mustache into the corner of his mouth and began to chew, his eyes narrowing in thought. "Other fella's paying five hundred."

Austin's stomach tightened into a hard ball. "What fella?"

The bartender nodded toward the back. "The fella at that table in the corner."

Austin turned and studied the man sitting at a distant table. Dressed in a black jacket and red brocade vest, he reminded Austin of a gambler. His fingers nimbly set one card after another on the table.

"Just sits there and plays cards by himself all day," the bartender offered.

"I'll take the bottle of whiskey," Austin said as he laid down his money and grabbed the neck of the bottle along with his glass. He ambled across the hardwood floor, his spurs jangling. He found comfort in the sound he'd been without for five years. "Hear you're looking for information on Boyd McQueen."

The man raised his eyes from the cards, pinning Austin with his dark gaze. "Yep."

"Found out anything so far?"

"Nope."

Not appreciating the man's brief answers, Austin tethered his temper. "Five hundred dollars is a lot of money—"

"Ain't coming out of my pocket."

Suspicion lurked in the back of Austin's mind. "Whose pocket is it coming out of?"

"Your brother's." With the toe of his boot, the man shoved a chair away from the table. "Have a seat."

"You're the detective Dallas hired?"

"Yep."

Cautiously Austin settled into the chair. "How did you know who I was?"

"You've got your brother's eyes."

Austin released a breath of disgust. "No wonder you haven't located the person who murdered Boyd. Dallas has brown eyes." He leaned forward, opening his eyes wide. "Mine are blue."

"They're shaped the same, and they both show a man of little patience. You've got his thick brows, his square chin, and a jaw that tightens when you're angry." With one hand, he swept up the cards spread over the table and rearranged them with a quiet shuffle. "And you walk like a man who just spent five years in prison and doesn't know if he can trust anyone."

Austin downed his whiskey, refilled his glass, and poured the amber liquid into the empty glass resting beside the man's arm. He didn't particularly like that the man had summed him up so easily and precisely. Between the town folk actually thinking him capable of murder and Becky's betrayal, he'd lost a great deal of his faith in his fellow man. Although Loree's touch had certainly made him want to believe in the worth of people. "Dallas didn't tell me your name."

"Wylan Alexander."

"What brought you to this town?"

"Your brother sent me a telegram."

Austin leaned forward. "What do you think of my theory that Boyd meant this town and not me when he wrote 'Austin' in the dirt?"

Wylan slapped the cards down on the table and swallowed all the whiskey in his glass before meeting Austin's gaze. "I'm here, ain't I?"

"But you think it's hogwash."

Wylan shook his head and patiently began laying the cards one face up, six face down. "I'll admit when I got your brother's telegram telling me what you thought, I laughed out loud, but I'm as desperate as you are and just as angry. It's never taken me more than six weeks to solve a case. This one's been hanging around too long and it's ruining my reputation, not to mention being hard on my pride. If McQueen hadn't written your name in the dirt, I'd say he was in the wrong place at the wrong time and some drifter got lucky."

Austin rubbed his hands up and down his face. "But he did write my name. Damn, I wish my parents had been living in Galveston when I was born."

Wylan chuckled. "Yep, might have saved us all some grief."

Austin took a sip of the whiskey. "You haven't learned anything at all?"

"Unfortunately, no."

"So what do we do?"

Wylan began to turn up cards and rearrange the ones on the table. "We wait."

WAITING HAD NEVER been Austin's strong suit. He had thought prison guards had beat patience into him, but now that he was once again his own man—no longer a slave of the state—impatience had become his companion.

He had spent three days walking the streets, talking to people in saloons. The seedier the saloon, the more hopeful he had been that he would glean some information. Although Boyd McQueen had appeared upstanding to many in the community, he had possessed a darker side that curdled Austin's gut. He had to admit that it didn't bother him that the man had come to an untimely end. His only regret was that he had been the one to pay for it.

He had hoped by now that he would have had a glimmer of information. He walked past the post office and approached the Griedenweiss stables. He had a need to ride fast and hard over the hills, to feel Black Thunder's hooves pounding the ground beneath him, taking him away from an elusive quest toward . . . an unknown future.

Out of the corner of his eye, he saw a slight movement and shifted his gaze. A boy no older than seven was pulling a wooden wagon along the boardwalk. A sign hung over the side of the wagon.

PUPYS 4 SALE
2 BITS

Austin changed directions, ambled across the street, and easily caught up with the boy. "What you got here?" he asked.

The boy ground to a halt and furrowed his brow. "Don't you read?"

Austin smiled. "Yeah, I do. What kind of dogs are these?"

Confusion filled the boy's brown eyes as he swiped his nose with his sleeve. "The kind that's got four legs and a tail."

Smothering a grin, Austin hunkered down beside the wagon. The boy obviously didn't know a lot about breeding. Austin peered at the two puppies tumbling over each other. The tiny brown and white one caught his fancy. He scooped it up and studied it from all angles.

"That one's a boy," the child told him.

"Yeah, I can see that. How big was his mama?"

The boy held his hand level with his waist. "'Bout this big."

"Think he'll be a good hunting dog?"

The boy nodded his head briskly. Austin figured he didn't know if the dog would be good at hunting, but he needed to get rid of him. The puppy squirmed, yipped, and gnawed on his thumb. A fighter. He liked that. "I'll take this one."

"The other one's better," the boy said.

"Why is that?"

"On account of the other one's a girl. If you git her, some day you can git more dogs that won't cost you nothing."

Grinning, Austin unfolded his body and reached into his pocket for a quarter. "I only need one."

He handed the silver coin to the boy. "Don't spend it all in one place," Austin said, tucking the dog beneath his arm.

Feeling more content than he had in days, Austin ambled to the livery and had one of the workers saddle Black Thunder. He mounted the horse and settled the dog into the crook of his thigh. Then he turned the stallion west and prodded him into an easy lope.

He reached his destination just as the sun began to paint its farewell across the sky. It had been a long time since he'd thought of the sunset as anything but the sun going down, yet he almost imagined he heard the fiery ball announcing the end of its daily journey.

His heart pounding as the weathered house came into view, he brought Black Thunder to a walk. He saw Loree sitting on the porch, her elbows on her knees, her chin cradled in her palms as she gazed into the distance. Her braid was draped over her shoulder, the bottom curling near her waist. As though sensing his presence, she straightened and looked in his direction. Slowly, she rose to her feet, a tentative smile playing across her lips. "Hello."

His heart felt as though someone had just closed

a meaty fist around it. He drew the horse to a halt near the porch. "Howdy."

She crossed one bare foot over the other and put her hands behind her back, causing the worn material of her dress to stretch taut across her breasts. Austin's mouth went as dry as the West Texas wind in August.

"Did you find the man you were looking for?"

"No."

She peered around Black Thunder, obvious curiosity furrowing her delicate brow. "What are you holding?"

Austin glanced at his thigh. "Dog."

Dismounting, he remembered a time when he could have spoken more than one word without his throat closing off. She'd urged him not to return, and he had been leery of the welcome she'd bestow upon him. He wouldn't have blamed her for leveling her rifle at him and pulling the trigger this time. Cradling the animal in his palm, he extended it toward her. "It's for you."

Tears welled in her eyes, and her smile faltered before returning brighter than before. She took the puppy and rubbed it against her cheek. "He's beautiful."

She dropped to the porch and set the dog on her lap, running her small hands over the brown and white fur, and Austin knew a pang of envy.

She leaned close to the dog. "Do you have a name?"

His pink tongue snaked out and licked her chin, her nose. Loree laughed and Austin felt a shaft of pure joy pierce his soul. She looked up at him. "Does he have a name?"

Austin eased down to the porch, keeping a respectful distance, knowing it was ludicrous to even worry about respectability after all they'd shared. "Between town and here, I was calling him Two-bits. That's what he cost me."

"Two-bits," she repeated as she scratched behind the dog's short ears. The dog's body visibly quivered, and it released a little sound deep in its throat that had Austin shifting his butt on the porch, wondering what it would take to get Loree to rub her hands over him.

She peered at him. "Thank you."

"My pleasure." It truly was his pleasure to see her eyes shining like gold touched by the sun, and he wished he had more to offer her. She turned her attention back to the dog, and Austin shifted his gaze to the sunset, realizing why he'd come here. In town, surrounded by people, the loneliness had sharpened and grown. But here on this porch, sitting beside this woman, the loneliness eased away.

"Were you and Becky engaged?"

He snapped his head around and met her hesitant gaze. She licked her lips. "I was just curious. I always thought I'd know everything there was to know about a man before I . . ."

Even in the fading light, he saw the embarrassment flaming her cheeks. He watched her swallow.

"It just seems to me that we . . . we got ahead of ourselves," she said softly.

She struggled to hold his gaze, and his heart

went out to her. He owed her. More than he could ever pay. Leaning forward, he planted his elbows on his thighs and clasped his hands tightly together. "No, we weren't engaged. We'd talked about getting married, but we never announced it. Guess I thought the talking about it etched it in stone, and that wasn't the way of it."

"Did you know the man she married?"

"He was my best friend."

Sympathy filled her eyes. "That must have been so hard—to lose Becky and your best friend."

He shrugged. "I always told Cameron that he needed to take care of Becky if I couldn't. Reckon he took my instructions to heart." He worked his jaw back and forth, knowing he should stop there, but this woman had a way about her that made him want to continue. "They've got a son. That hurt, seeing him for the first time. Until then, I thought . . ."

She leaned toward him. "What did you think?"

His mouth grew dry, and he stared at the scuffed toes of his boots. "That maybe she wasn't lying in Cameron's arms at night." He unclasped his hands, afraid the tension radiating through him would snap a bone.

"Do you think she's happy?"

He wiped his sweating hands on his thighs. "I hope she is." Peering over at her, he gave her a sad smile. "Truly I hope she is."

Reaching out, she threaded her fingers through his. "I imagine she wishes the same for you."

Strangely, he thought she was probably right. He

closed his fingers gently around hers and rubbed the thumb of his free hand back and forth across her knuckles. "So tell me about Jake."

She drew her brows together. "Jake?"

Unwarranted joy shot through him, and he had to fight like the devil to keep the smile buried deep within his chest, to keep his face serious. He'd suspected that there had been no Jake in her life. "Yeah, Jake. Remember? You were thinking about him—"

Her eyes widened. "Oh, Jake."

She tried to pull her hand from his, but Austin tightened his grip. "So tell me about him."

The dog tumbled out of her lap, hit the ground with a yip, and pounced after a bug. Loree stopped struggling and lowered her gaze to her bare toes. "There is no Jake."

Austin slipped his finger beneath her chin and tilted her face back until her gaze met his. "I suspected as much."

"Why? Because I'm so plain?"

"You're not plain, Loree. There's something about you—a sweetness that just bubbles up from deep inside you. It touches your eyes, your lips. Once a man had gained your affections, he'd be a fool to leave you." He grazed his thumb over her full lower lip. "I have been known to be a fool."

"You say that as though you had gained my affections. If you believe that, you assume too much. I don't even know you. I was hurting and needed comfort. You offered, and as wrong as it was, I took. That's all."

"Was it wrong, Loree?"

In the encroaching darkness, he still saw the tears welling in her eyes as she nodded briskly.

"Why did you have to say her name?" she rasped. "Now, I can't even pretend you wanted me. I *know* you were thinking of someone else." She shot off the porch like a bullet fired from a rifle. She waved her hand dismissively in the air. "It doesn't matter. You used me. I used you." She scooped up the dog and hugged it close against her breast. "You don't owe me anything."

But it did matter, and he did owe her because he didn't think Loree Grant could *use* someone if her life depended on it. He came slowly to his feet, his gaze never leaving hers. "Maybe I owe me something."

"What does that mean?" she asked.

"I'm not sure." He mounted Black Thunder and touched his finger to the brim of his hat. "Take care, Miss Grant."

He set his heels to his horse's sides and sent him into a lope. Austin had spent five years thinking about an auburn-haired, blue-eyed beauty. He didn't intend to spend the rest of his life thinking about a golden-eyed, blond-haired woman who had touched him one night and sent all his common sense to perdition.

He'd given her the damn dog. He had nothing else to offer her. And she was right. Even his heart wasn't free.

Chapter Six

Austin Leigh owed her nothing. Loree repeated that litany in the following days as she watched Two-bits romp through her garden. The dog was a fierce protector. As she watched him attack the worms he uncovered, she couldn't remember when she'd laughed so hard.

Two-bits would never replace Digger in her heart, but he was slowly earning his own place, different but just as precious. She wondered if any woman would ever replace the woman Austin held in his heart. She thought it unlikely. She doubted that his heart even held room for another.

She wished she had kept her hurt buried deep inside and hadn't shown it to him when he visited her. She had driven him away with her accusations. He'd never return now. She knew it was for the best, but the loneliness increased because for some unfathomable reason when she had seen him sitting astride his horse, it felt as though a part of her had come home.

Standing in her garden, she heard the rapid

clop of horses' hooves and the whirl of wheels. She spun around, her heart imitating the rapid motion of the buggy as it approached, two matching bay horses trotting before it. Austin pulled back on the reins, jumped out of the black buggy, and swept his hat from his head. "Morning, Miss Grant."

Her breath hitched at the warm smile he bestowed upon her. "What are you doing?"

"Well . . ." He turned his hat in his hands as he walked toward her. "I told you my parents had lived near Austin. My brother drew a map of the area for me before I left. I woke up this morning with a hankering to see the old homestead. I was hoping you'd give me the pleasure of your company."

He halted his steps and his fingers tightened around the brim of his hat. "But I'm not courting you, Loree. I've got nothing to offer you so I want to make that clear at the outset, but since you'd mentioned not knowing me well . . . and thinking that you should, I just thought you might like to come." His smile lessened. "And I'd like for you to be there with me."

"I could pack some food and we could have a picnic."

His smile returned, deeper than before. "I had the kitchen staff at the hotel fix us something and I bundled up the blankets from my bed . . ." His gaze slowly roamed over her. "So you wouldn't have to get your britches dirty."

"Oh." She glanced down at her brother's clothes. "Do you have time for me to change into a dress?"

He settled his hat into place. "I have time for you to do anything you want."

"I won't be long," she assured him as she hurried past him and scurried into the house, her heart beating so hard she was certain he'd been able to hear it. He had come back. His reasons didn't matter, and she didn't care that he wasn't courting her. She would spend the day without the loneliness eating at her.

She washed up quickly before donning the faded yellow dress. She rolled the stockings over her calloused feet and up her calves before reaching beneath the bed and dragging out her black shoes. She worked her feet into the hated leather, reached for the button hook, and sealed her feet into what she'd always considered an instrument of torture.

But for reasons she couldn't understand, today, she was glad she'd kept them. She almost twisted her ankle with the first step she took toward the mirror. She gazed at her reflection, wishing the dress were a bit more fashionable, her hair more colorful. She wasn't a beauty. Yet Austin had rented a buggy and two horses and driven out here, seeking her company, when surely he had met women in town.

She tossed the braid over her shoulder, hating the way it made her look like a little girl. But she had never tried to sweep it up into a womanly fashion and had no idea where to begin. With a sigh, she grabbed a ragged shawl just in case they didn't get back before nightfall and headed out the door.

Austin shoved himself away from the porch beam as she closed the door, the shawl draped over her arm. She hadn't noticed before how his shirt appeared to be freshly laundered, recently ironed. His hair no longer curled around his collar, but was slightly shorter, cut even along the edges, and when the breeze blew by him and traveled to her, she smelled soap and a scent that was uniquely his. For a man who wasn't courting, he'd gone to a lot of trouble. When she had finished her slow perusal, she lifted her gaze to his sparkling blue eyes.

"You're wearing shoes," he said quietly, but she heard the amusement in his voice. "I was beginning to wonder if you owned a pair."

"I wear them in winter . . . and on special occasions." The heat warmed her cheeks. "I've never taken a ride in a buggy."

"Then you're in for a treat. This buggy rides well."

She stepped off the porch, and he fell in step beside her, his hand coming to rest easily on the small of her back. The buggy had two seats. The bench in the back held two boxes.

"What's in the boxes?" she asked.

"Our lunch is in one, and your dog is in the other."

Looking up at him, she nearly tripped over her feet. He steadied her and smiled. "Didn't figure you'd want to leave him here alone. I put him in the box with some blankets and my pocket watch. He went right to sleep."

He took her hand, helped her into the carriage,

and settled beside her, his thigh brushing hers. She pressed her knees together and clenched her hands in her lap. He lifted the reins and gave the horses a gentle rap on the backside. In unison, they surged forward into a trot.

They rode in silence for several moments, the countryside unfolding before them, bathed in the blue of bluebonnets.

"I love this time of year," Loree said wistfully, "when the flowers coat the hills."

"Their fragrance reminds me of you."

Peering at him, finding his gaze fastened on her, she released a self-conscious laugh. "I gather them up, dry them out, and sprinkle the petals around the house. Sometimes I put them in my bath water."

His eyes darkened and she wondered if he was thinking of the night when he'd washed her. His gaze drifted down to her lips and she knew he was.

"How far away is your old home?" she asked hastily.

"If my brother's map is accurate, I figure an hour or so."

The journey took a little over two hours, and Loree thought it was the most pleasant two hours of her life, even though they spoke little. When he finally drew the buggy to a halt, Loree felt a somberness come over him. She couldn't say that she blamed him. Weeds, overgrowth, and a dilapidated structure that might have once been a one-room cabin greeted them.

Although she had grown up with little, she

knew she'd had more than he might have possessed here. The buggy rocked as he climbed out. He walked around the horses and came to her side, extending his hand. He helped her out, then reached beneath the seat and gathered up a handful of bluebonnets. She was surprised to feel the slight trembling in his hand as he wrapped it around hers.

"I don't remember much about the place," he said quietly as he led her away from the buggy.

"How old were you when you left?" she asked.

"Five."

They walked until they reached a towering oak tree, the branches spreading out gracefully, the abundant leaves whispering in the breeze. Hanging from the lowest branch, a swing made of fraying rope and weathered wood swayed slightly. On the ground to the right of it, among the weeds and briars, stood a wooden marker.

Lovita Leigh.
Wife and Mother.
Deeply Loved, Sorely Missed
1829–1865

Austin released Loree's hand, removed his hat, dropped to one knee beside the grave, pulled at the weeds until he'd made a small clearing, and placed the flowers in front of the marker. He braced his forearm on his thigh and bowed his head.

Loree knew a moment's hesitation, feeling awkward because she was familiar with every aspect of the outer man and understood so little of the man who dwelled inside. Yet from the beginning, she had been drawn to him and the anguish in his eyes that spoke when his voice didn't.

She knelt beside him and laid her hand on his forearm, squeezing gently. He turned his hand slightly and moved it back until he was able to intertwine his fingers with hers.

"I don't remember what she looked like," he said quietly. "A man should remember his mother."

"You do remember her or you wouldn't have felt a need to come here." She touched the blue petals of the flowers he'd set on the ground. "I bet you picked flowers for her."

A faraway look came into his eyes and a corner of his mouth quirked up. "Yeah, I did. She laughed. Not because she thought it was funny, but because it made her happy." He closed his eyes. "Lord, she had a pretty laugh . . . like music."

"Did she tell you stories at bedtime?"

He opened his eyes, and it gladdened her heart to see that a small portion of the sadness had melted away.

"She told me stories, but not with words. She used songs. I remember she'd sit on the edge of my bed, and I'd watch her fingers caress the violin strings as she moved the bow and the most beautiful sounds flowed from the wood through the strings. I tried so hard not to fall asleep so I could keep watching her hands. I loved watching her hands." Turning his head slightly, he smiled warmly. "I remember her hands. She had the longest fingers—"

"Like yours."

Surprise flitted across his face. He lifted the hand she wasn't holding, turned it, and studied it from all angles. "I reckon so. I never noticed before."

"You should learn to play the violin."

She felt his hand stiffen within hers.

"You have to hear the music in your heart before you can create it with a fiddle. I can't do that," he said.

"You could try—"

"I can't."

He surged to his feet, pulling her up with him, his fingers tightening around hers as he walked away from the grave. Loree stumbled as she followed. He swung around, caught, and steadied her.

"You all right?" he asked, concern clearly reflected in his eyes.

Her cheeks grew warm, and she suddenly wished she'd spent the last five years practicing to be a lady as her mother had wanted instead of a hoyden thinking no man would ever look at her the way Austin Leigh was looking at her now. She nodded jerkily and gave him a wan smile. "I'm just used to ground beneath my feet instead of leather."

As though amused, he slowly shook his head and glanced at her scuffed shoes. Unexpectedly he dropped to one knee and slapped his raised thigh. "Put your foot up here."

"What are you going to do?"

He grabbed her ankle and lifted her foot. Thrown off-balance, she clamped her fingers onto his shoulder to brace herself. She watched in amazement as he freed the buttons on her shoe. She thought about jerking her foot back, insisting the shoes stay where they were, but he dropped his head back and she fell into the depths of his blue, blue eyes. How many times during the past week had she caught herself staring into the flames of a fire, searching for the warmth of his gaze?

He worked her shoe off, and when she would have removed her stockinged foot from his thigh, he covered it with his palm and held it in place. His gaze holding hers, he slowly guided his hands over her ankle, beneath her skirt, up her calf, past her knee, until his fingers grazed the bare flesh of her thigh just above her stockings. Scalding heat shot through her, and she dug her fingers into his shoulders.

Using his thumbs, he rolled her stocking down her leg, while his fingers trailed over her skin, his gaze never leaving hers, the blue darkening until she felt as though he had ignited something within her. Her heart beat so hard that she was certain he'd be able to feel the pounding in her toes. He skimmed her stocking over her foot, and finally lowered his gaze to her bare foot. He rubbed his finger over the top of her foot.

"You've got the cutest toes."

"They're crooked," she told him as though he didn't have a clear view of her toes as he massaged each toe thoroughly before moving onto the next.

Feeling as though every bone in her body was melting, she was surprised she still had the ability to stand.

"Did you break this toe?" he asked when he reached the toe next to her biggest toe.

"No. My pa had toes like that. He called it a hammer toe. See, it looks like a hammer."

He gave her a grin that very nearly caused all the breath to leave her body. She was too aware of him. Memories of his touching her in the ways that a man touched a woman threatened to turn from cold ashes into a blazing fire. She jerked her foot off his thigh.

As though he knew exactly what she'd been remembering, he patted his thigh and his smile grew. "Other foot."

She took a deep calming breath. "I can take it off." To her embarrassment, her voice hitched, but he didn't laugh. He just turned those blue eyes on her, challenging her. "Come on, Sugar. Give me your other foot before you break your pretty neck."

She had never been able to resist a challenge. She stomped her foot onto his thigh. He laughed deeply, richly, like a man remembering what it was to enjoy life.

"So you've got a bit of a temper," he said as he attacked the buttons.

"Sometimes." She watched the deftness with which his fingers worked. "Not often."

He dropped her shoe to the ground and started gliding his hands over her leg. She wasn't certain she could survive his removing the other stocking, and when he lifted his gaze to hers, she was certain she wouldn't.

"Where's your father?" she blurted, to distract

herself from the heavenly sensation of his fingers sliding beneath her skirt.

He blinked, halting his hands behind her knee. "He died at Chickamauga."

"So he fought in the war."

"Yep."

"Who raised you then?"

"My brothers."

He had mentioned the one. "How many do you have?"

"Two. They're considerably older than me. Both fought in the war alongside my pa. I don't remember my pa at all, but my oldest brother supposedly looks just like him."

He began to massage her knee.

"Aren't you getting tired of kneeling?"

He smiled warmly. "Nope."

"I'm getting tired of standing on one leg."

He barely looked contrite as he apologized and rolled down her stocking. As soon as her stocking cleared her toes, she removed her foot from his thigh. He didn't appear offended as he stuffed her stocking into her shoe.

Loree took a moment to relish the feel of the grass beneath her soles, but it somehow paled in comparison to his warm thigh against her foot. He grabbed her shoes and unfolded his long, lanky body.

"I'll put these in the carriage," he offered.

She watched him walk to the carriage, wishing she didn't have so many mixed emotions where he was concerned. Dreading the feelings his touch stirred within her, desperately wanting the easing of the loneliness that his presence caused. As often as Dewayne visited, he never managed to take the loneliness away.

Austin scooped Two-bits out of the box and set him on the ground, laughing as the dog scampered after a butterfly. She liked the rumble of his laughter, the glow in his eyes as he walked to her, the slight curving of his lips, and the warmth of his hand as he wrapped it around hers before they continued their journey into his past.

NIGHT HAD FALLEN by the time Austin brought the buggy to a halt in front of Loree's house. He set the box containing the sleeping puppy on the table, lit a lamp, and walked through the house as though he owned it, checking all the dark corners and closets.

"Everything seems to be in order," he said, his voice low, and Loree wondered why everyone always talked quieter at night.

Her gaze drifted toward the bedroom door, and she wondered what, if anything, he expected now. Once an intimacy had been shared, how did one establish boundaries?

"I appreciate that you went with me today."

She snapped her gaze to his. "I enjoyed it."

"Did you?" he asked, turning his hat in his hands.

She smiled softly. "Yes, I did."

"Good." He glanced quickly around the room. "I'd best get back to town, get the buggy and horses turned into the livery."

With long strides he crossed the room and opened the door. Loree followed him onto the porch, the pale light from the lamp spilling through the doorway and across his face. Within the shadows, she saw his fingers working the brim of his hat.

"Loree . . ."

Her breath caught and held. She didn't know where she'd find the strength to refuse him if he asked to come back inside. He took a step nearer and rubbed his knuckles across her cheek.

"Loree, I'm not courting you," he said quietly.

"You told me that earlier today. I haven't forgotten."

"I just want to make sure that you understand that."

"I do."

"Good."

His mouth swooped down to cover hers, his arm snaking around her waist, drawing her flush against his body. Hot, moist, and hungry, his lips taunted and teased. Of their own accord, her arms wound around his neck, and she returned his kiss with equal fervor. She knew it was wrong. She had nothing of permanence to offer him.

When he finally drew away, Loree was surprised her legs were able to support her.

"Get inside before I do something we both regret," he rasped in a ragged voice.

She nodded, slipped inside, and closed the door. She pressed her ear against it. It was long moments before she heard his boots hitting the porch, carrying him away, before she heard the buggy roll into the night.

She sank to the floor and buried her face in her hands, but she couldn't hide from the truth. Had he asked, she would have invited him to stay.

Chapter Seven

Austin stared at the five cards in his hand. The queen of hearts looked damned lonely with no other face cards to keep her company. He understood that feeling. Christ, loneliness had been his companion for most of his life. He loved his brothers, but hanging on to their shirttails, he'd found little affection and when it came, it had been little more than a quick nod of the head for a job well done. He didn't resent that. A man's world was decidedly different from a woman's.

Amelia had taught him that affection deepened with a touch: slender fingers on a clenched fist, a hand rubbing a shoulder, a hug, or a kiss on the cheek. Small things that breached the mighty wall of lonesomeness. But Amelia had belonged first to Dallas, then to Houston, never to Austin. As much as she had eased his forlorn heart, she had also left him wanting. Until he'd first set eyes on Becky.

She had been his: to look at, to smile at, to laugh with—whenever he wanted. But he'd kept his hands and lips to himself, waiting until she was old enough. She had been nearly seventeen, the first time he'd kissed her. And nine months later, he was sitting in a cold barren cell with nothing but the memories. And the loneliness had increased because he had known what it was to live without it.

He told himself that it was loneliness that had him riding out to Loree Grant's house late into the night. He'd simply sit astride Black Thunder and stare at the shadowed house. More than once he had to stop himself from dismounting and knocking on her door. He didn't imagine she'd appreciate being disturbed from her slumber at two o'clock in the morning. And what could he have said?

I can't sleep without holding you, smelling you, listening to your breath whispering into the night.

He'd gone so far as to pull bluebonnets from the fields and stuff them beneath his pillow at the hotel just so he could pretend she was near.

It had been a week since he'd taken her to the old homestead and his loneliness had increased with each passing day. He wasn't in a position to court her, had nothing to offer her, and even though he'd told her that, he had seen a measure of hope reflected in her golden eyes. He couldn't bear the thought of disappointing her, and he feared if he spent much more time with her, he might do just that.

"You in or out?"

Austin snapped his gaze up to the detective's. Wylan had lifted a brow. Austin tossed down his cards. "I feel like we're wasting our time. Or at least I am. I might as well be spitting in a high wind for all the good I'm doing here."

Wylan gathered up the cards and began his infuriating silent shuffle. "I finished visiting the last of the brothels last night. Didn't glean any information."

"You've been visiting brothels?"

"Yep. No telling what a man might say in the heat of passion."

Austin knew too well the truth of that statement. "I could have saved you the trouble."

Wylan smiled. "Oh, it was no trouble."

The man's easy attitude was beginning to wear thin. Austin planted his elbows on the table and leaned forward. "Boyd McQueen had a preference for boys."

The cards Wylan had been shuffling went flying out of his hands and disbelief swept over his face. "What?"

Austin rubbed his jaw wondering how much he could say without causing harm. He'd learned of Boyd's perversions from Rawley. Furious over a past he'd been unable to change, Austin had shot a bullet over Boyd's head in the saloon and announced that nothing would have brought him greater pleasure than to rid the ground of Boyd's shadow. Those words had served to condemn him as much as Boyd writing "Austin" in the dirt. Austin sighed deeply. "Boyd took pleasure in hurting boys, among other things."

"Your brother's son?"

"I didn't say that."

"You didn't have to. The boy has a haunted

look in his eyes. I just couldn't figure out what had put it there." Wylan poured himself a whiskey and downed it in one swallow. "I gotta tell you, the more I learn about Boyd McQueen the more I hope I don't find the man who killed him. But then there's the matter of your innocence."

Austin fingered his glass of whiskey. "I spent five years thinking someone had killed him and purposely put the blame on me. The thought of getting even burned inside me. Now, I'm beginning to think I just got unlucky. No one set out to hurt me. Someone murdered Boyd, and I got blamed for it. If it hadn't destroyed my life, I'd be applauding whoever killed him."

"Which is the reason I'll keep looking, but this gives me a different angle: an irate father, a young boy McQueen might have hurt who finally grew to manhood . . . People will be less likely to share that sort of information, but I'll keep that in mind as I'm digging."

"I'm thinking of heading home. I can't see that I'm doing any good here. Boyd stole five years of my life. I don't want him taking any more."

Wylan gathered up his scattered cards and began to play a game of solitaire. "I'm going to stay here a few more days, then head back to Kansas, see if this new information brings anything to the surface."

The McQueens had moved to Texas from Kansas several years back. If Dee hadn't brought such joy to Dallas's life, Austin would have wished they'd never left Kansas.

"Mr. Leigh?"

Austin glanced up at the hesitant voice. Recognition dawned and he slowly came to his feet. "Dewayne, isn't it?"

"Yes, sir. I was out visiting Loree today. She looks a might poorly. I have a feeling you're the cause, but she said it ain't my place to judge."

Guilt cut through him like a rusty knife. He should have honored her request that he never return. "That was mighty generous of her."

"She's a generous sort—to a fault, if you want to know the truth. I don't like to see her hurt."

"I have no intention of hurting her." It was that intention that had kept him away from her when everything inside him wanted to see her again.

"Well, see that you don't 'cuz you'd have to answer to me if you did."

Dewayne spun on his heel. Austin dropped into his chair and met Wylan's speculative gaze.

"What was all that about?"

"Personal," Austin said just before he downed his whiskey, relishing the burning in his gut. Dewayne obviously had a soft spot for Loree. Hell, who wouldn't?

"Nothing that might help me find Boyd's killer?"

"No, but what would it cost me to have you search for another killer?"

"Not a cent. Your brother is paying me enough to find ten killers."

"What information would you need?"

"Name helps. Description. Anything at all. What do you know about him?"

"Not much. He killed a family—"

"Mr. Leigh?"

Austin jerked his head around. Dewayne held out an envelope. "I forgot that Loree asked me to drop this off at the Driskill for you, but reckon I can just give it to you here."

Austin took the envelope, studying the scrawl on the paper that looked as though it had been written with a trembling hand. "'Preciate it."

Dewayne gave him a slow nod before sauntering away.

"That from your Loree?"

"She's not *my* Loree." Austin tore open the envelope and pulled out the letter she'd written. The words had joy, fear, and dread weaving through him. He surged to his feet, knocking the chair over.

"What is it?"

"I was wrong. She is my Loree. Do whatever it takes to find Boyd's killer. I'm headin' back to Dallas's ranch."

His Loree. Austin stood in the doorway of her bedroom, watching her. She was too trusting, leaving the front door and the door to her bedroom open. And the dog wasn't a damn bit of good. It had neither heard nor smelled his approach, but just continued to gnaw on one of Loree's black shoes near the bed, growling at it as though it were a threat when the real threat was leaning against her doorjamb.

In her daisy colored dress, she sat on the floor, her legs tucked beneath her, her toes peering out from under her backside. Her thick braid was draped over her shoulder. She had opened a wooden chest and was slowly removing tiny pieces of clothing, spreading them over her lap, and pressing them flat with her fingers, as though each garment was precious—as precious as the child growing within her.

His child.

His knees felt like a couple of strawberries left too long on the vine, until they were soft and worthless. Her note had asked nothing of him. She expected nothing from him. She had simply wanted him to know that she was carrying his child.

He'd gathered up his belongings at the hotel, saddled Black Thunder, and ridden hard, every word of her letter emblazoned on his mind, echoing through his heart. He wished he could offer her more than an uncertain future and broken dreams.

He shoved himself away from the doorjamb. His boot heels echoed through the room as he walked toward her, his stomach knotted as though someone had lassoed it and given the rope a hard tug. She jerked her head around, the wariness in her golden eyes remaining as he neared. Sweeping his hat from his head, he hunkered down beside her. "Howdy."

She gave him a tentative smile, her fingers wrinkling the tiny gown she'd just smoothed across her lap. "Hello."

"Dewayne gave me your letter."

"You didn't have to come."

A shaft of deep sadness pierced his soul. "You don't know me at all, Loree, if you believe that."

Tears welled in her eyes as she dropped her gaze to the delicate clothing in her lap. Reaching out with his thumb, he captured a teardrop that slowly rolled from the corner of her eye. "I'm going home, Loree."

She snapped her gaze up to his. "You found the man you were looking for?"

"No, but I think it's unlikely that I ever will, after all this time. I spent the past five years dying. I want to start living again."

She gave him a hesitant smile. "I don't even know where your home is."

"West Texas. My brother has a ranch. For as long as I can remember, I've helped him work his spread, herd his cattle."

Her smile grew. "I guessed that you were a cowboy."

Not by choice. He'd always hated ranching, had always dreamed of leaving, but the places life had taken him weren't exactly what he'd had in mind. His gaze drifted to her stomach, flat as a board. He was about to travel another trail he hadn't knowingly chosen, but oddly, he had a feeling this one would leave him with no regrets.

"I'd be real honored if you'd marry me," he said, his voice low.

More tears filled her eyes just before she averted her gaze. He wished the blue flowers hadn't disappeared from the hills. He would have liked to have brought her some. Maybe he should have settled for the red and yellow flowers that remained. Or maybe he should have brought her a bright yellow ribbon for her hair, anything to accompany the words that sounded as cold as a river in January. He watched helplessly as she swiped the tears from her eyes, knowing he was the cause.

She peered at him and gave him the saddest smile he'd ever seen. "No."

He felt as though she'd just hit him in the chest with an iron skillet. "What do you mean no?"

"I mean I don't want to get married."

"Then why did you send me the note?"

"I just thought you had a right to know about the child."

"I have more than the right to know. I have the responsibility to care for it. I'm not gonna have him labeled a bastard."

She flinched and angled her chin. "Her."

"What?"

"I think it's a girl."

That made sense to him since it seemed the Leigh men were only capable of producing girls. "All right, fine. It's a girl. You want her whispered about 'cuz that's what'll happen." He softened his voice. "And they'll whisper about you, too, and don't tell me that there's nobody around to notice. You can't live like a hermit with a child. You can't deny her the world just because you've seen the ugliest side of it. Marry me, Loree."

"Do you love me?"

Her quietly spoken question was like a fist closing around his heart. "I like you well enough," he answered honestly. "Don't you like me?"

"I like what I know of you, but what do I really know? Until a few minutes ago, your home could have been on the moon as far as I knew."

"Well, I *don't* live on the moon. I live in West Texas, and I have the means to provide for you—not in as grand a fashion as I'd like, but I think it'd be tolerable."

"Tolerable?"

"Dammit, Loree! I wronged you and I'm willing to do whatever it takes to make it right."

"How does convincing me to marry a man who doesn't love me make it right?"

"Maybe it doesn't make it right for us, but it'll make it right for the baby. We have to put her first."

"Do you still love Becky?"

His stomach tightened, and he clenched his jaw. Wylan had certainly been right about words spoken in the heat of passion. He'd uttered one word, and this woman was going to hold it against him for the rest of his life. He surged to his feet and stormed from the house. He headed for the woodpile, worked the ax out of the stump, lifted a log, and slammed the ax into it.

He tried to put himself in Loree's place, remembering the relief he'd felt when she'd confessed there was no Jake. Only for her, there would always be a Becky. His first love.

"What are you doing?" she asked from behind him.

He tossed the split wood onto the pile and hefted another log to the stump. "Chopping you twenty years worth of wood. I'm gonna repair your house, paint it, and do anything else around here that needs to be done. You don't want to marry me? Fine. But I'll be damned before a child of mine is gonna suffer because of mistakes I made."

I'LL BE DAMNED before a child of mine is gonna suffer because of mistakes I made.

Those words echoed through Loree's mind as she lay in her bed unable to sleep. They told her a lot about the man. He accepted responsibility for his actions.

But then, if she were honest with herself, she'd already known that, had learned that fact about him the first night when he'd chopped wood for a bowl of stew.

She didn't know the little things about him: his favorite foods, preferred colors. She didn't know if he danced or sang.

But she knew the important things: He was a rare man who thought more with his heart than his head. When he loved, he loved deeply and years didn't diminish his affections even when memories faded. She had seen him weep over the loss of a woman, had watched him place flowers on the twenty-year-old grave of his mother. Had welcomed his gifts of a burned barn and a puppy.

But above all else, she had welcomed the comfort of his presence, the warmth of his touch. For a while, he had eased the sorrow and the loneliness.

For the past two hours, she had heard Austin tromping around her house. He had no barn in which to sleep. She had left the front door unbolted, the door to her room ajar, a portion of her hoping that he would sleep with her—just sleep with her, his arm around her, his breath skimming over the nape of her neck.

She strained her ears for several moments, but no longer heard him stirring outside. He had probably stretched out in the wagon he'd brought along with his plans to pack her up and haul her to West Texas as his wife.

She pressed her hand to her stomach. It wasn't the first time that the actions of one night would forever change her life, but their actions were reaching out to touch an innocent child.

Austin was right. Their child would suffer because of their mistake. Born out of wedlock, she would carry the burden of shame that rightfully belonged to them.

She threw off the blankets and scrambled out of bed. In bare feet, wearing nothing but her nightgown, she padded through the house, opened the front door, and saw Austin sitting on the porch steps. He glanced over his shoulder. She felt his gaze travel from the top of her head to the tips of her toes before he turned his attention back to the blackness stretching across the sky.

She knew that rejecting his proposal had hurt him. He hadn't joined her for supper. He'd prepared a bath for her, but hadn't indulged himself in the luxury. He seemed intent on giving all to her and taking nothing from her.

Her mouth grew as dry as cotton. She crossed the porch and sat beside him. His knees were widespread, his elbows resting on his thighs, his hands clamped together before him, his gaze trained on the distance. In the shadows of the night, she saw the slight breeze brushing his black hair over his collar.

"Lot of stars falling from the sky tonight," he said, his voice low.

She followed the direction of his gaze. A ball of light arced through the black void and disappeared like a dream that was never meant to be.

"Make a wish, Loree," he said quietly.

She closed her eyes. One wish. If she were allowed only one wish, she wished she could unburden her past on this man sitting beside her. She thought he, of all people, would understand all that she had done, the things the killer had goaded her into doing. She wished she could tell him and not risk losing any of the affection he might hold for her.

"What did you wish?" he asked.

Opening her eyes, she peered at him. He watched her, and even in the darkness, she felt the intensity of his gaze. "If I tell you, it won't come true. Did you make a wish?"

He leaned toward her, propping himself up on an elbow. "I wished that you would marry me."

Her heart beat faster, harder than the hind foot of a rabbit. He took the curling end of her braid and carried it to his lips. She almost imagined she felt his breath fanning over it, his soft lips brushing over it.

"I want you to marry me for the sake of our daughter—"

"Son."

His hand stilled, the locks of her hair resting against his chin. "Earlier you said—"

"Well, now I'm thinking it's a boy." She rolled her head to her shoulder. "I can't decide what it is."

He chuckled low. "Marry me because you make me smile when I haven't in a long time."

"Less than a week ago, you told me that you weren't courting me, that you had nothing to offer me."

"That was before I knew you needed my name." He cradled her cheek. "I'd give you the world if I could, Loree, but I made a decision five years ago that's gonna limit the things I can offer you. The only thing I have that I can give you is my name, and I hate like hell that I can't give it to you untarnished. But I'll work hard. I think I can give you—and our children—a good life. I know I can give you a better life than the one you have here. At least with me, you won't have the loneliness."

During the past month, she could count the number of days that contained a promise of happiness. The promise always arrived when he did. Her child could have a father who had been in prison or no father at all. Was the past more important than the present? And who was she to judge? Her past was as tarnished as his.

"Will you promise me something?" she asked hesitantly.

"Anything."

Her stomach quivered, and she clasped her hands tightly together. "Will you promise never to make love to me if you're thinking of Becky?"

A profound silence stretched between them. Earlier he had mentioned children, not child, and she knew he expected more than a marriage in name only. She also knew that she could easily come to care for this man, perhaps she already did more than she should. Her heart would shatter if he ever again whispered another's name while joining his body to hers.

"I promise," he rasped.

"Then I'll marry you—for the sake of the child."

A warm smile crept over his face, and he grazed his knuckles over her cheek. "I'll make it good for you, Sugar. You won't regret that you had to marry me."

He drew her face toward his and kissed her. Not with passion, not with fire. But with an apology and understanding.

She knew she'd never regret marrying him, and she hoped he would never discover what she had done, the actions that had prompted her to settle for a life of solitude. For if he did, she feared that he would deeply regret marrying her.

Chapter Eight

~∘≈⊰⊱≈∘~

Oh my goodness!"

As the wagon rolled along, Loree shifted Two-bits on her lap and stared at the massive adobe structure. Turrets in the corners. A crenellated roof. She'd never seen anything like it. "Is that an inn?"

Beside her on the wagon seat, Austin chuckled. "Nope. That's my brother's house."

Loree pressed her hand against her stomach as though to protect the child. "It's so big."

"I think it's god-awful ugly."

"Well, it's not exactly what I would want in a house—"

"What do you want, Loree?"

She turned at the serious tone of his voice. They had been married in Austin, with only Dewayne and his family in attendance. She had worn a white dress and new soft leather shoes that Austin had purchased for her. She'd carried a bouquet of wild-flowers that he had picked for her.

As nervous as she'd been, she'd also felt a

spark of happiness because he treated her with reverence and respect, and he constantly worried over her. Too many years had passed since anyone other than Dewayne had worried over her.

He had packed up her belongings, loaded them on the wagon, and traveled slower than a snail's pace for fear the jarring wagon would cause her to lose the baby. At night, they slept within each other's arms, beneath the stars, but he never attempted to exercise his husbandly rights.

"Something smaller," she assured him. Then she smiled brightly. "Something much smaller."

He returned her smile. "I ought to be able to give you that."

She slipped Two-bits into his box on the floorboards. He no longer looked like a puppy and was rapidly outgrowing the box. Austin had promised to build a shelter for the dog as soon as they arrived.

"Are we going to stay with your brother?"

"For a while. Till we get settled. Decide what we want, where we want to live. I have a little money saved up, but it won't get us far."

The wagon rolled past a huge barn that bore no resemblance to the one that had sat on her property. She heard the clanging of iron from the blacksmith who worked near the barn. Horses trotted around a large corral. In the distance, she saw a long narrow clapboard house and a brick building. She felt as though she were traveling through a miniature town. Men wearing chaps and dusty hats sauntered between the buildings. Only a couple acknowledged Austin as he drove the wagon by them.

She might have thought he didn't know the others if it weren't for the tightening in his jaw. He brought the wagon to a halt in front of the veranda. A man and woman sitting on a bench swing slowly came to their feet. The man stood as tall as Austin did, and she knew from the facial features that he was Austin's brother. The woman was nearly as tall. Slender, she moved gracefully across the porch.

"You should have sent word that you were on your way home," she said as she floated down the steps.

Austin leapt from the wagon, walked briskly to her, and hugged her fiercely. "Didn't know how long we'd be. Didn't want you worrying about us."

"Did you find out anything?" his brother asked, and Loree sensed in the tone of his voice that he was a man who gave no quarter.

"Not a damn thing," Austin said as he stepped toward the wagon and held his arms up to her.

Loree wiped her sweating palms on her skirt before she placed her hands on his shoulders. He grabbed her waist, and she felt his trembling through her clothes. She met his gaze and saw the worry in his eyes. She tried to give him a smile of reassurance, but feared that she had failed miserably.

He brought her to the ground and slipped his arm around her. "This is my brother Dallas and his wife, Dee."

Dee smiled prettily and Dallas looked as though he were waiting for a clap of thunder to sound.

"Did your parents name all their sons after towns?" Loree asked.

"Yeah, they did." Austin met his brother's darkening gaze. "This is Loree. My wife."

Dallas narrowed his eyes. "Your wife?"

Shock rippled across Dee's face, before her eyes warmed, and she gave Loree a sincere smile. Stepping forward, she wrapped her arms around Loree's shoulders. "How wonderful! Welcome to the family."

As Dee released her hold, a wave of nausea hit Loree, and the world suddenly spun around her. She staggered backward. Austin reached out, steadying her. Her cheeks burned as concern swept over Dee's face.

"Are you all right?" Dee asked.

Loree nodded. "It's just the baby. I get light-headed when I go too long without eating."

"The baby?" Dallas ground out in a clipped voice. "And when is this blessed event to take place?"

From the tone of his voice, Loree wasn't certain he truly considered it to be a blessed event, but she wasn't going to let him think she was ashamed of carrying his brother's child. She angled her chin. "End of January."

"Dee, why don't you take Loree inside and get her something cool to drink?" Austin suggested. "I'm afraid I might have pushed us a little too hard trying to get here before nightfall."

Dee wrapped her arm around Loree's waist. "I'd love to get her out of this heat. Come on inside."

Loree glanced over her shoulder at Austin.

"Go on," he urged.

Austin watched Dee guide his wife into the house. Then he met Dallas's blazing glare.

"She's your wife and she didn't know your brother's name?" he asked.

"I told her I had brothers. I mentioned Houston to her. Guess I just never got around to mentioning your name. Don't take it personal." Austin stepped onto the porch. Dallas grabbed his arm and jerked him back down.

"Let me get this straight," Dallas said, his voice seething. "Five years ago, you bedded Becky Oliver and to protect her reputation, you kept your mouth shut and ended up in prison. Now, you've been gone less than four months and show up at my door with a wife—a pregnant wife at that. Do you have a problem keeping your trousers buttoned or do you just have a tendency to get involved with women who have no morals—"

Dallas's tirade ended the instant Austin's fist made contact with his jaw and sent him staggering backward. He landed hard in the dirt. It took every ounce of control Austin could muster not to pound his brother into a bloody pulp. "You don't know a goddamn thing about any of it, and until you do, keep your goddamn mouth shut!"

Austin stormed up the steps and threw open the door. "Loree, we're leaving!"

He stalked down the steps, taking deep breaths, trying to calm himself before Loree got outside. Dallas worked his way to his feet, backhanding the blood trailing from the corner of his mouth.

"Where in the hell do you think you're going, boy?" Dallas demanded.

"I'm not a boy. If prison does nothing else, it beats the boy right out of you. Where I'm going is none of your damn business," Austin snarled. He spun around at the sound of footsteps and held his hand toward Loree. "Come on, Sugar."

Worry etched creases into her brow. "Is something wrong?" she asked, her gaze darting between him and Dallas.

"No, I just decided we'd be better off staying at the hotel in town." The anxiety didn't ease from her face. He squeezed her hand. "Honest."

He helped her into the wagon, then climbed up, released the brake, and slapped the reins. He'd expected coming home with a wife to be difficult. He just hadn't expected it to rip away the last bonds he had with his family.

STARING AT THE night sky through the window of his office, Dallas felt a need to ride across the plains, climb to the top of one of his windmills, and listen to the clatter created by the constant breeze. Instead, he quietly sipped on his whiskey and wondered where he had gone wrong.

He heard the quiet footsteps, downed the remaining whiskey, and set his glass aside.

"Are you ready to tell me why Austin hit you?" Dee asked softly.

"I questioned his wife's morals."

"Then, I'm glad he hit you. It says a lot about his feelings for the woman."

"And I questioned his ability to keep his trousers buttoned."

"Oh, Dallas, you didn't."

He spun around and faced his wife. "Dammit, Dee, by my reckoning, he must have bedded her two minutes after he met her. He's given himself a life sentence with a woman he barely knows—"

She angled her head and lifted a dark brow.

"Dammit! Our situation was different."

"I realize that. You didn't know me *at all* when we married."

He twisted around, gazing back into the night, into the past. "I raised him, Dee. From the time he was five, I was more of a father than a brother. I hate seeing him waste his life, making decisions that lead him nowhere."

She placed her hand on his shoulder, a habit she'd acquired once she realized his back had little feeling in it after the beating he'd received five years before as a result of her oldest brother's greed. "You gave him a good foundation. Now you have to give him the freedom to build on it."

He snapped his head around. "And if I don't like the life he's building on it?"

"As hard as it is, you have to learn to accept it. Someday Rawley and Faith will leave us. All we can do is hope that the foundation we give them is strong enough to sustain their dreams . . . and their failures."

He drew her into his embrace and pressed his cheek against the top of her head. "I remember coming home from the war and finding him living like an animal. I don't know how long our ma had been dead before we got there or how Austin managed to survive. It took me and Houston weeks to earn his trust. Then he looked at everything we gave him as though he were afraid we'd snatch it away. I always expected him to dream bigger dreams, go farther than I ever dared. I feel as though I've failed him."

She leaned back and cradled his face between her hands. "Do you know what Cameron's biggest fear was?"

Dallas blinked at the abrupt change of subject. "I've got no idea."

"Once Austin realized that Cameron and Becky were married, he'd post a public announcement telling the town that he had been with Becky the night Boyd was killed. Neither he nor Becky would have blamed him had he done so, but he didn't. Becky trusted him that night and he won't betray that trust. How can you have failed him when you raised him to be such a fine young man, to accept responsibility for his actions?

"Loree and I didn't have much of an opportunity to talk, but I know he met her on his way to Austin. She didn't even know where he lived until today. He could have ridden out of her life and never looked back. Instead he convinced her to marry him. You didn't fail him, Dallas. You raised him to be the kind of man you can be proud to call 'brother.'"

Dallas heaved a weary sigh. "If I didn't fail him in the twenty years I raised him, I'm afraid I may have failed him today."

"Only if you let what happened this afternoon

fester between you. He needs us more now than he ever has before, and I'm sure tomorrow he'll wake up with a few regrets of his own. Go talk to him first thing in the morning."

"What in the world did I do to deserve such a wise wife?"

She smiled seductively. "Come to bed, and we'll try to figure it out."

Laughing, he scooped her into his arms and hoped his youngest brother hadn't made the biggest mistake of his life.

HOLDING THE CURTAIN aside, Austin gazed into the quiet street where lanterns fought to hold the darkness at bay. He'd never felt so unsure of himself in his life.

He heard his wife's movements as she changed into her nightgown behind the screen. The day they were married, they'd returned to her house and slept in her bed. Just slept. Holding each other.

They'd continued that ritual through the journey, but tonight he needed more. The only family he had left was sharing this room with him, and the memories they'd created spanned only a few weeks.

Memories of Dallas spanned years.

He wanted—needed—Loree's touch on his skin, her scent filling his nostrils, her taste on his lips. And dammit, he didn't know how to go about getting it.

He'd made love twice in his life. Neither time had been planned. He'd sought comfort, given comfort.

The one time he'd stood in a room with a woman knowing he had the right to her body, he'd walked out because no matter how much he'd paid her, he couldn't make himself want her.

"I've never been in so fine a place," Loree said quietly.

Austin released his death grip on the curtain and faced his wife. Her hands were clasped in front of her. He smiled, hoping to ease her nervousness as much as his own. "Dee would only settle for the best."

"Why didn't we stay with your brother?"

Austin plowed his hands through his hair. "Because he still sees me as a boy. He never noticed that I grew up."

"He's angry that you married me."

The sadness in her voice had him crossing the room with only one thought: to comfort her. He cradled her delicate face between his large hands. "It doesn't matter. He ain't got a dog in this fight."

She blinked, one corner of her mouth curling up. "What does that mean?"

"It means you—our marriage—is none of his business." He traced the edge of his thumbs across her brow, down her temple, across her cheek. "My reasons for marrying you are my business." Her eyes lured him the way gold lured miners, and he felt as though he were traveling into a mine, guided by light and darkness, searching for the treasures that lay within. He touched his thumbs to the corners of her mouth. He'd given her a perfunctory kiss after they'd exchanged vows. It had been less than satisfying. He wasn't certain what she expected of this marriage, but he damn sure knew what he wanted.

He lowered his mouth to hers, tasting her sweetness on his tongue. Her small hands pressed against his chest, and he wondered if she felt the heavy pounding of his heart. He guided her toward the bed and they fell together into the deep softness of the mattress. He'd have to remember to compliment Dee on her taste in furnishings.

Austin tucked Loree's finely boned body beneath his. He'd take his time tonight, go slowly, savoring every moment, every inch of her, making certain he caused her no discomfort. He trailed his lips along the slender column of her throat and dipped his tongue into the hollow at the base of her throat.

"Remember your promise," she pleaded softly.

His promise? He'd made so many of late. To find the man who murdered Boyd. To love Loree, honor, and cherish her . . .

To never touch her if he was thinking of Becky.

Groaning, he rolled off her and draped his arm over his eyes, his body aching with need and desires that would go unfulfilled. He felt the stiffness of her body as she lay beside him. She hadn't moved—not a finger, not a toe. He wasn't even certain if she was still breathing.

He peered out from beneath his arm and watched a solitary tear escape from her tightly closed eyes and trail toward her ear. Anger, sadness, guilt swamped him.

He swung his legs off the bed, sat up, and rubbed his hands up and down his face. Then he stood, jerked his hat off the bedpost, and headed for the door.

"Where are you going?"

"I need some fresh air." He yanked open the door, stopped, and looked over his shoulder at the woman who was now sitting up in the bed, her face a mask of anguish. "I wasn't thinking of her, Loree," he said, his voice low. "But I'm not going to make that announcement every time I touch you. You're gonna have to learn to trust me to keep my promises." He forced his tense body not to slam the door in his wake.

He strode from the hotel. The sultry summer night wrapped around him, offering no comfort. His boot heels echoed over the boardwalk. He stepped off the planks and allowed the dirt to muffle his passing.

He came to an abrupt halt in front of the general store. He saw a pale light glowing within a window upstairs. He wondered where the boy slept. He wondered where Becky and Cameron held each other through the night.

He started walking again, toward the far end of town. He heard the tinny sound of an off-key piano wafting out of the saloon. A bottle of whiskey appealed to him, but he'd never enjoyed drinking alone.

And the drinking companion of his youth was probably making passionate love to Becky right about now. He went to the livery, saddled Black Thunder, and rode into the night, trying to escape the invisible prison that surrounded his heart.

He felt the terror that had engulfed him when

they'd put him in solitary confinement. The loneliness had been absolute, frightening. Just as it was now. Loving Becky had been so easy. They had never argued, she had never questioned.

But as he rode, it wasn't Becky who haunted his thoughts. It was Loree with golden eyes that didn't quite trust him and a heart that might never be his.

"So you're figuring to make this place your home?" Dallas asked.

"I'd like to, but it depends on Loree. Her family was murdered a few years back and she's been living alone ever since. I thought she'd find it easier living here where she could get used to having people around—and I wanted to get her away from the memories."

"Sounds like I stepped knee-deep into a fool's pasture yesterday. I owe you an apology for that."

Austin had always known his brother was a big man, but he'd never seemed bigger than he did at this moment. Austin's throat tightened. "I realize now that I should have sent a telegram—"

"Might have made things a little easier on Loree. A wife and baby tie a man down whether he wants to be tied down or not."

"I accepted that before I ever asked Loree to marry me. She deserves better than the life I can give her."

Dallas looked off into the distance. "Dee taught me the only thing that matters is what you give her from your heart."

"My heart's not entirely free."

Dallas pierced him with a darkening gaze. "Then I'd say you wronged her pretty damn bad."

"You'll get no argument from me on that, but I aim to make it up to her."

Dallas gave him a long slow nod. "Well, this spread is getting too big for one man to handle. Reckon I could use some help."

"Same pay as before?"

A corner of Dallas's mouth lifted up, carrying the end of his mustache with it. "Those were a boy's wages." He rubbed the bruise on his jaw. "As you so tactfully pointed out to me yesterday, it's time I realized you were a man. Let's head back to the house, and we'll settle the particulars."

LOREE STOOD ON the boardwalk outside the hotel. The town had grown. She never would have recognized it if it weren't for the hotel. As they'd ridden in last night, the massive silhouette of the building had loomed before them, throwing her back in time to a night five years before.

"Why this town?" she whispered beneath her breath. As vast as West Texas was, why couldn't Austin have settled somewhere else?

Fate had a cruel streak running through her. No doubt about that.

The town hadn't possessed a sign when she'd been here before. She hadn't known its name. She hadn't cared. But it proudly bore a sign on the outskirts now: Leighton.

Named for her husband's family. Why had Fate chosen to bring a man to her door who lived in the one place she had never again wanted to see?

But more, she wondered if Fate would be kind enough to bring the man back to her?

He hadn't returned to the hotel room last night, and she wondered where he was, if he'd abandoned her. She wished she'd kept her insecurities to herself. What did it matter if he thought of someone else as long as he held her?

Stupid, stupid girl! she chastised herself. She

had known by the pain reflected in his gaze that she'd hurt him to the core. She wanted to trust him, but life had taught her to value caution. And because of life's lessons, she knew she needed a gun.

She strolled along the boardwalk, her stomach quivering as people skirted past her. The men touched their fingers to the brim of their hats, some even smiled at her, but she refused to look any of them in the eye.

She was grateful when she saw the sign for Oliver's General Store. She slipped inside, cringing when the cowbell above the door announced her arrival.

A woman standing behind the counter looked up and smiled warmly. "Hello. Can I help you?"

Loree wiped her damp palms on her skirt. "I'd just like to look around."

"Let me know if I can help you with anything."

Loree nodded her appreciation of the offer and strolled down the nearest aisle. Toys of all shapes and sizes greeted her. She hadn't seen many children in the town, but she'd noticed the red schoolhouse near the hotel. She supposed her child would attend school there. She and Austin might purchase toys here. Or would he carve the toys himself?

She picked up a wooden rattle. Did her husband whittle? What hidden talents did he possess? The sparse knowledge she possessed grew frustrating with each passing day. She supposed it should be enough that she didn't fear him and that he was for the most part considerate of her.

Yet she couldn't help but feel that he held a part

of himself back. She wondered if he'd always been distant with people or if prison had reshaped him.

How could it have not reshaped him?

Her heart picked up its tempo, beating unsteadily with the thought of iron bars and brick walls and guards. How had he survived five years without freedom? She knew it would very likely have killed her.

Carefully, she placed the rattle back onto the shelf. She'd have to find out if he planned to make one before she purchased it. And she'd have to find out if they had the means for her to purchase it. She needed the little money she possessed for something more important.

She walked to the counter. The woman stopped dusting the shelves behind the counter and turned. Her burnished hair was pulled back into a stylish bun. The color reminded Loree of the locks she'd discovered in Austin's saddlebags. The woman had eyes the blue of a summer sky.

"Did you find what you were looking for?" she asked in a soft voice.

Loree tightened her fingers around her reticule. "I was looking for a small gun, something like a derringer."

The woman's delicate brow furrowed. "We don't carry guns anymore, not since the gunsmith came to town. You'll find his shop—"

"Becky!"

Loree's heart felt as though an iron fist had just clamped around it. How many Beckies could reside in this town? How many with hair the shade of autumn leaves?

A tall man stormed through the curtain behind the counter. With his hand he combed his blond hair off his brow. "I just saw Austin."

"He's back?"

"Yep, and it's the dangdest thing. He got married."

Loree watched the blood drain from Becky's face, and she hoped her own feelings weren't as visible.

"Married? Who in the world did he marry?" she whispered, her voice achingly low. Then as though just remembering she had a customer, she blinked several times and returned her attention to Loree. "I'm sorry. You wanted the gunsmith. You'll find him at the end of Main Street, near the saloon. I know Mr. Wesson will be able to help you." She turned back to the man. "Cameron, did he tell you about his wife?"

Loree didn't want to hear the answer. She hurried out of the general store. Once outside, she slumped against the front of the building. The woman inside the store was beautiful. How in the world could she expect Austin not to think of that woman when his wife was incredibly plain?

Then she remembered what the man had said. He'd just seen Austin. She hurried along the boardwalk, back to the hotel. She rushed inside and up the stairs, bursting through the door to their room.

Austin stood near the bed, stuffing her clothes into her suitcase on the bed. He jerked back, his brow deeply furrowed. "Where have you been?"

She closed the door more quietly than she'd opened it and eased into the room. "I needed something. I went to the general store."

He reached across the bed, grabbed her nightgown, and shoved it into the bag. "We're going back to Dallas's."

"I met a woman at the general store. A Becky." He stiffened. Her heart pounded so hard that she was sure he heard it. "Is she your Becky?"

"No, she is not *my* Becky," he replied through a clenched jaw. He grabbed her hairbrush from the bedside table and threw it into the bag.

"*Was* she your Becky?" she asked, unable to let it go for reasons she couldn't understand.

With one rapid-fire movement, he sent her bag and everything in it crashing to the floor. She stumbled back. She'd never seen him truly angry and wondered if she'd pushed him too far.

He dropped onto the bed, planted his elbows on his thighs, leaned forward, and buried his face in his hands. She heard his harsh breathing, saw the tenseness in his shoulders. He held out a hand. "Come here."

But her feet remained rooted to the spot. She knew nothing about how he acted in anger. If he gave as much of himself to anger as he did to passion . . .

He looked up, the torment in his eyes deepening as he met her gaze. "Come here, Loree. Please."

The anguish in his voice had her walking toward him, seeking to comfort him for the painful memories her constant badgering brought him. As she neared, he reached out, clamped his hand on her waist, and brought her to stand between his thighs.

He took a deep shuddering breath, staring at a

button on her bodice. "Yes, she *was* my Becky." He tilted his head back, his deep blue gaze capturing hers. "But she's not anymore, and she never will be again."

He pressed a kiss to her slightly rounded stomach, to the place where their child grew. "I need you, Loree," he rasped.

She wrapped her arms around him, pressing his head against her belly. How could the woman have not waited for Austin? With demons haunting her and no family, the past five years had been an eternity, but at least she'd had the stars at night, the sunrise at dawn, and the freedom to walk wherever she wanted. "I hate her because she hurt you," she said, her voice seething.

"She doesn't deserve your hate."

"She doesn't deserve your loyalty or your love."

He tipped his head back, meeting her gaze. "Five years is a long time."

"I would have waited," she said, surprised by the conviction in her voice, more surprised to realize the words were true. If she were fortunate enough to possess his love, she'd wait forever.

A corner of his mouth quirked up and he brushed the stray strands of her hair behind her ear. "You know, I do believe you would have."

"I hate that she hurt you."

"And I hate that I've hurt you."

"You didn't hurt me on purpose. I know that."

"But I don't imagine it lessened the pain."

No, the pain had been sharp, agonizing, but she was tired of letting the wound fester. She needed to lance it, clean it, and let it heal.

"She's very pretty," she admitted reluctantly.

He smiled broadly. "She is that."

He tugged her down until she sat on his lap. He cradled her cheek. "But then so are you."

She shoved his hand away and averted her gaze, the heat flaming her face. "No, I'm not. I'm uglier than the back end of a mule."

When he didn't jump to her defense, she dared to peer at him. Narrowing his eyes, he scrutinized her features. "Don't go staring at me."

"How else am I gonna find the ugly?"

"It's there for the whole world to see."

"Where?"

She pursed her lips. "My nose for one thing. The end tips up like a broken twig."

"And here I thought it looked like a petal unfurling."

His eyes grew warm, a touch of humor twinkling in the centers.

"And my lips. I don't hardly have a top lip and my bottom lip looks swollen like a bee stung it."

"It reminds me of a plump, ripe strawberry just waiting to be tasted."

She felt the heat suffuse her face as his eyes darkened.

"My hair," she said in a rush, desperate to convince him of her flaws. "It's got no color."

He took her braid and carried the end to his lips. "I always thought it looked like it had been woven from moonbeams. Reckon that's why I stole some of it."

She furrowed her brow. "What?"

He leaned back slightly, dug his hand into his

pocket, and brought out several locks of her hair, tied together with a dainty ribbon.

"When did you do that?"

"That first night I slept with you, after you'd fallen asleep."

Tears stung her eyes as she pressed her hand to her mouth. "Oh, Austin. You must like me some to carry my hair around."

"I like you more than some, Loree. I wouldn't have married you otherwise."

She knew she shouldn't ask, knew she risked angering him again, but she had to know. "What about the locks of Becky's hair that you carried around?"

"I know words can't undo actions, but I'm hoping actions can undo the harm caused by a careless word." She watched his Adam's apple slowly slide up and down as he swallowed. "I burned them . . . the day we burned the barn."

She studied him, trying to understand the significance of his actions. "Why? You didn't have to punish yourself—"

"I wasn't punishing myself. Burning the barn was a way for you to put the past behind you. Thought it was time for me to put the past to rest, too."

"But you still love her."

His thumb stroked her cheek. "I love the memory of her."

The difference sounded slight to her, if it existed at all. She was no longer competing against a woman—only a memory. Perhaps if she'd loved someone before Austin came into her life, she could better understand how difficult it was to let go. As it was, all she knew was that she wished there'd been no one before her.

"Last night, I was afraid you weren't going to come back," she confessed quietly.

His lips spread into a smile that had warmth swirling through her, from her head to her toes.

"Missed me, did you?" he asked, and she heard the slight teasing in his voice.

"Where did you go?" she asked, not ready to admit how very much she'd missed him.

"Riding." He sighed deeply. "I just needed to ride."

"All night?"

"All night."

She realized then how tired he looked. Shadows rested beneath his eyes. His face remained unshaven. "I'll finish packing if you want to get a little sleep before we leave," she offered.

"What I want is a little kiss." He brought her face closer to his. "I know it's hard, but trust me, Loree."

She nodded hesitantly. "I'm trying."

He joined his lips to hers and rolled back onto the bed, holding her close, bringing her down with him, his mouth never leaving hers. He cradled her head, holding her in place as he plunged his tongue into her mouth.

Awkwardly, she straddled his thighs as his lips worked their magic. The warmth grew through her, and she hoped he'd kiss her forever.

He moaned low in his throat and shifted his mouth from hers. "So sweet," he murmured.

He pressed her face into the crook of his shoulder. She heard his soft even breathing. She lifted her head slightly to gaze at him. He'd fallen asleep.

She eased off him. He tightened his hold, turning onto his side and bringing his legs onto the bed, forming a cocoon around her. "Don't leave yet," he mumbled.

"I won't," she whispered, snuggling against him. She was determined to stop feeling jealousy over the beautiful woman who worked in the general store. She was part of Austin's past. Loree was his future.

TREPIDATION SLICED THROUGH Loree as they neared Dallas's house. She saw Austin's brother standing by the corral, a young boy standing by his side. As Austin brought the wagon to a halt in front of the house, they both turned and headed toward them. Loree knew beyond a doubt that the boy was Dallas's son. He had his father's walk.

"Expected you to show up sooner," Dallas said, an authoritative ring to his voice that made Loree think the man always got what he expected.

"I fell asleep," Austin said as he helped Loree climb down from the wagon.

"During the day?" Dallas asked.

"Yep, not everyone works from dawn till midnight building empires," Austin said, giving her a wink.

"Nothing wrong with building empires," Dallas informed him.

"Didn't say there was," Austin said. "Only pointing out that not everybody does it."

Once she was firmly on the ground, Loree glanced around, feeling like a bush surrounded by mighty oak trees. Even Dallas's son stood inches above her.

Dallas swept his hat from his head. "Think I forgot to welcome you to the family yesterday."

Before she knew what he was about, he'd taken her hand, leaned forward, and kissed her cheek.

"It's a pleasure to have you here," he said as he released her hand. "This is my son, Rawley."

The boy swept off his hat in much the same manner as his father had. "We're right pleased to have you here, Aunt Loree."

He cast a furtive glance at his father who gave him a nod of approval, and she wondered how many times they'd practiced his greeting. Two-bits chose that moment to make his presence known. He leapt up, placed his paws on the side of the wagon, and began barking.

A broad smile split Rawley's face as he rushed to the wagon. "You got a dog?"

"Yep. Why don't you take him out?" Austin suggested. "He's probably ready to do some running around."

Rawley lifted Two-bits into his arms. The dog squirmed, snaking out his tongue to get a taste of Rawley's nose. Rawley set Two-bits on the ground and dropped to his knees to rub the dog's stomach as he rolled onto his back.

"What's his name?" Rawley asked.

"Two-bits," Loree told him, an ache in her heart. The boy very much reminded her of her brother.

She judged him to be near her brother's age before he died.

Rawley glanced over his shoulder, his face skewed up. "Who named him that?"

"I did," Austin said. "Why don't you take him around to the back? We'll probably need to tie him up for the night so he won't run off," Austin said.

"He can stay in my room," Rawley suggested.

"I don't think so," Dallas said.

Rawley's face fell even as he gave his father a brusque nod. "Come on, Two-bits," he called out as he began running. The dog chased after him like he'd found a new friend.

"Rawley!" Dallas yelled.

The boy stumbled to a stop and spun around. "Yes, sir?"

"It's warm enough, you can bed down on the back porch tonight if you've a mind to."

Rawley smiled brightly. "Thanks, Mr. D!"

Loree turned her attention back to Dallas in time to catch a glimpse of a grimace before he wiped it from his face.

"Still can't get him to call you 'Pa'?" Austin asked.

Dallas shook his head. "Nope, but it doesn't matter. He's my son. I'll find Dee. She's bound to have an empty room or two that you can put your belongings in," Dallas said.

Loree waited until Dallas disappeared into the house before asking, "Why doesn't Rawley call him 'Pa'?"

"Dallas and Dee adopted him. He wasn't treated too kindly before they took him under their wing. Think he still finds it difficult to trust men."

"Did someone beat him?"

"Among other things." As though signaling an end to the conversation, Austin took her hand. "Come on. I'll show you around the house."

Had he not told her, Loree still would have known which bedroom had belonged to Austin. Smiling, she picked his rumpled shirt and britches off the floor.

"Guess Dee hasn't been in here since I left," he said as he set her suitcase on the bed.

She didn't think anyone had been in the room. It carried his lingering scent, faint because of his absences, but ingrained because of the years he had slept here.

He jerked the blankets on the bed up to cover his pillows and grinned sheepishly. "Never saw much point in making a bed in the morning just to unmake it at night."

He wiped his hands on his backside. "Let me talk to Dee about some clean sheets."

He headed out the door, and Loree wandered around the room. She imagined it to be a reflection of the man he'd been before prison. It was sparsely furnished as though he'd never planned to stay: a bed, a bureau, a dresser.

No portraits adorned the walls. Nothing hinted at permanence, but it was his room and on the dresser rested a violin. Reverently, Loree trailed her finger over the dull varnish. A chip here, a scratch there did not diminish the beauty of the instrument. Still, it looked forlorn and lonely.

"Dee thought the maid had cleaned in here," Austin said as he came back into the room. "She said she'll send Maria in to take care of it for us."

"I can change the bed—"

"Enjoy the luxury of being waited on because you'll only get it while you're here."

"Your brother is very wealthy, isn't he?"

"Yep, but I don't envy him that. He worked hard for every penny."

She turned her attention back to his dresser. "Is this the violin your mother played for you?"

Stuffing his hands in his pockets, he slowly approached her. "Yeah, it is."

"My father played the violin. He thought music was important. He'd take me into Austin once a week so I could have a piano lesson. I had no natural talent, but I tried to learn. I could teach you what I know. You could play your mother's violin."

"No."

"But it would be a tribute to your mother, a way—"

"No. I can't play and you can't teach me."

"But how do you know if you don't try?"

"Trust me. I know."

Baffled, she watched him turn for the door. She didn't want the moment to end with disappointment. "Austin?"

He glanced over his shoulder. "I'm just going to get the rest of our things."

She gave him a hesitant smile. "Do you think you could draw me a map of the house so I don't get lost when I wander through it?"

He grinned. "It's god-awful big, isn't it? Dallas doesn't do anything in small measures."

"I guess they're planning to have a large family," she offered.

His grin eased away. "They were planning on it, but Dee had an accident a few years ago. She won't be giving Dallas any more children."

She wrapped her arms around herself. "I'm so sorry. Will my being here and having a baby upset her?"

Austin shook his head. "One thing about the Leigh men, they tend to marry generous women."

He disappeared through the door. Loree crossed the room, opened a double set of doors, and stepped onto the balcony. She was glad they'd left the town. It had stirred up memories that had kept her from sleeping the night before.

She hoped that tonight Austin's presence would hold the nightmares at bay.

Chapter Ten

Blood. It was everywhere. Rich, red, warm, glistening in the night. Coating her hands, soaking through her clothes.

She couldn't stop it from flowing like a raging river. She was drowning, drowning in the blood.

The scream ripped through the tranquil night. Dallas jerked upright as Dee rolled away from his side and turned up the flame in the lamp.

"What in the hell was that?" Dallas asked.

The terrorized shriek came again.

"It came from Austin's room," Dee said as she headed for the door.

Dallas bolted from bed, rushed after her into the hallway, and grabbed her arm. "Where do you think you're going?"

"To help."

"Let me go first," he ordered, taking the lamp from her. No telling what was waiting on the other side. The woman was always rushing into places where she shouldn't.

Quietly he opened the door to Austin's room

and peered inside. The light from the lamp cast a pale glow around the room. He heard a woman's harsh sobs.

Dee edged past him and walked into the room, giving him no choice but to follow.

Sitting in bed, the blankets draped around his waist, Austin held Loree. "It's all right, Loree. It was just a bad dream," he said, his voice low as he rocked back and forth, stroking her back.

"I didn't know where you lived. I didn't know. I shouldn't have come here," she wailed.

"It's all right, Sugar. No one's gonna hurt you here."

She tilted her head away from his shoulder and the light from the lamp glistened over her tears. "I'm so scared, Austin."

He pressed her face back into the nook of his shoulder. "I know you are, but I'm gonna make things good for you, Loree. You'll see."

Dee eased toward the bed. "Why don't I warm up some milk for Loree?" she whispered. "It always helps the children get back to sleep when they wake up with a bad dream."

Austin glanced over his shoulder at her, gratitude etched over his features. "And put a lot of sugar in it."

Dee strolled to Dallas and placed her hand on his arm. "Light their lamp for them, then give them a little privacy while I warm some milk."

When she left his side, Dallas walked to the bedside table and lit the lamp. "Need anything else?"

Shaking his head, Austin settled down on the

bed, carrying his wife with him. Dallas heard her stifling sobs and Austin's repeated words of comfort. He strode back to his own room, jerked open the door to the balcony, and stepped into the night. He was trembling almost as much as he imagined Loree was. Taking several deep breaths, he stared at the canopy of stars overhead.

Long moments passed before he heard Dee's soft footsteps. She joined him on the balcony and rubbed her hand up and down his bare arm. "Loree's sleeping. Come back to bed."

"Did you see his back? They beat him in prison."

It wasn't a question, but she answered anyway. "It looks like it."

"When we find the man who killed your brother, I'm gonna string him up from the nearest tree."

"You need to let the law handle—"

He spun around. "The law sent my brother to prison."

"The law isn't perfect, but you have to trust it to serve justice. You have to let the law send the real murderer to prison."

"They had better damn well hang the man, and I want a front row seat."

Austin held Loree as she sipped on the warm milk Dee had prepared for her. She was trembling so hard that the bed shook.

After all she'd lived through, he wasn't surprised she still had nightmares. On the journey, he'd heard her whimper a few times in her sleep. It seemed the farther they traveled from Austin, the more restless she was when she slept. He hoped bringing her here wasn't a mistake, but he'd feared she'd continue living as a hermit if they'd stayed at her home.

She gave him a shaky smile and handed the empty cup to him. "Thank you," she whispered.

He set the cup aside, and with his thumb, he wiped the milky mustache away from her lip. "You're welcome."

She released an awkward chuckle. "I am so embarrassed. Your brother must think—"

"He doesn't think anything," he assured her, lying her down and tucking her against his body. Lord, she fit so nicely, even though she was beginning to swell with his child. As it rested against his chest, her hand curled like the petals of a flower closing for the night. He wrapped one hand around it, while the other lazily stroked her back. He kissed her forehead. "Were you dreaming about your family?"

She moved her head up and down against his chest.

"And the man who killed them. There was so much blood," she whispered hoarsely.

"What did he look like?"

He felt the shiver course through her body.

"I don't want to talk about him."

"While I was in Austin, I talked with a detective about hunting the man down—"

She jerked away and stared at him, fear reflected in her eyes. "What?"

"I thought it would put your mind at peace if the man was found and hanged for what he did to your family. But I couldn't give the detective enough information. If you tell me what you know about him—"

She shook her head violently. "No, no, I don't want him looking."

"Sugar, I'm not gonna let the man hurt you—"

"No!" She buried her face against his chest. "It's been over five years. Please just let it be."

"It's not right that he murdered three people and got away with it."

He felt her tense within his arms as she shook her head. He drew her closer. "I won't press you on this, Loree, but think about it. What if he's out killing others?"

Loree squeezed her eyes shut. She should have told Austin everything before they were married even though she might have sacrificed any affection he held for her. But she'd wanted what he was offering for her baby.

Strange how a little one, not yet born, could bring so many responsibilities with him. She had to do what was best for the baby. She had to put him first. So she held her silence.

A detective searching for the man who had killed her family was a worse nightmare than the one that had woken her up screaming. If anyone tracked down the man who had killed her family, he'd no doubt discover things about her father that Loree wanted to remain a secret.

The only peace of mind she found resided in the fact that she knew the murderer wasn't going to kill anyone else.

"LOREE? IS THAT short for Lorena?" Dallas asked.

Austin watched his wife jerk to attention and glance down the breakfast table at his brother. Shadows rested beneath her eyes. He wished he had the power to rid her of the nightmares.

"Yes, it is," she said. "My father told me it was a favorite song around the campfire during the war."

"Not in my unit," Dallas said. "I forbid my men to play it, sing it, or think about it."

"How come?" Rawley asked.

"Because it made the men miss home so much that they'd end up deserting. Can't tolerate a man shirking his responsibilities."

Loree flicked her gaze to Austin, and he noticed the crimson fanning her cheeks. He gave her a wink. Dallas tolerated less than most men, and Austin was glad Loree hadn't shared her father's military history with his brother.

"Can I add taking care of Aunt Loree's dog to my list of chores?" Rawley asked.

Austin sipped on his coffee, watching Rawley wait expectantly for his father's permission.

"Don't you think you got enough chores?" Dallas asked as he scooped up his eggs.

"But I like taking care of dogs, and I don't have one to watch over since Ma's went to live with her friends."

Out of the corner of his eye, Austin saw his wife lean forward and glance down the table at Dee.

"While she carried her litter, she got a bit testy, so I thought it was best to set her free. She still comes up to the house, but not as often," Dee said.

Loree shook her head. "I don't understand why you set it free—"

"It was a prairie dog," Dallas said with disgust.

Loree blinked, confusion mirrored in her eyes. "You had a prairie dog as a pet?"

"Yep," Austin said, grinning broadly. "Dallas even made it a leash. Carved the dog's name right into it."

"Me 'n Wrawley wanna dog," Faith piped in from her high chair beside Dee.

"Maybe you can borrow your Aunt Loree's for a spell," Dallas suggested.

"Can we, Aunt Loree?" Rawley asked. "I'll take real good care of him."

Loree smiled softly. "I'd appreciate the help."

"Now that that's settled," Dallas began.

Austin listened with half an ear as Dallas rattled off all the things that Austin needed to tend to that day. He remembered a time when he'd handled his chores and still had time to go into town and visit with Becky.

Right now, it seemed his list of responsibilities would leave him with little time to visit his wife. He watched as she sprinkled two spoons of sugar into her coffee and began to stir. Austin reached across the table and took her cup from her. When she started to protest, he silenced her with a lifted brow. Then he scooped four more spoons of sugar into the brew before handing it back to her. "There's no shortage of sugar around here."

Her cheeks took on the hue of a sunrise. "Most people don't use as much sugar as I do."

"Maybe if they did, they'd be as sweet as you are."

Her blush deepened and she lowered her gaze to her plate.

"Have you heard a damn word I've said?" Dallas asked.

Austin shifted his gaze to the end of the table. "Heard every word. I want to take Loree over to Houston's this morning so she can pick out a horse."

Narrowing his eyes, Dallas rubbed his thumb and forefinger over his mustache. "Reckon Amelia will have your hide if you don't take Loree out and introduce her."

Austin gave his brother a nod. "I figured the same thing. I'd rather face your wrath than Amelia's."

Dallas leaned back in his chair and laughed.

AUSTIN DREW DALLAS'S buggy to a halt, unable to do little more than stare at the huge unfamiliar house. A balcony jutted out from a room on the second floor. Some sort of fancy railing circled the porch that circled the house. One side of the house eased out into a half circle. Bright yellow curtains billowed out from large windows.

"What's wrong?" Loree asked.

"Houston has always preferred solitude. I just never expected to see him with neighbors."

"It certainly is a fancy house," Loree said.

"Yep," Austin responded, apprehension taking hold of his gut. He slapped the reins, sending the two black mares into a trot. Beyond the corral where Houston worked with a palomino mustang,

Austin saw the house he had helped to build. It appeared abandoned. Austin shifted his gaze back to the larger house.

A woman stepped onto the porch and waved, a tiny girl planted on her hip, another girl clinging to her skirt.

"Good Lord," Austin muttered.

Loree leaned toward him. "What?"

He shook his head. "I never would have believed it." He brought the horses and buggy to a halt near the corral just as Houston slipped through the slats. Austin set the brake and climbed out of the buggy. "Tell me that isn't your house?" he ordered.

Houston grimaced. "Disgusting, ain't it? I wasn't looking for it, but success found me. Figured the least I could do was give the woman a fancy house." He rubbed the scarred side of his face. "I hear tell Cupid's cramp got a hold of you."

Inwardly, Austin cringed at his brother's phrasing. Cowboys used it whenever they got an urge to marry. "Yeah, you might say that." Turning to Loree, Austin helped her out of the buggy and slipped his arm protectively around her. "My wife needs a horse."

"Not gonna bother with introductions?" Houston asked.

"I figured it was obvious you're my brother and this is my wife."

Houston swept his hat from his head. Austin heard Loree's tiny gasp. He'd grown up with Houston's scars. He hadn't thought to warn Loree about them.

"Welcome to the family," Houston said quietly.

Loree's lips spread into the most understanding smile Austin had ever seen. "I'm very happy to be here," she said.

Houston gave her a distorted grin. "You have to be the most forgiving soul on earth to say that after meeting Dallas."

"I think our announcement took him by surprise," she said.

"Yeah, you might say it took us all unawares, but then Austin always did have a hard time figuring out when to open his mouth and when to keep it shut."

"How long were you planning to stay out here with the horses instead of bringing your wife to the house so I can meet her?"

Austin spun around at Amelia's welcoming voice. She waddled toward him, a girl in each arm. Houston strode toward her and took both girls from her.

"I told you not to carry them," he said.

"You tell me a lot of things," she said, her voice laced with teasing.

Austin grinned at her swollen stomach. "I'll be. When I was home before, Dallas said you had to be carrying another one 'cuz you weren't eating."

Amelia laughed. "I can't eat anything for the first three months. You'd think I'd get skinny, but I just keep getting more plump with each girl we have." She turned slightly and smiled. "You must be Loree. I'm so grateful Austin has someone to love."

Austin watched his wife's face blush becomingly. "Well, I'm not certain—" she began.

"I am," Amelia said, interrupting her. She threw her arms around Loree and hugged her closely. "Welcome to the family."

Then she stepped back, grinning. "And look at this. Someone I can actually reach. Dee's as tall as a tree, and these men here are no different." She slipped her arm through Loree's. "Why don't you come into the house for a spell? Our other two girls are baking cookies. They won't be edible, but we can pretend to nibble on them."

Austin listened to his wife's laughter as she walked toward the house with Amelia. Amelia had always had a way of putting people at ease. He'd never been more grateful for it than he was now. He glanced at Houston. "Want me to take one of those girls?"

"Sure." Houston handed the smallest one over.

"Which one is this?" he asked.

"A. J."

Austin shifted her in his arms. "Hello, A. J. I bet you don't remember your Uncle Austin, do you?"

She covered her eyes and buried her tiny nose against his shoulder. Lord, she was incredibly small and warm. A knot rose in his throat with the thought that he'd soon have one of these of his own.

"Since you came in Dallas's buggy, I reckon the two of you mended your fence," Houston said.

"He told you about that, did he?" Austin asked.

Houston gave him a lopsided grin. "Yep."

"What's so funny?"

"The whole world is afraid of Dallas. He's only been hit twice in his life—and both times the fist was attached to one of his brothers."

Austin chuckled. "I'd forgotten that you'd hit him. I never knew why."

Houston shrugged and started walking toward the house. Austin took off after him. "Why *did* you hit him?"

"He questioned Amelia's virtue. I took exception to his doubts."

Austin was relieved to know Loree wasn't the only one whose virtue Dallas had doubted, but he also knew that Amelia had been long married before she began to swell with a child. Austin swallowed hard. "Loree's pregnant."

Houston glanced over at him. "I know."

"She's a decent woman—"

"Never doubted that for a minute. Hell, Austin, I took you to your first whorehouse, and you walked out as pure as you were before you went in. Decent women are the only kind that ever appealed to you."

"Don't suppose you happened to mention that to Dallas when he came by."

"Figured he knew since he told me if anyone dared to look at your wife with anything but admiration, they'd answer to him."

The knot in Austin's throat tightened a little. "I wasn't sure how he felt—"

"You're his baby brother. He would have sheltered you from the world if he could have, and that's probably where he went wrong. Some lessons have simply got to be learned the hard way."

LOREE FOLDED THE blanket, placed it in the box, and lifted her gaze to the woman standing on the other side of the bed who was doing the same thing. "I hope we haven't hurt your feelings."

Dee glanced up. "Of course not. Why ever would you think that?"

Loree shrugged. "You made me feel so welcome, and here we are, after only one night, moving out."

Dee smiled with understanding. "I'm glad that Amelia and Houston offered to let you live in their vacant house. I know it's difficult to marry someone you've only known a short time. I didn't know Dallas at all when I married him. If my family had been underfoot, I don't think I ever would have gotten to know him."

"I feel badly taking the furniture from this room."

"It's always been Austin's. I often thought of replacing it, but I wanted him to come home to something familiar. I was afraid all the other changes would overwhelm him."

Loree picked at a loose thread on the blanket. "You must love him very much to accept what he did."

"I understand why he did it. I hated to see him go to prison, but the decision was his to make, and I respect that."

Understanding, respect, acceptance. She wondered if Austin would give those as easily to her if he knew the entire truth about her past. She supposed one had to build a foundation of love before one's faults could be laid bare and accepted.

"Dallas and Austin should have the table moved out of the shed by now. Do you want to run outside and let them know that we're almost finished here?" Dee asked.

Loree nodded, walked to the doorway, and halted. "Dee?"

Dee glanced over at her, and Loree nibbled on her lower lip. "I appreciate that you don't seem to be sitting in judgment of me."

Dee's brown eyes widened. "Because of the baby?"

Loree jerked her head quickly.

A wealth of understanding and sympathy filled Dee's brown eyes. "A child is a gift, Loree, regardless of the circumstances. And Austin's child at that. We will spoil the baby rotten, I promise you."

Loree didn't doubt it. She'd already seen evidence that every child in this family was considered precious.

She walked into the hallway and down the wide sweeping staircase. The discordant notes of a piano traveled from the front parlor. She ambled toward the room, the off-key chords grating on her nerves before they fell into silence. She peered into the room.

"Did you practice one hour every day like I told you?" a rotund woman asked Rawley.

He shrugged.

"Stand up, young man," she ordered.

Slower than ice melting in winter he slid off the bench and stood.

"Hold out your hand."

She saw Rawley tense as he extended his hand, palm up. The woman picked up a thin wooden stick and raised it.

"Don't you even think about striking him," Loree snarled as she stormed into the room.

Rawley spun around so fast that he lost his

balance and dropped onto the bench. The woman's eyes protruded farther than her nose.

"How dare you interfere with this lesson—"

"I'm interfering with your cruelty, not the lesson."

"Mr. Leigh is paying me good money—"

"To teach his son, not to beat him."

"He is lazy and irresponsible—"

"Irresponsible? What time did you get out of bed this morning?"

"I don't see that that's any of your business."

"This child was up before the sun tending to his chores, and he'll sneak in a few more after everyone thinks he's in bed, so don't tell me he's irresponsible. You are irresponsible." Loree snatched the stick out of the woman's hand and snapped it in two.

The woman's jowls shook. "How dare you! Wait until Mr. Leigh hears about this." She stormed from the room.

Loree slid onto the bench beside Rawley, gave him a warm smile, and began to play "Greensleeves."

"MR. LEIGH! MR. LEIGH!"

Standing in the wagon, holding one end of the heavy table, Austin glanced over his shoulder to see something that looked like the beginnings of a dust storm hurling toward them.

"Drop it!" Dallas ordered, and Austin gladly obliged, hearing the wagon groan beneath the weight.

The banker's wife staggered to a stop. "She broke my stick!"

"Who did?" Dallas asked.

She pointed her finger at Austin. "I believe she's his wife."

Austin settled his butt on the side of the wagon. "If Loree broke your stick"—he swallowed his laughter—"I'm sure she had good reason."

"I will not tolerate interference from that hoyden when I'm teaching," the woman said.

"I'll talk to her," Dallas said.

"The hell you will," Austin said. He glared at the woman. "And she's not a hoyden."

"She's married to a murderer—"

"My brother's not a murderer."

"I was at the trial—"

"That'll be enough, Mrs. Henderson. Why don't you head on home, and we'll take this up tomorrow?" Dallas suggested.

She stuck her nose in the air. "I don't think I can teach Rawley. That boy is as lazy as his father—"

"I'm his father."

"Not by blood—"

"By all that matters." Dallas shoved on the table and sent it crashing against the back of the wagon. "Jackson!"

A tall lanky man hurried out of the barn. "Yes, sir?"

"Escort Mrs. Henderson home."

Leaving the woman to huff and puff, Dallas strode toward the house. Austin leapt off the wagon and caught up to him. "You gotta pity poor Lester being married to that."

Dallas just snorted.

"What are you aiming to do?" Austin asked as Dallas stalked through the front door.

"Find out what really happened."

Austin heard the music filtering out of the parlor. Dallas ground to a stop in the parlor doorway. Wanting to ensure that he could get between Dallas and Loree if the need arose, Austin slipped past his brother and froze.

Loree was playing the piano with Rawley sitting beside her, watching as her hands moved over the keys. She struck the final chord and folded her hands in her lap.

"I could never play like that," Rawley said, his voice filled with awe.

"You could if you wanted," Loree said. "But the secret is—do you want to?"

Rawley shook his head. "I'd rather be out tending cattle."

"Then that's what you should do."

"But I don't want to disappoint Mr. D. He ain't gonna like what happened with Miz Henderson at all," Rawley said quietly.

"Of course, he won't like it," Loree said. "She's lucky I walked into this room and not your father. He would have snatched her baldheaded if he'd seen that she was going to strike you."

"You really think so?"

"I know so." She shifted on the bench. "Rawley, he loves you very much."

"I know he does, but I ain't really his son. His son is buried out by the windmill. He died on account of me." Ducking his head, Rawley rubbed his finger along the edge of the piano. "I ain't never said that out loud, but I know it to be true."

"Rawley!"

Rawley came off the bench at his father's booming voice, and Loree looked as though she'd jumped out of her skin.

"Yes, sir?"

"I need to talk to you, son," Dallas said more quietly. "Outside."

Dallas turned abruptly and headed down the hallway. Rawley hurried after him. Austin ambled into the room and sprawled in a chair near the piano.

"What do you think he's going to say to Rawley?" Loree asked, worry etched deeply between her brows.

"Imagine he's going to explain to the boy that he is indeed Dallas's son."

"How long were you there?"

"Long enough to know Rawley will be herding cattle instead of banging on a piano."

Loree breathed a sigh of relief. "I'm beginning to think your brother is more bark than bite."

"Only where family is concerned. Make no mistake about that."

AUSTIN HEARD LOREE'S laughter as he prodded his horse into the corral. Moving into their own place had seemed to put Loree more at ease with her new surroundings. He sauntered to the house, rounded the corner, and leaned against the beam supporting the eve. Contentment stole over him as his gaze fell on Loree, sitting on the ground, her bare toes peeking out from beneath her skirt. Rawley was hunkered beside her while Two-bits yelped and wagged his tail like there was no tomorrow.

"Sit!" Rawley ordered, deepening his voice.

The dog got his shaking butt halfway to the ground before he lifted it back up and began wagging his tail again.

"Sit!" Rawley repeated. Austin thought he sounded a great deal like Dallas.

This time, the dog plopped his butt onto the ground. Loree smiled brightly and clapped while Rawley tossed the dog a scrap of food. Loree glanced Austin's way, and her smile grew warm. "You're home."

He ambled to her, extended his hand, and helped her to her feet. "Yep. What are you two doing?"

"Teaching Two-bits how to sit," Rawley explained as he tossed the dog another morsel. The dog devoured it like he hadn't eaten in weeks when Austin knew that wasn't the case.

"Rawley made him a collar," Loree said as she reached down and petted the dog.

"Used an old belt. Mr. D taught me how to carve into the leather." Rawley pointed. "See, I did the dog's name."

"You did a good job," Austin said, glad to see how his words pleased Rawley. The boy had received too little praise before he'd come to live with Dallas.

"Mr. D said when Two-bits fathers some pups, I can have one."

"That might be a while," Austin said.

"Mr. D said the same thing. Said he'd git me a dog now if I wanted, but I decided to wait on account I want a dog like Two-bits." Rawley backed up a step. "Well, I'd best git home."

"Tell your pa that I'll be checking on the north range tomorrow."

Rawley gave him a quick nod. "Yes, sir. Bye, Aunt Loree."

"Thank you for the collar," she said warmly.

"You're welcome." He hurried to his horse, mounted up, and kicked his horse into a gallop.

Austin watched the dust settle back into place.

"You did that on purpose didn't you?" Loree asked.

He shifted his gaze to her. "Did what?"

"Gave him a message to take to 'his pa.' My guess is Dallas already knows you'll be checking the north range tomorrow."

Austin rubbed the side of his nose. "Was it that obvious I want the boy to realize Dallas is his father?"

"Probably not to him, but I'm beginning to know you a little more. Dallas tells people what he wants. You have a tendency to try and guide them without letting them know that you're guiding them."

Reaching out, he took her hand and tugged her to him until her toes crept over his boots. "So if I wanted to guide you toward an 'I'm glad that you're home' kiss, what would I do?"

"What you do every evening. Put my hands on your shoulders and your hands on my waist. Then lean down—"

He didn't let her finish, just planted his lips over hers, allowing the seed for love to begin taking root. He wished like hell that she hadn't been forced to marry him, but if she hadn't—she'd be in Austin and he'd be here, wishing he were with her.

He kept the kiss sweet and short because his resolve was weakening. What he really wanted was to lift her into his arms, guide her into the bedroom, and make love to her until dawn—but that damn promise stopped him because he hadn't figured out how to convince her that he was only thinking of her.

Loree bit back the whimper when his mouth left hers. She did so look forward to his coming home in the evening. She smiled warmly. "Are you ready for supper?"

"Starving."

Loree strolled into the house. A main living area on the first floor opened into a kitchen area. The bedroom she and Austin shared was off to the side. Stairs within that bedroom led to the second floor where two other rooms waited for them to decide how best to use them.

She had brought a few things from her home near Austin: a rocking chair, her vanity, her music boxes. They had Austin's bedroom furniture, Dee and Dallas's table, and a sofa from Amelia and Houston.

Nothing to hint at permanence . . . and yet, she felt contentment. She was learning a good deal about her husband. He was a man of simple habits. He awoke each morning before dawn and sat on the front porch, waiting for the sunrise, his hands wrapped around a tin cup that held his black coffee. He never started the day with a meal, always ate lunch with the cowhands, and returned in the evening with a voracious appetite.

Night had fallen by the time they finished their meal, and she joined Austin on the porch. She enjoyed these moments when he seemed most relaxed and content. She sat on the top step. "How was your day?" she asked quietly.

A corner of Austin's mouth quirked up. "Tiring. I sure don't remember feeling this tired in the evenings before. Must be age catching up with me."

She laughed lightly. "You are so incredibly old."

Turning, he pressed his back against the beam, straightened his legs, and brought her feet to his lap. He rubbed his thumbs over her sole. "How was your day?"

"Amelia visited."

"Not being a pesky neighbor, is she?"

"No, I think she's purposefully trying to leave us alone. She told me you had helped build the house."

"Helped to add the bedroom and the rooms upstairs."

"I like the thought of our children playing on a floor you may have hammered into place." She gnawed on her lower lip, raised a hand, and squinted into the setting sun. "You see that tree over there?"

Austin glanced over his shoulder. "Yeah?"

The tree was not what she would call beautiful. Bent, gnarled, and crooked, it looked as though it had spent much of its time fighting the lonesome winds and seldom winning.

"Can we hang a swing from it?"

"We can hang anything from it that you want, Sugar."

Two-bits leapt on the porch, wagged his tail, and yipped before settling down beside her hip.

Austin chuckled. "He's such a ferocious guardian."

"He's good company, and he gives Rawley an excuse to visit. He reminds me so much of my brother."

Austin's fingers stilled their soothing journey over the soles of her feet. "You really miss your brother, don't you?"

"Some days are harder than others, but I guess it's always like that when you lose someone you love."

He started rubbing her feet again. "Speaking of someone you love, they're putting the ones they love to bed."

Night had swept over the land. Loree gazed at the house in the distance. Lights spilled out from the windows on the second floor. A window fell into darkness.

"That'll be A. J.," Austin said.

"What does the A. J. stand for?" Loree asked.

"Anita June. Amanda's middle name is April. When it suits their fancy, they have a tendency to name their daughters after the month in which they were born. Hope you're not planning to do that."

"What if I was?" she challenged.

"Then that's what we'd do." Austin pointed toward the house. "They're coming to my favorite window."

Loree glanced back over her shoulder. Two other windows were now ensconced in darkness. She watched as the light from the last window disappeared.

"That was Maggie's room. Give her a minute . . ." The light again burned within the window. Austin chuckled.

"What's she doing?" Loree asked.

"No idea, but she turns that lamp back up every night."

"You love her so much."

"I love 'em all, but I know Maggie . . . and Rawley. But I'm slowly getting to know the others." He yawned and patted her feet. "Guess I'd best get to bed."

He unfolded his body, took her hand, and brought her to her feet. "Don't know if you noticed the theater Dee built in town. It's gonna have its first performance next week. She's invited the whole family to go."

"That should be fun."

"Yeah," he replied, but she thought she heard doubt in his voice. "You go on in. I'll be there directly."

Following their nightly ritual, she went to their bedroom, slipped into her nightgown, crawled into bed, turned down the lamp, and waited. She heard her husband walking the perimeter of the house as though he loathed giving up another day. He joined her a little sooner than he had the night before. Pressing a kiss to her temple, he drew her into the circle of his arms.

As she lay there, listening to his breathing, knowing he was giving as much as he could without dishonoring his vow, she cursed the night she'd extracted a promise from him.

Chapter Eleven

$\mathcal{L}$oree glanced at her reflection in the mirror. The yellow ribbon at the end of her braid looked incredibly childish, even if it had been a gift from Austin. She yanked it from her hair and dropped onto the bed, pulling the ribbon through her fingers, over and over.

Austin had gone to Houston's as soon as he'd seen Dallas and his family arrive in their buggy, leaving Loree to finish getting dressed on her own. She didn't want to embarrass him by looking like a little girl when they attended the play at the theater. Only she had no idea how to make herself look grown up. She heard the soft knock on her door. "Come in."

Dee poked her head around the door. "How's it coming?"

Loree held up the ribbon. "I just need to figure out what to do with this ribbon. I don't want to hurt Austin's feelings by not wearing it."

Dee stepped into the room, and Loree wished she could come up with a plausible excuse to get out of going to this affair. Dee's red gown complemented her pale complexion, black hair, and brown eyes, leaving her devastatingly beautiful. "Oh, I'm sure we can think of something to do with it. Don't you think, Amelia?"

Smiling warmly and holding a large box, Amelia waltzed in behind Dee. Amelia's golden hair was swept up into a graceful bouquet of curls. The green of her dress emphasized the green of her eyes. She looked radiant.

Dee pulled out the chair in front of the mirrored vanity. "Loree, why don't you sit here?"

"Why don't we put on the gown first?" Amelia suggested.

Incredibly embarrassed, Loree glanced at her best dress. "I am wearing my dress."

Amelia walked to the bed, set the box down, and ripped off the lid. "I thought you'd want to wear the gown Austin ordered for you."

Loree took a hesitant step forward. "What gown?"

With a flourish, Amelia pulled a rustle of lace and silk out of the box and held it up for Loree to see. "This one."

Tears stung Loree's eyes. The pale yellow bodice dipped down to form a V. Lace decorated the area between the V and ran up along the shoulders. A top skirt was split down the middle and pulled back, held in place with yellow ribbons, to reveal a pleated lace skirt beneath.

"Austin ordered this gown?" Loree asked, touching the soft material with awe.

"In a way," Amelia admitted. "He told me you

needed something to wear. He insisted it be yellow because you look beautiful in yellow—"

"He said that?" Loree asked. "That I looked beautiful?"

Amelia smiled warmly. "He said that. But not knowing how his taste in women's clothing runs . . . and having had an unfortunate experience with Dallas's tastes in women's attire, I oversaw the dress maker's efforts."

"I had no idea—" Loree began.

"I think he wanted it to be a surprise."

"Oh, it is."

"Why don't you slip it on," Dee suggested, "and then we'll see about arranging your hair."

Loree grabbed her braid. "I don't suppose we could pile it on top of my head."

"We can do anything you want."

AUSTIN SAT IN Houston's parlor, sprawled in the chair, gazing out the window, wishing he could think of a way to get out of his family obligation.

The way Rawley was crunching his face, Austin figured he was searching for an excuse, too. Rawley dug his finger behind the collar of his starched white shirt, looking like he might choke at any minute. Then his face brightened. "I should probably check on the herd."

Dallas shifted his gaze from the window and nodded slowly. "You probably should."

Relief washed over Rawley's face as he strode for the door.

"If the herd means more to you than your mother does," Dallas added.

Rawley stumbled to a stop and glanced over his shoulder.

"The theater is one of your mother's dreams. She's a little nervous about tonight," Dallas said.

Rawley took a deep breath. "Then I reckon I oughta be there."

"Reckon so."

Rawley reached into his shirt pocket and pulled out a sarsaparilla stick. Daintily, Faith walked up to him. "Gimme."

"It's my last one," Rawley said, even as he broke it in half and handed a piece to her. Then he glared at Maggie as she sat in the corner, watching over her three sisters. "Reckon you want some, too."

She held up a bag. "We still have the lemon drops Uncle Dallas brought."

"If those women don't hurry, the girls are all gonna have belly aches before we get out of here," Houston said.

"As long as they're riding in your wagon, that's not a problem for me," Dallas said.

"What's keeping them?" Austin asked.

"Hell, you never know with women," Dallas said.

Austin heard the patter of footsteps on the front porch. The door swung open. Amelia and Dee rushed in, looking like little girls trying to hold in an enormous secret. Then Loree stepped through the doorway and Austin felt as though a wild mustang had just kicked him in the chest. Sweet Lord, the little darling he'd married was going to catch the eye of every man in town.

Slowly he came to his feet. Loree's smile faltered

and she touched her gloved hand to the nape of her neck.

"You don't like it?" she asked.

"I like it just fine," he said, wondering where that raspy voice had come from.

"Amelia said you purchased the gown."

"I did. I just didn't know it was gonna look like that."

"I could change—"

"No!" three male voices sounded at once.

LOREE HAD SEEN the outside of the theater from the hotel, but she had never imagined the opulence that had been hidden inside. Candles flickered within crystal chandeliers. A thick red carpet with designs running through it covered every inch of the floor. Gilded mirrors adorned the walls. Wide sweeping stairs on either side of the foyer led to the balconies.

At one end of the foyer was a room where parents could leave their children in the capable hands of women paid to care for them. As far as Loree could determine, Dee had thought of everything and designed the theater to give the people of Leighton a night they'd never forget.

It seemed everyone within a thousand miles had come for the opening performance. Loree had never been in one room with so many people.

Austin took her elbow and leaned low. "They're serving champagne over there. Do you want some?"

"Do you think they have some water?"

Smiling, he tucked a stray strand of hair behind

her ear. "If they don't, I'll find some. Why don't you wait here with Rawley until Dee and Dallas get back from taking Faith to that baby room?"

She nodded slightly.

"Rawley, I'm leaving your aunt in your care. You watch after her, now."

Rawley straightened his shoulders. "Yes, sir."

Loree's heart swelled as she watched her husband make his way through the crowd. Tall, lean, he looked incredibly handsome in his black jacket and white starched shirt.

"How long is a play anyway?" Rawley asked, drawing her attention away from Austin.

"A couple of hours I imagine."

"Think there's any chance *Romeo and Juliet* is a story about a boy and his dog?" Rawley asked.

Loree fought back her smile. "No, it's a love story."

"A boy could love his dog," he said hopefully.

Loree's smile broke free. "In this story, he loves a woman."

Rawley grimaced. "They ain't gonna do any kissing, are they?"

"Don't you like kissing?"

"Ain't never tried it, but can't see where it'd be much fun. From what I can tell, looks to me like the two people are just swapping spit. I'd rather swap marbles."

"Rawley!"

Loree turned just as Maggie plowed into Rawley. Breathless, she squeezed his arm. "Rawley, one of the actors is over there showing people his sword. His honest to gosh sword! Come on!"

She tugged on his arm, but Rawley pulled back. He cast a quick glance at Loree, and she saw the longing in his eyes. "I can't. Told Uncle Austin I'd stay here with Aunt Loree."

Maggie wasn't as discreet in her disappointment. "Heck fire, Rawley, we won't be that far away."

Rawley hesitated, then shook his head. "Can't do it. Gave my word."

Loree placed her hand on his shoulder. "Go on. I'll be all right."

"Uncle Austin might not like it."

"I'll explain it to him so he does."

"Suppose I could just run over and take a quick look-see."

Maggie grabbed his hand. "Come on, Rawley. You won't believe how shiny his sword is. Looks like it's sharp enough to cut the head off a Longhorn."

Loree watched them work their way through the crowd. Her brother had been around Rawley's age when he'd died. She couldn't remember if he'd ever looked at a sword.

She felt a light tap on her arm and turned. Her stomach dropped to her knees at the sight of the man and woman standing before her.

"Hello," Becky said smiling warmly. "I didn't know you were still in town."

Loree gave her a jerky nod. "Yes. Yes, I live here now."

"How wonderful! You'll have to come visit some Sunday when the store is closed. Did you find the gun you were looking for?"

"Why would she need a gun?" Austin asked from behind her.

Loree's heart pounded so heavily she was certain he felt it as he clamped his hand possessively onto her waist. "Here's your water," he said quietly.

With a trembling hand, Loree took the glass from him. "Thank you. I was already beginning to miss you."

Austin smiled warmly, dipped his head, and brushed a quick kiss across her lips. "I was missing you, too."

Loree shifted her gaze and watched as understanding dawned in Becky's eyes and the blood drained from her face.

"Austin, it's so good to see you again," Becky said, her voice faltering. "How are you?"

"Wiser."

"Cameron told me you'd gotten married . . . I just . . . I just didn't realize . . . I'd met your wife," Becky stammered.

"She mentioned meeting you. Loree, Sugar, did you meet Cameron?"

"I saw him, but I don't think we actually met."

"He's Dee's brother. I'm not sure I ever mentioned that," Austin said.

"No, you didn't. You only mentioned that he'd been your best friend."

Cameron looked as though he might fall ill at any moment. "Austin—"

"If you'll excuse us," Austin said, "we need to find our seats. Dee would never forgive us for missing the opening scene."

Austin held out his arm. Loree grabbed onto it, afraid she'd sink to the floor if she didn't have his support. The crowd parted as they walked to the sweeping staircase. She heard a mumbled "murderer," and her heart tripped over itself. She glanced at her husband, saw his clenched jaw, and realized people were murmuring about him. She angled her chin proudly.

"I've never watched a play before. I've always wanted to attend one."

Austin glanced down at her.

She smiled with her heart in her eyes. "I'm very glad that you're the one who's taking me."

"Sugar, I don't think I would have made it up these stairs without you by my side."

He took her hand at the top of the stairs. They walked along the landing, passing several curtained entrances before Austin swept back the drapery and led Loree into the darkness of a balcony.

"Thank you, Loree, for looking like you were proud to have me by your side," he whispered.

"I was proud."

She sensed a moment's hesitation before he took her into his arms and lowered his mouth to hers. She twined her arms around his neck, returning his kiss with a fervor that surprised her. She had wanted to scratch out eyes and yank out hair. She'd wanted to ask those two people how they could have betrayed her husband, the father of her child, the man she was coming to love.

Austin grunted and stumbled to the side, taking her with him. The curtain was drawn aside, and Dallas was silhouetted in the doorway.

"What are you doing?" Dallas demanded.

"Looking for our seats," Austin said, his hand skimming over hers before latching securely onto it.

Then mayhem erupted as the family crowded inside the small balcony.

"Everyone take your seats," Dee said excitedly. "They'll be opening the curtains any minute."

"Which chair is mine?" Maggie asked. "I wanna sit in the front."

"Ladies in the front," Dallas said, "Men in the back."

"Loree sits by me," Austin said.

"Yeah, and I want to sit by Amelia," Houston added.

"Fine," Dallas ground out.

"We'll put the children, Austin, and Loree in the back—" Dallas began.

"Then the children won't be able to see," Amelia pointed out.

"I don't care if I can't see," Rawley said.

"But then you won't see the sword fight," Maggie told him. "You gotta see the sword fight."

"I don't mind sitting in the back—"

"Houston and I will sit in the back," Amelia said.

"No, Dallas and I are taller. We'll sit in the back," Dee offered.

"No, Dee, this is your dream—"

"But I want you to see—"

Austin tugged on Loree's hand. "Come on," he whispered. "We'll just sit in the back."

He guided her toward the far side. As they sat,

he kept his hand wrapped around hers. She heard his low chuckle. "Guess I started this by wanting to sit by you."

"I'm grateful you did because I really didn't want to sit by anyone else."

He trailed his finger along her jaw. "I'm glad. Loree, I'm sorry it was so awkward down there, with people staring and whispering. They're just not used to me being home yet."

"My home could give us the things we need."

"I want you to have things that you *want* not just things that you need."

"That's it!" Dallas roared. "Everyone has five seconds to plant their butts in a seat. Anyone left standing at the end of that time goes over the balcony."

A mad scramble ensued.

"Come on, Rawley," Maggie cried as she pulled him to a seat in front.

She plopped down in front of Austin. He tapped her shoulder. "Trade places with Rawley so your Aunt Loree can see."

She and Rawley switched chairs. While the remaining adults discussed the seating arrangements, Maggie turned and looked at Austin. "Can me and Rawley spit over the side of the balcony?"

"Sure, especially if your Uncle Cameron is sitting down there."

"He ain't. They got balcony seats, too." She pointed to the side. "They're right there."

Loree watched as Austin's gaze followed the direction of Maggie's finger. He stiffened. Cameron and Becky were sitting alone in the balcony next to theirs.

"You don't like Uncle Cameron anymore, do you?" Maggie asked.

Austin jerked his head around and stared at her. Amelia put her hand on her daughter's shoulder. "Turn around, young lady." She gave Austin an apologetic smile before taking her seat beside Maggie. Houston settled in beside her.

Dee sat beside Loree and laughed lightly. "I didn't realize that was going to be such an ordeal." She patted Dallas's knee. "You handled the situation very well."

"Next time, everybody gets their own balcony."

A man walked onto the stage, and a hush fell over the audience.

"Ladies and gentlemen! The Royal Shakespearean Theater is honored to be in your lovely town. Tonight's performance is *Romeo and Juliet*."

He walked off the stage. The curtains slowly began to open, but Loree found she had no interest in the play. She wondered what thoughts preyed on her husband's mind. His hand had tightened around hers when Maggie had asked her question. His grip had yet to loosen. He stared straight ahead, but she didn't think he was paying any more attention to the play than she was. She leaned toward him. "I want to go outside."

He jerked his head around, and even in the shadows, she saw the concern etched in his face. His hand closed more tightly around hers. "You all right?"

She nodded slightly. "I just need a breath of fresh air."

He leaned low around her and whispered to Dallas, "We're gonna step outside for a few minutes."

Rawley twisted around in his chair. "Can I go?"

Dallas gave a quick nod and stood. Austin helped Loree to her feet and they worked their way between the chairs.

"I'm sorry," she whispered as she stepped on Dee's foot. But Dee didn't seem to notice as she waved them past, her gaze riveted on the stage. They stepped between the curtains, and Loree took a deep breath.

"You sure you're all right?" Austin asked.

"I just felt a little faint."

"You wanna go sit in the buggy?"

"Could we take a walk?"

"Sure." He wrapped his hand around hers, and they descended the stairs.

"Could you understand anything them actors was saying?" Rawley asked as he tromped along behind them.

"Not a word," Austin said.

They walked through the foyer, and Austin swung open the front door. Loree walked through. Austin glanced over his shoulder. "You coming?"

Loree noticed Rawley's hesitation. She peered back inside. At the far end, in the baby room, Faith had her nose pressed to the pane of glass.

"Reckon I'll go be with Faith," Rawley muttered.

"There's women inside watching them," Austin assured him. "She's fine."

"She don't look fine. She looks downright miserable," Rawley said. "I don't like for my sister to be unhappy."

He stalked toward the room. Austin chuckled. "I reckon Faith couldn't have asked for a better brother." He glanced at Loree. "I couldn't have asked for a finer wife."

Loree felt herself blush as she stepped onto the boardwalk. Austin followed her outside and took her hand. "Where do you want to walk?"

"Doesn't matter."

"We'll head for the far end of town, then."

He'd taken four long strides before he adjusted the length of his walk to accommodate her.

"So why did you need a gun?" he asked quietly.

Her step faltered, and she glanced up at him. "I was hoping you'd forgotten about that."

"There's not a lot I forget."

She sighed heavily. "I was in a strange town, I didn't know if you'd come back—"

He came to an abrupt halt and spun her around to face him, hurt evident in his eyes. "You thought I'd abandoned you?"

"No, not really. I was just . . . I was just scared."

She felt him searching her face, searching for something she could never let him see.

"What is it exactly that you fear?"

"The past. I'm afraid it has a stronger hold on us than either of us realizes."

"Because of Becky?"

"Because of a lot of things."

"I can't change my past."

Unfortunately, she couldn't change hers either.

She could only hope that it would never lift its ugly head to touch Austin or their children. "Share something good with me."

His blue eyes darkened, and his lips spread into a warm smile filled with impassioned promises. He placed his hands on either side of her waist and drew her against him. "What exactly did you have in mind?"

"A story. Tell me a good story from your past."

Laughing, he released her waist, took her hand, and began walking. "I'm no good at telling stories."

The night closed in around them. The lamps along the street threw ashen light over the abandoned boardwalk. The town seemed almost deserted with most of the residents attending the play. She saw pale lamplight spilling out from the saloon at the far end of town, along with boisterous laughter, and the echo of a tinny piano.

She stumbled when the heel of her shoe hit a loose plank in the boardwalk. Austin steadied her, then knelt and slapped his thigh. "Give me your foot."

"What are you going to do?"

He glanced up at her and she saw the answer in his gaze.

"I'm dressed all fancy. I can't go barefooted."

He angled his head and lifted a brow. "Are we going back into the theater to watch the play?"

She remembered how tense he'd been inside the building, how his body and his hold on her had relaxed once they'd stepped outside. "No."

"Then get your foot up here."

Placing her hands on his shoulders, she planted her foot on his thigh and watched as he nimbly worked her buttons free and removed the shoe from her foot. "You have such nice fingers," she said as he rolled her stocking off.

"You think so?"

"Mmm-uh." She relished the feel of the boardwalk beneath her bare sole and placed her other foot on his thigh. "I wish you'd let me teach you to play your mother's violin."

His hands stilled.

"It takes time and patience, but I have both," she assured him.

He worked her shoe free, grabbed the other shoe, and unfolded his body. "I can't play the violin, Loree."

"If you tried—"

"I can't."

His words were spoken with absolute finality.

"Can't never could," she muttered.

"What?"

She shook her head. "Just something my ma used to tell me."

He shifted her shoes to one hand, wrapped his free hand around hers, and began walking.

"Dallas has his cattle, Houston has his horses. What do you have?"

"You."

His smile was warm, and her heart fluttered.

"Before me, what did you have? What were your dreams?"

His steps slowed as though they followed his thinking, back to a time when he had dreams.

"Dallas is a man of powerful influence." He pierced her with his gaze. "I love and admire him, Loree. Don't ever think that I don't."

"I wouldn't."

He gave a curt nod. "I wanted to go someplace where people had never heard of him. I wanted to make a name for myself, knowing I had earned the recognition because of me, not him. Does that make any sense?"

She nodded with complete understanding. "Where would you have gone?"

He shook his head slowly. "Never got that far in my thinking. Once I . . . Once I met Becky, the thought of leaving went straight out of my head."

"She became your dream then."

He stopped walking, leaned one shoulder against the side of the building, and brought her close. "No. No, she didn't. She just made me stop thinking about it." He trailed his long fingers along her jaw. "You made me start thinking about dreams again."

He dipped his head and brushed his lips over hers. "You make me think about a lot of things. You have from the first moment I realized you weren't a boy."

He settled his mouth over hers, drawing her up onto her toes. Her feet crept over his boots, taking her higher. His arm came around her, holding her close while he cradled her cheek with his other hand and tilted her head back. He trailed his hot mouth along her throat.

"Sweet, sweet Loree. God, I need you," he rasped.

Heat swirled through her, around her, over her. Her head dropped back. "Tell me . . . tell me what you would have done to make a name for yourself."

"I woulda—"

He made a guttural sound and stumbled back. Loree went flying off him and landed hard on her backside.

"You goddamn murdering son of a bitch!" a man yelled as he slammed Austin into the brick building.

Austin grunted and slid in a heap to the ground.

"They shoulda hanged you!" The man kicked him in the side. Groaning, Austin curled into a ball.

"No!" Loree screamed as she crawled toward one of the shoes Austin had dropped. She threw it at the man, hitting him squarely on the side of the head.

The man jerked back. She heaved the other shoe at him, grateful to see him run into the shadows.

Loree scrambled across the boardwalk. "Austin?"

He moaned as she rolled him over and gently placed his head in her lap. She felt the warm, sticky wetness coating her hands and released a blood-curdling scream.

Chapter Twelve

❧

I can't get the blood off," Loree ground out through clenched teeth as she washed her hands in the bowl of warm water that the doctor had brought her.

Austin heard the tremor of panic in her voice, watched the way she scrubbed viciously at her hands, and was afraid she was going to peel off her skin. He moved away from the doctor who was examining his head.

"Hey, young fella—" Dr. Freeman began.

Austin held up a hand. "Just a minute."

He crossed the room and took Loree's hands. She snapped her gaze up to his, and he could almost see the horrific memories mirrored in her golden eyes.

"I can't get the blood off," she rasped.

He remembered how she'd continued to scrub herself the night Digger had died, even though she'd washed away all the blood. "I can get it off," he said quietly. He dipped his hand into the water, then slowly, gently trailed his fingers over her clean hands. Tenderly, he wiped them dry. "There, see? The blood's all gone."

Her brow furrowed, Loree glanced at her hands, then lifted one to touch the back of his head. He grabbed her hand before she could get blood on it again. Tears welled in her eyes. "Someone hurt you."

He kissed the tips of her fingers. "I'm gonna be all right. You go sit in the front room with Dee."

She nodded before leaving the room, closing the door in her wake. He wished he'd been able to spare her the sight of his blood. Austin crossed back to the chair and sat. He grimaced as the doctor dabbed something against his head. "Damn! That burns."

"I just want to make certain the gash is clean before I stitch it up. We don't need any infection," Dr. Freeman said, his tall skeletal frame thinner than Austin remembered.

"Are you sure Loree is all right?" he asked. Afraid she might have been hurt earlier, he had insisted Dr. Freeman examine her first.

"She's fine," Dr. Freeman said. "She just doesn't have much stomach for blood is all."

Austin figured he wouldn't either if he'd watched someone murder his family.

"Who attacked you?" Dallas asked from his place near the doorway.

"I don't know."

"Duncan?"

Austin glared at his brother. "I said, I don't know. He came at me from behind and slammed my head against the wall. Everything went from black to blacker."

"I'll ride out and talk to Duncan tomorrow—"

"And what? Tell him to stay away from me when you don't even know it was him? He's not the only one in town who thinks I should have hanged."

Dallas's eyes narrowed. "Who else?"

"Most of the town."

"Then I'll set them all straight."

"It's your word against a verdict of guilty. Just stay clear of this. You're only asking for trouble if you get involved."

"Goddamn it! This started with me!"

"And it'll finish with me." He heaved a weary sigh. "I appreciate your willingness to take a stand, but the truth of the matter is that I did some stupid things without thinking them through. They were my mistakes, and I'm the one that has to pay for them. Without those mistakes, no jury would have ever found me guilty."

He expected a further argument. Instead, he saw abiding respect delve into his oldest brother's eyes. "Christ, you did grow up, didn't you?"

Austin gave him a halfhearted smile. "Yeah."

The door opened and Dee poked her head through the opening. "Dr. Freeman, Loree said something is happening with the baby."

Austin shot off the table. "Dammit! I thought you looked her over."

"I did," Dr. Freeman said as he shuffled from the room, following in Austin's wake.

Loree was sitting in a stuffed chair in Dr. Freeman's front parlor. Austin knelt beside her and wrapped his hand around her tightened fist. "Loree?"

Tears shimmered in her eyes. "Oh, Austin, I think I'm losing the baby."

Austin heard bones creak as Dr. Freeman made his way to his knees. "How badly did it hurt?" he asked.

A look of surprise swept over Loree's face. "Well, it didn't hurt exactly."

"What exactly did it do?" Dr. Freeman asked.

Loree cast a sidelong glance at Austin before turning her attention back to Dr. Freeman. "Well, it sorta felt like"—she gnawed on her lower lip and furrowed her brow—"you know when you jump into a creek and air gets trapped in your pantaloons and sorta sits there for a minute after you hit the water and then it bubbles out and tickles? That's what it felt like."

Austin thought Dr. Freeman looked as though he were on the verge of busting a gut, his face turned crimson and Austin could tell he was fighting to hold back his laughter. "Can't say I've ever had air get trapped in my pantaloons." He glanced over his shoulder at Dee. "Think she just felt the baby roll over?"

Dee smiled warmly. "I think so."

With wonder reflected in her golden eyes, Loree pressed her hand against her stomach. "I felt the baby roll over? She's all right?"

"I'm certain she's just fine," Dr. Freeman said.

THE STYMIED LATE August air hung outside the open window, doing little to cool Austin's sweating body. The moon spilled into the bedroom, waltzing with the darkness.

He saw the shadow of his violin as it rested on the top of his bureau. Once he'd been able to hear the music long before he ever touched the strings.

Once, he had dreamed of a special violin—created with his own hands—that made the sweetest music ever heard.

Now, he would be content to play his mother's scarred and scratched violin—if only he once again had the ability to bring the music to life within his heart.

"Austin, what are you doing?" Loree whispered sleepily.

He walked to the bed, stretched out beside her, and spread his fingers over her stomach. "Just couldn't sleep."

"Does your head hurt?"

"Nah, it's fine."

"The man you went to prison for killing—"

"Was a sorry son of a bitch not worth worrying over."

"He must have meant something to someone for a man to attack you. I heard him say you should have hanged."

He cradled her cheek. "I'll tell you how worthless he was. One night behind the hotel, he shoved some wooden crates over on top of Dee and lit out without a backward glance. Dee lost the baby she was carrying and dang near lost her life. Then he paid Rawley's father to kill Dallas. I don't regret his dying. I only regret that I went to prison because of it." Tenderly, he brushed his lips over hers. "I'm gonna be the one waking up with nightmares if we keep following this trail. Let's talk about something else. Tell me again what it felt like when the baby moved inside you."

"It scared me at first because I thought something was wrong. My ma never told me things about having a baby. I didn't know I'd feel her roll over . . . or that it would feel so wonderful." She turned to her side, burying her face in the crook of his shoulder. "I'm glad we're gonna have her. I was embarrassed at first . . . even ashamed—"

He tilted her face back. He couldn't see the gold in her eyes, but it didn't stop him from searching for it. "Loree, the shame is mine, not yours, never yours."

"Austin, I wanted you close to me that night. I'd never felt so alone in my whole life."

He reached through the darkness, found her hand, and brought it to his lips. "In prison . . ."

"What?"

He swallowed hard. If only removing the shackles had removed the memories. "There was this box. The inside was black as tar. If the guard had a toothache or was in the mood to be mean, he'd shove someone into that box." He felt the sweat break out on his skin and he shivered, even though the night was warm. Her fingers tightened around his. "I couldn't breathe in that box. I thought I'd go crazy. The night I got home and Dallas told me Becky had gotten married, I felt like he'd shoved me inside that box."

She pressed a kiss against his chest. "I'm sorry."

"That first night I held you, I felt a flicker of hope that I might be able to escape."

He felt her warm tears slide down his chest.

"One of these nights, Loree, I'm gonna leave every memory I have outside that door. When that happens I'm gonna make love to you until dawn." Her arms slid around him and she scooted her body close enough to his that he felt every curve. "Lord, I love it when you do that," he whispered, drawing her closer.

"They're nice people, aren't they?"

His chest muffled her words, but he knew without asking to whom she referred. Becky and Cameron. "Yeah, they are. That's what makes this so much harder. I can't find it in me to hate them."

Her hold on him tightened, and he felt slight tremors racing through her. "I'm glad," she whispered hoarsely. "Hate can eat at you . . . make you do things . . ."

He pressed a kiss to her temple and tasted the salt of a tear. "What do you know of hate, Loree?"

"The man who murdered my family. I wanted him dead. I wanted him dead so bad that it was like he'd crawled inside me."

She started gasping for breath, and he heard a broken sob escape. "Shh. Shh. Loree, don't upset yourself. It's been a bad night. Don't think about the past. Think about the future." He continued to coo to her, feeling her body relaxing within his arms. Her gasping gave way to slow even breathing. "That's it, Sugar. Think about that little girl—"

She sniffed. "Boy."

He chuckled low. "Oh, it's a boy now, is it?"

"I think so."

He drew her closer. The night was warm, unbearably hot, but he kept her within the circle of his arms. He hadn't been lying when he'd told her he'd be the one to wake up with nightmares, but he'd discovered that as long as she was nestled against him, he could hold the hated memories at bay.

"TELL ME ABOUT your wedding."

Loree stopped kneading the bread dough and glanced up at Maggie's expectant face. The child sat at the end of the table, her legs tucked up beneath her bottom on the chair, the hand holding the stub of her pencil poised above the journal.

"My wedding?"

Maggie nodded briskly. "I want to write a story about it."

Loree glanced at the window. She saw the gray skies. She could not believe how quickly autumn had given way to winter. She turned her attention back to Maggie. "Do you write lots of stories?"

Maggie bobbed her head.

"When do you write all these stories?"

"Nighttime is the best. It's usually the quietest 'cept when Pa gets a hankering for a bunch of kisses. He'll say he wants to see Ma's toes curl, and she'll start giggling. Then suddenly, it gets really quiet. Do your toes curl when Uncle Austin kisses you?"

Loree felt her face warm. She had to admit Maggie wasn't a shy child, but she couldn't wait to tell Austin that she knew what Maggie was doing at night when her light again became visible in her room. She started pounding the bread dough. "Sometimes."

"I bet Aunt Becky's toes curl. When Uncle Cameron married her, he kissed her a really long time. Until Uncle Dallas cleared his throat real loud. Made me jump outta my skin."

Loree imagined any noise Dallas made on purpose would startle her. "Was their wedding nice?"

Maggie shrugged. "It was tiny. There was just us. And Aunt Becky was so silly. She started crying. She said she didn't think we'd come on account of her lovin' Uncle Austin first and then lovin' Uncle Cameron." Maggie rolled her eyes. "But once you love someone, you don't stop lovin' 'em."

"No, I guess you don't." Loree wondered where the child had gained her wisdom, and if she'd lose it once she grew older.

A brief knock sounded on the door before Houston opened it, a panicked expression on his face. His other three daughters were with him, their eyes wide. "Amelia's having the baby. Can I leave the young 'uns with you?"

"Certainly." Wiping her hands on her apron, Loree crossed the room and ushered the children inside.

THE COLD NOVEMBER winds whipped around Austin as he guided Black Thunder home. He drew up the collar on his sheepskin jacket and pulled his hat lower over his brow. Night was closing in, and he relished its arrival.

Evenings had become his favorite time of day. Loree welcomed him with arms open wide, a warm meal, and a warmer kiss. They sat in front of the fire, curled around each other, waiting for their child to move.

Austin had grown up around a brother who bred cattle, a brother who bred horses . . . and yet the wonder of a child that he'd helped to create growing within a woman he cherished . . . humbled him.

He brought Black Thunder to a halt, dismounted, and impatiently set about the task of tending to his horse before seeing to his own needs. He saw the lamplight spilling out from the window, and the chill of the night gave way to an unexpected warmth.

He finished his task and strode to the house, anticipation hurrying his step. He threw open the door and froze.

"Uncle Austin," three little magpies chirped and raced across the room to wrap themselves around his legs.

"We're makin' baby cookies," Laurel said. "Want one?"

The one she extended toward him had a bite taken from it. Loree strolled across the room and began to tug the girls back. "Come on, girls. At least let Uncle Austin get his jacket off."

He met Loree's eyes as he shrugged out of his jacket. She looked at him imploringly. "Amelia went into labor this morning. Houston brought the girls over so I could watch them."

Austin looked past her to the table laden with cookies. "I said we'd bake cookies until the baby was born. I didn't know it would take all day."

The door swung open catching Austin in the middle of his back. Maggie pushed her way through. "Not yet. Pa says anytime. So can we bake some more cookies?"

"Don't you think you have enough cookies?" Austin asked.

"But Aunt Loree said—"

"She didn't know your ma would take so long," Austin explained. "And Aunt Loree looks mighty tired to me."

"We could play Go Fish," Maggie suggested.

"It's a little late to go fishing," Austin said.

Maggie laughed. "You're so silly, Uncle Austin. It's a game."

Loree sat in the rocking chair, watching her husband play a card game with his nieces. They sat in a circle, drawing cards, laying down cards. She suspected he was cheating because tiny A. J. who sat in his lap while he held her cards, as well as his own, was winning several hands while Austin was repeatedly ending up with no cards to his credit. It was a strange moment to come to the realization that she had fallen in love with him.

Her father had cheated as well—but it was always to his benefit . . . and she had yet to see Austin do anything that put him ahead at anyone else's expense.

As night wore on, he carried each sleeping girl to the bed. Near midnight, a knock finally sounded on the door. Looking exhausted Houston stepped into the house.

"It's a girl. Gracie."

"How's Amelia?" Austin asked.

"She had a hard time of it. Dr. Freeman says this will probably be the last one. Let me gather up the girls—"

"Why don't you let them stay?" Loree said quietly. "They're already asleep. I'll bring them over in the morning."

"If you're sure?"

"We're sure."

"If Maggie turns up the lamp after you've gone to sleep, will you ignore it? I know she slipped into the house and got her journal earlier. She likes to write in it after everyone else is asleep. We're not supposed to know."

Austin patted his brother's shoulder. "Go on. You look like you're ready to collapse."

Houston walked out the door. Austin turned to Loree. "Lie with me by the fire for a little while."

He stretched out on the sofa, and she curled against his side, watching the flames dance within the hearth.

"I'm almost out of sugar," Loree said quietly.

"I'll pick up another ten pounds tomorrow."

"I'm not that bad," she said, knowing he was teasing her.

"You're not bad at all."

Silence wove around them. Reaching down, Austin splayed his fingers over her swollen stomach. "You're tinier than Amelia."

"My mother was tiny. She didn't have any problems."

"Dallas wanted to be a father. Houston wanted to be a father. It's not that I don't want to be a father, but the thought of this little fella coming into the world scares the hell out of me."

"Scares me, too," she admitted.

He wrapped his hand around hers. "I've made a lot of mistakes in my life, Loree. I want you to know that I don't consider this child to be one of them."

She met his gaze, the love she held for him deepening. "I never thought that you did."

Chapter Thirteen

Austin stood against the wall in Dallas's dining area and watched the bustling activity with interest. Christmas had always been his favorite time of year.

Beside him, Loree jostled Gracie. Six weeks had passed since her birth, and it was evident that Houston had finally fathered a daughter who resembled him, with black hair and dark eyes. Austin enjoyed watching Loree care for the children.

He couldn't remember what she thought their baby was going to be this week, but whether it was a boy or a girl, he wanted it to have the one thing he'd grown up without: the comfort of a mother. And he knew beyond a doubt that with Loree, his children would have the best.

"When is Uncle Cameron going to get here?" Maggie asked as she plucked a pecan out of a bright red bowl and popped it into her mouth.

Dee stilled, the dish of applesauce halfway to the table. She cast a furtive glance at Austin before answering. "He's not going to celebrate Christmas with us this year."

A look of horror swept over Maggie's face. "But what about the special reindeer hay?"

Clearing her throat, Dee set the dish on the table between pumpkin pies and candles that smelled of cinnamon. "I'm sure Santa Claus will come even if we don't have the hay."

"No, he won't," Maggie said as she crossed her arms over her chest and pushed out her lower lip.

"Somebody ought to tell her the truth: There ain't no Santa Claus," Rawley whispered beside Austin.

Austin watched Rawley saunter to Maggie and put his hand on her shoulder. He didn't know if he could stand to watch the disappointment reshape Maggie's face when she heard the truth.

"Hey, Brat, we could probably use some of the hay from the barn," Rawley told her in a comforting voice.

Maggie wrinkled her nose. "It's not reindeer hay. What if it gives them a belly ache?"

"Then we'd know for sure there's a Santa Claus."

Maggie laughed, her green eyes sparkling like the candles lit upon the evergreen tree that stood in the corner of the front parlor. Rawley shoved on her shoulder. "Come on. Maybe we can find some that'll work."

"Get your jackets," Dee ordered as she headed back to the kitchen.

As they walked toward the door, Faith scrambled to her feet and raced after them. "Wawley, I wanna go, too."

"Come on then, Shorty."

She squealed as he swung her up into his arms.

"It's a wonder that girl ever learned to walk," Amelia said as she came to stand beside Austin. "The way her brother carts her around."

He shifted his gaze and found Amelia studying him. "Don't look at me like that," he ordered.

"Like what?" she asked, her green eyes containing an innocence he didn't believe.

"Like you know what I'm thinking. It's damn aggravating when you do that, and you've done it for as long as I've known you. Hell, you probably figured out that I lied about Houston's horse breaking its leg all those years ago."

She smiled at him the way he supposed mothers smiled at their errant children. "I suspected it at the time."

"Then why didn't you say something back then?"

"Because I figured it was a dilemma you needed to work out for yourself—just like now." She patted his shoulder before taking her daughter from Loree.

Austin spun on his heel and caught up with the children as they were shoving their arms into the sleeves of their coats. He opened the door and followed them outside, leaned against the veranda beam, and watched them trudge into the barn. The cold wind whipping around him felt warmer than his heart.

He heard the door open quietly and glanced over his shoulder. The woman had a way of walking into his life when he needed her the most.

Reaching out, he grabbed Loree's hand and pulled her against his side, her arms forming a cocoon around his chest.

"Special hay for reindeer." He snorted. "Where did Cameron come up with that?" Although she held her silence while he stared at the barn, he felt her scrutinizing gaze delving clear into his soul.

"I love those children," he finally managed to force past the knot that had risen in his throat. "I'd do anything for them." He shifted his gaze to her, taking his time, needing to gauge her reaction in order to find the truth. "I won't go into town and get Cameron and his family if it'll hurt you to have them here."

Warmth and reassurance caused the gold of her eyes to glisten like a miner's treasure as she rose up on her toes. He dipped his head, welcoming the light brush of her lips over his.

"I'll get your jacket," she said, stepping away from him.

He drew her back into his arms, lowered his mouth to hers, and kissed her like a man who had lived too long in the bowels of hell and was only just beginning to see a glimpse of heaven.

STANDING ON THE second floor landing, Austin turned up the collar on his sheepskin jacket. Through the paned glass window, he saw the scraggly boughs of a tree that looked as though it might have been left over from a past Christmas— or brought in quickly to accommodate last minute plans.

Cameron had never celebrated Christmas at

Dallas's house before Austin had gone to prison, but he supposed since he was Dee's brother, his family had welcomed him into their home after Austin left. He shoved his trembling, damp hands into his jacket pockets. He should have brought Loree with him. Sometimes he thought he could face anything if Loree stood beside him. What was it Houston had said to Amelia the day he married her? "With you by my side, I'm a better man than I've ever been alone." Austin hadn't understood the significance of the words at the time—but they were certainly beginning to make sense now.

Taking a deep breath, he pounded on the door. The heavy footsteps echoed on the other side. Cameron opened the door, and Austin watched as shock quickly gave way to concern.

"Has something happened to Dee?" Cameron asked.

"Nope. To Maggie."

"Ah, Jesus. What do you need us to do?"

Austin turned away as memories swamped him, and the stinging in his eyes had little to do with the bitter wind. Cameron had been his first—his best—friend, the kind of man who had always put others before himself.

"Let me get the keys to the store and I'll open it up. You can just take what you need—"

"I need reindeer hay."

Cameron's mouth fell open. "What? You said something had happened to Maggie."

"Yep. She got her heart broke when she found out you weren't coming with your special reindeer hay so pack up your family. I want to get back before dark."

"You don't need me. Just put some hay in burlap sacks and tell them it's reindeer hay. I've got some sacks in the store that I can get for you." Cameron turned to go back into the house.

"Not good enough," Austin said. Cameron halted and glanced over his shoulder. "They think you're the only one who can deliver special hay."

"Look, Austin—"

"I figure you've got two choices. You can either come with me now or go with Dallas later because as soon as he sees the sad faces on those children—"

"Becky, pack up!" Cameron called out. "We're going to spend Christmas with my sister."

Austin chuckled low as Cameron disappeared into the house. It felt good after all this time to find something that had remained exactly the same over the years: Cameron was still scared to death of Dallas.

"Uncle Cameron, you came!" Maggie cried as she hopped up from the floor, spilling the bowl of popcorn she'd been threading. "Did you bring the reindeer hay?"

Standing in the doorway of the front parlor, Austin watched with interest as his family welcomed the visitors into their midst. Smiles grew bigger. Laughter erupted along with hugs and backslapping.

Wearing a wide grin, Dee strolled over and

kissed his cheek. "Thank you. I know it was hard for you."

He glanced at Loree as she greeted Becky with a warm smile and held a cookie out to Drew.

"You've got no idea," Austin said roughly. "I need to unhitch the horses."

He went outside, taking his time drawing the buggy into the barn and unhitching the horses. The wind howling through the cracks wasn't strong enough to drown the sound of laughter he'd heard inside the house. He slapped each horse on the rump, sending it into the corral through the side door of the barn.

Twilight was closing in. Dallas would have a house full of people tonight. He wondered if he and Loree should head back to their own place rather than sleep in his old room with the new furniture as they'd planned.

"Are you all right?" a quiet voice asked from behind him.

Turning he smiled, took Loree's hand, and drew her near. "I am now."

Her cheeks took on a rosy hue as though she'd spent the afternoon sitting before a cozy fire. Suddenly he wished that they were home, sitting before the crackling hearth, wrapped around each other.

"Was the journey back awkward?" she asked.

He shrugged. "We didn't talk. You would have thought we were heading for a funeral if Drew hadn't been bouncing on the seat, singing 'Jingle Bells' the whole way."

Her eyes widened. "Becky said he's only eighteen months old. I think it's impressive that he can sing a song—"

Austin shook his head. "Not a song. Only two words. Jingle bells, jingle bells, jingle bells. Over and over. All the way here."

"The children are so excited—" she began.

"Yeah. They sounded like a herd of stampeding wild horses when Cameron walked in."

She placed her hand over his heart. "Even if they hadn't come, this Christmas seems difficult for you."

"The last Christmas I had here . . ." His voice trailed off as he shook his head. "It was so different. Dee had just lost the baby. Rawley had been living here for a couple of weeks, but he was still afraid." He grazed his knuckles over her cheek and smiled. "The only niece I had was Maggie. It truly was a silent night. I have a feeling tonight will be anything but quiet."

"My family died shortly after Christmas. I haven't celebrated Christmas in the years since."

He wrapped his arms around her and pressed his cheek to the top of her head. "Ah, Loree, I'm so sorry. I haven't given any thought to what this time of year must mean to you."

She tilted her head back and met his gaze. "It's wonderful to have children around, snitching the candies and shaking presents." Taking his hand, she placed it on her swollen stomach. "I'm glad to be here."

"Ah, Sugar, I'm—" The movement beneath his hand halted his words. He gave his wife a warm slow smile. "Lord, I love it when he does that."

His knees creaked as he hunkered down and placed his cheek against Loree's stomach. She intertwined her fingers through his hair, and he realized that contentment existed in the smallest of moments. Suddenly it didn't matter that he had never before celebrated Christmas with over half the people in his brother's house.

What mattered was that he would be sharing the day with Loree and with a child that was not yet born.

"Uncle Austin!" Maggie staggered to a stop right after she rounded the corner of the stall. Her eyes turned into two big circles of green. "Can I listen?" She didn't wait for an answer but hurried over, two burlap sacks clutched in one hand, and pressed her ear against Loree's stomach. Austin glanced up to see Loree's startled expression.

Maggie drew her brows together. "It don't sound like a girl," she announced.

"I reckon you'd be the one to know," Austin said.

Maggie nodded her head enthusiastically, her blond curls bouncing. "Ma always lets me and Pa listen. Pa even talks to the baby before it's born!"

"I don't believe that," Austin told her.

She jerked her head up and down. "He does so. I 'member when he talked to me before I was born. He told me he loved me better than anything." She thrust a burlap sack into his hand. "We need to get the reindeer hay put out. Come on!"

She raced out of the barn. Austin slowly unfolded his body and took his wife's hand, escorting her outside.

"I cannot picture Houston making a fool of himself and talking to his wife's belly," Austin said.

"He was talking to the baby."

Austin snapped his head around. "You say that like you think the baby could hear him."

Loree shrugged. "Maybe. I don't know."

He glanced down at his wife's rounded stomach. He'd feel silly talking to it. He met her gaze. "I'll just wait until he's born."

He closed his fingers more firmly around hers as they approached the house. Giggling children were digging into burlap sacks and tossing hay over the yard, the veranda, and each other.

"Is there a trick to this?" he asked as he neared Dallas.

"Don't put it in the hands of a three-year-old," Dallas warned as he waited patiently while Faith carefully picked a single piece of straw from the pile he held in his hand. She bent down and placed it on the ground. Then she meticulously sifted through the straw in his hand, searching for another piece to her liking.

Austin cleared his throat. "You'll be here all night."

"Yep, and this ain't the worst part. We gotta remember where they put all the damn hay so we can pick it up in the morning before they wake up." He lifted a brow. "So they'll think the dadgum reindeer ate it."

Austin knelt beside his niece. She stilled, the straw pressed between her tiny forefinger and thumb, her brown eyes huge. He smiled broadly.

"You want to put out my hay for the reindeer, too?"

She bobbed her head, took his sack, and held it up to her father. Dallas scowled and ground out his warning through his clenched teeth, "You just wait until next year."

Austin threw back his head and laughed. God, it was good to be home . . . to know there would be a Christmas next year . . . and he would be here.

Breathless, Maggie rushed over, Rawley in her wake. "Uncle Dallas, can me and Rawley go put some on the balcony outside his room?"

"Sure."

"Me, too," Faith said as she held her arms out to Rawley.

He lifted her into his arms. "Get her bags, Brat."

Maggie relieved Dallas of his burden and rushed after Rawley, her short legs unable to keep up with his long strides.

"She never seems to mind that he calls her a brat," Loree said quietly. "Why does he call her that?"

"I think because she's like her mother and speaks what's on her mind—even when he wishes she wouldn't. When Rawley first started going to school, he somehow got on the teacher's bad side. Teacher was punishing him for not learning quickly enough. Rawley was too ashamed to tell me about it. Reckon he thought he deserved it. Maggie thought differently and told me about it."

"So you talked with the teacher and worked things out?" Loree asked.

"Hell, no. Gave him his wages and sent him on

his way. Hired another teacher. Nobody, but nobody punishes my children but me. And you were right. I would have snatched that piano teacher baldheaded if I'd seen her lifting a hand to my boy. Never did thank you for interfering there." He walked off, with Loree staring after him.

"I wouldn't want to get on his bad side," she said quietly.

"I don't think you have to worry. That's the closest thing to an 'I owe you' that I've ever heard from Dallas," Austin said.

AUSTIN STUDIED THE abundance of food that stretched the length of the heavy oak table. Every time he turned around, Dee or Amelia came through the door that led to the kitchen, carrying more food. He picked up something that looked like a tiny pie, held it beneath his nose, and sniffed. It smelled like raisins. "What's this?"

Amelia stopped slicing off pieces of pound cake and looked up. "Mincemeat pie."

Austin gave her a slow nod and popped it into his mouth. A combination of tangy and sweet hit his tongue. "Pretty good," he said as he swallowed and reached for another one.

"Would you do me a favor and tell Maggie she can come decorate the cookies now?"

"Sure," he said as he snitched another pie and headed toward the parlor. He never would have believed that Dallas's big old adobe house would seem so warm and cozy. Dee had added so many small touches. Wreathes on the doors, greenery here and there, red ribbons, and satiny bows.

He rounded the corner to go into the parlor and staggered to a stop in the doorway, his path blocked by Becky, who had obviously been planning to leave the parlor. Her face burned crimson, reminding him of the stockings Dee had hung over the fireplace. Then her pale blue gaze shot upward. He slowly shifted his gaze to the arch above his head and his stomach tightened like a ribbon wound too tight around a package.

Damn mistletoe!

If it had been anyone else standing there—Dee or Amelia—he would have laughed heartily and given her a sound kiss on the lips. But not Becky. Five long years had passed since he'd held her, kissed her, been close enough to smell her vanilla scent, and count the freckles on her nose.

He didn't have to look into the parlor to know that they'd managed to gain everyone's attention. His mouth went as dry as a dust storm. Becky gave him a shaky smile, and he recognized the silent plea in her pretty blue eyes, but damn if he could figure out what she was asking for.

He swallowed hard, lowered his head, bussed a quick kiss across her cheek, and turned to the side, giving her the freedom to slip past him. He'd never been so glad to hear anything as he was to hear the rapid click of her shoes as she left the room.

Reaching up, he snatched the mistletoe from its mooring and glared briefly at his oldest brother, daring him to say anything about what he'd just done.

"Maggie—" his voice sounded like that of a

drowning man coming up for the last time. He cleared his throat. "Maggie, your ma says the cookies are ready for decorating."

Maggie shoved the present she'd been shaking back under the tree and raced out of the parlor.

Austin crossed the room and hunkered down beside the rocking chair. Loree stilled her gentle swaying and met his gaze. He brushed a stray curl away from her cheek. "Think you can give Houston back his daughter and come with me for a minute?"

She nodded slightly and eased up on the seat. Austin slipped his hand beneath her elbow and helped her stand. Houston stopped helping his other three daughters paste bits of colored paper into a chain and stood.

"'Preciate your getting her to sleep. Sometimes there's nothing like a woman's touch."

"Kin Aunt Loree rock me?" Amanda asked.

"Maybe after a while," Houston said patiently. "I think your uncle Austin needs her right now."

His brother couldn't have spoken truer words. Austin wrapped his hand around Loree's and guided her from the room. The women's laughter spilled out of the dining room. He cast a hesitant glance at Loree. "Did you want to join them?"

"Maybe later. I thought you needed something."

"I do," he admitted as he opened the door to Dallas's study.

A low fire burning within the hearth served as the only light in the room. The drapes were drawn back to reveal the cloudless night sky, a thousand stars, and a bright golden moon. "I just needed a little solitude. I'd take you outside if it weren't so cold," he said as he led her to the window that covered most of the wall.

"I like being in here where it's warm, knowing that it's cold out there," she said quietly.

He trailed his fingers along her cheek and cupped her chin. "I wanted to apologize for earlier, kissing Becky in the doorway . . . I didn't know what to do . . . if I hurt you—"

"You didn't. She and Cameron were friends, now they're family. Our paths are going to cross constantly, and not always in ways we'd prefer, but I can accept that." She lowered her lashes. "Besides, she looked as uncomfortable as you did."

"Guess you could kiss Cameron to get even with me."

"Now, why would I want to kiss Cameron when I love you?"

She ducked her head as though embarrassed while his heart pounded like an untamed stallion thundering over the plains. He'd heard those three little words before, in his youth, but they hadn't managed then to bring him to his knees. Right now, he wasn't certain how long he could remain standing. She loved him. This sweet little woman loved him.

"Loree?"

Loree glanced up and watched Austin dangle the mistletoe in front of her nose. She smiled warmly. "You don't need that."

She raised up on her toes, entwined her arms around his neck, and pressed her lips against his. He welcomed her as he had that first night when they had each needed comfort. His mouth was hot and devouring as though he couldn't get enough of tasting her.

She hadn't planned to tell him that she'd come to love him, but she had thought he needed to hear the words as badly as she did. She knew she couldn't compete with his memories, but she'd grown weary of worrying how the past—his and hers—might affect their future.

She had this moment, when he held her as though he would never release her, this moment, when the world contained all that mattered: warmth, security, and the possibility of love. She had no doubts that he cared for her and treasured her. Maybe not in the same manner that he had Becky, but he had been younger then. Now and then, she would catch glimpses of the young man he might have been. She could not return to him his youth, but she could give him her love—unconditionally.

And if he continued to love another, she would not allow her love for him to diminish.

He trailed his mouth along the sensitive area below her ear. She felt as though the fire had jumped from the hearth and was surrounding her, flames licking at her flesh. He nimbly unbuttoned the top buttons on her bodice and dipped his tongue into the hollow at the base of her throat. She dug her fingers into his shoulders, needing his strength to prevent her from melting into the floor.

"Ah, Sugar," he rasped, his breath skimming along the curve of her bosom, "why don't we ever do this at home?"

She dropped her head back, giving him easier access. "Your promise, I guess."

"My promise?" His lips moved lower. "My promise? Dammit to hell!" He pressed his mouth to the valley between her breasts. "I was only thinking of you, Loree. I swear to God, I was only thinking of you."

He pulled away from her, braced his forearm on the window, and pressed his forehead against the glass, his breathing harsh and labored. Studying his tortured profile, she watched his Adam's apple rise and fall as he swallowed. Tears stung her eyes. Without thought she had answered his question with the excuse that she gave herself each night when he simply held her and didn't ask for more.

"Austin—"

Reaching out, he took her hand, brought it to his lips, and pressed a kiss to her fingertips. "We probably ought to get back to the others. I'll need to pass out the presents soon."

Turning he gave her a wayward smile and began to button her bodice. "You make me forget all about propriety, Loree . . . and promises." He slipped the last button through its loop and straightened her collar. "One of these days, Sugar, I'm gonna kiss you until *you* forget about promises."

"Promise?" she asked, a hint of teasing in her voice.

His eyes grew warm. "Promise."

He slipped his fingers between hers, pressing his rough palm against hers. "Come on. My favorite part of Christmas is nearly here."

His excitement was infectious as he led her from Dallas's office. They'd create new memories to replace the old, and she imagined each Christmas would simply be more wonderful than the one that had come before.

They walked into the parlor. Someone had lit the candles on the branches of the evergreen tree. The flames flickered, making the shadows dance around the room.

The drapes were drawn open. The night eased inside. The fire in the hearth burned brightly. Everyone had gathered inside the room, some sitting, some standing, many of the children sprawled over the floor.

"Oh, there you are," Dee said smiling. She took Loree's free hand. "We have a tradition of singing a song before we open presents. We were wondering if you'd play the piano while we sang."

Loree felt the comfort of belonging slip around her like a warm blanket as Austin squeezed her hand. "I'd love to. What should I play?"

"'Silent Night'?"

"One of my favorites," Loree said as she released Austin's hand and walked to the piano. She sat on the bench and swiped her damp palms along her skirt. Austin came to stand beside her.

"You'll do fine," he mouthed.

She smiled and nodded. "Hope so."

"All right, everyone, Loree is going to play 'Silent Night.' Everyone stand so we can sing together as a family," Dee commanded.

Loree glanced over her shoulder. The husbands and wives had gathered their children around them, distinct families that came together to form one. Where was a photographer when they needed one?

She wiped her hands again on her skirt before placing her fingers on the ivory keys. The notes sounded and the room filled with off-key voices— and for the first time ever, she heard her husband's voice lifted in song. He carried the tune like no one else in the room, as though the melody were part of him.

His gaze captured hers, holding her entranced, and she wished the song would never end, but eventually it drifted away, leaving a moment of respectful silence in its wake.

Austin smiled at her, rubbed his hands together as though in anticipation, and took a step away from the piano. Loree twisted around on the piano bench to watch the exchange of gifts.

"You can help me pass out presents, Brat," Rawley said as he knelt in front of the tree.

"You don't have to tell me," Maggie countered as she dropped beside him. "I've been helping you forever."

Austin still smiling, stepped back, and sank onto the bench beside Loree, his gaze focused on the tree. He took her hand. "Thought you played really nice," he said, his voice low.

She thought her heart might break as she remembered him saying earlier that he needed to pass out the presents. In the years while he was away, the responsibility had obviously fallen to Rawley until everyone had forgotten a time when anyone else had passed them out.

She squeezed Austin's arm. "It surprised me, hearing how well you sang."

He shrugged. "Use to enjoy music."

"I wish you'd let me teach you to play—"

"Here, Uncle Austin, this one's for you," Maggie said, holding out a large package.

"Well, I'll be," Austin said with a smile as he shook the box. "This is almost as big as the box Rawley got the first year that you helped me pass out the presents. You remember that?"

Maggie furrowed her brow and shook her head. "What'd he get?"

"A saddle."

"I don't 'member."

Austin touched her nose. "Doesn't matter. You'd better get back to helping him."

She scurried away. Loree leaned close and whispered, "She couldn't have been very old when you left—"

"Three."

He looked at her and smiled sadly. "Guess we can't always choose which memories we keep when we start growing up."

But she knew she would forever hold the memory of her husband's first Christmas after his release from prison. Even with her by his side, she thought he'd never looked more lonely.

Chapter Fourteen

Austin awoke as he had for several months, long before the sun came up, with his wife curled against his side, her furled hand resting on the center of his bare chest. He loved these first moments of awareness, hearing Loree's breathing, feeling her warmth, knowing they would be his for the remainder of his life.

He pressed a kiss to her forehead and gingerly moved away from her. She sighed softly and shifted over until she was nestled in the spot where he had been. He brought the blankets over her shoulders.

He carried the lamp to the dresser and increased the flame by a hair's breadth. He glanced toward the bed. Loree hadn't stirred. He turned back to his task and ran his hand over the wooden violin case she'd given him for Christmas. On the top, someone had carved his name in fancy script. His gift to her—a small music box—had paled in comparison.

"If you're not going to play your mother's violin, you need to keep it protected," Loree had told him. "Someday, maybe your son will play it."

His son. He thought of Drew's tiny fingers and wondered when a child's fingers would be long enough to play a violin. Houston's daughter Laurel could probably play. She was five now, but still she'd need a smaller violin.

He imagined the joys of teaching a child the wonders of music. He could teach his own children . . . He unfolded one of the sheets of music Loree had given him. All the black dots looked like bugs crawling over the page. Reading them was nothing like reading a book. Loree could teach his children to play.

Quietly he donned his clothes and slipped into the hallway. The house seemed incredibly quiet after all the festivity the night before. The children had finally fallen asleep around midnight, giving up their quest to actually see Santa Claus. Their stockings were now filled with goodies and additional presents were waiting under the tree in the parlor.

He crept down the wide winding staircase and grabbed his sheepskin jacket from the coat rack by the front door. Then he walked into the kitchen, prepared his morning coffee, and stepped onto the back porch.

He settled onto the top step, wrapped his hands around the warm tin cup, and waited . . . waited for the first ray of sun to touch the sky and reveal its beauty . . . waited to hear the music in his soul that had always accompanied the sunrise before he'd gone to prison.

He heard the door open and glanced over his shoulder, anticipating the sight of his wife, rumpled from sleep.

"What are you doing?" Cameron asked.

He averted his gaze and tightened his hold on the cup. "I *was* enjoying the sunrise."

"Mind if I join you?"

Austin shrugged. "It ain't my porch."

Cameron dropped beside him and wrapped his arms around his middle. "Cold out this morning."

Austin watched the steam rise from his coffee.

"Loree seems nice," Cameron said.

Austin sliced his gaze over to Cameron. "She is nice."

Cameron nodded. "She doesn't look like she's got much longer to go."

Austin narrowed his eyes. "You counting the months? 'Cuz if you are, I'll have to take you out behind the barn and teach you a lesson in minding your own business."

"Nah, I wasn't counting. I was just saying. That's all."

"Good, 'cuz I wouldn't like it at all if you were counting months." Austin extended the cup toward Cameron. "Take a sip on that before your clattering teeth wake everyone up. It'll help warm you."

Cameron took the cup without hesitating and downed a long swallow before handing it back. "Thanks."

"Becky would probably never forgive me if I let you freeze to death out here," Austin said, squinting into the distance, searching for that first hint of sunlight.

"She missed you like hell while you were in prison." Cameron clasped his hands between his knees. "So did I."

Austin laughed mirthlessly. "You two had a hell of a way of showing me that."

A suffocating silence wove itself between them, around them. Austin saw dawn's feathery fingers pushing back the night.

"After Boyd died, my pa didn't want anything to do with me since I didn't approve of what Boyd had done—paying someone to kill Dallas. Dallas offered me a job—"

Austin turned his attention toward Cameron. "You would have wet your britches every time he gave you an order."

A smile tugged on the corner of Cameron's mouth. "Yeah, that's what I figured so I went to work for Becky's pa. She and I put a box in the storage room. Every time we got in some new contraption, we'd put it in the box because she knew how much you loved new contraptions."

Austin took a sip on his coffee before handing the cup back to Cameron. "Didn't really care about them one way or the other. They were just an excuse to go into town and see Becky."

Cameron gulped on the black brew and passed it back. "She wrote you some letters. Couldn't bring herself to address them to you in prison, though. She couldn't stand to think of you being there so she just put them in the box so they'd be waiting for you when you got home."

Austin cut his blue-eyed glare over to Cameron. "One of those letters tell me how she fell in love with you?"

"I doubt it . . . since she never fell in love with me." He watched Cameron swallow. "We'd been married a little over eight months when Drew was born."

"Babies come early."

"He didn't. My pa was dying. He asked to see me. I always had the feeling he didn't like me much. Never knew why, but he didn't want to die without telling me that I didn't come from his loins. It took him six years to realize my mother had fallen in love with the foreman. His name was Joe Armstrong. My pa—I can't stop thinking of him as my pa—said he shot Joe Armstrong through the heart and buried him where no one would ever find him."

"You believe him?"

Cameron nodded. "Yeah. Dee remembered the foreman. Said I'd always reminded her of him, but she was so innocent she never put things together."

"And when you found out the truth, you turned to Becky."

Cameron gave him a jerky nod. "Her pa had died a few months before so I guess she knew how I was grieving. I'd loved her forever, but I didn't mean for things to turn out the way they did." He planted his elbows on his thighs and buried his face in his hands. "Christ, I never wanted her to *have* to marry me."

Austin looked toward the golden light sweeping

across the horizon—as brilliant a hue as Loree's eyes. He wondered if she was awake yet. It was past time for her to join him on the porch. Lord, he missed her.

"Drew seems like a good kid," he said quietly.

Cameron's head came up. "Oh, he's great. And Becky adores him. I was afraid she might resent him—like my pa resented me—but she doesn't. She loves him with all her heart."

"She loves you, too, Cameron." The words cut deeply, lancing the wound that had been left to fester too long.

Doubt plunged into Cameron's eyes. "You're just saying that."

"Why in the hell would I tell you that if it weren't true? Don't you think it would ease my pride to think she still loved me?"

"I haven't touched her since you got out of prison. I was afraid . . . afraid she'd wish it was you. I couldn't stand the thought that maybe she was thinking of you while I was loving her."

Austin tossed the remaining coffee over the cold ground. He'd made Loree a promise and suddenly, it didn't seem as though it would be difficult to keep. Whatever he and Becky had once had . . . was nothing more than a distant memory.

"A blind fool could see that she loves you more than she ever loved me. Why in the hell do you think I've been so angry all these months? Not because she married you. But because she didn't love me as much as she loves you."

"Yeah?"

Austin gave a brisk nod. "Yeah." He studied

Cameron a minute. "You said your pa killed your real father?"

Cameron gave a slow hesitant nod. "Hard to believe I lived with a murderer all those years and never knew it."

"You think there's a chance he might have killed Boyd?"

"It occurred to me, more than once, but why would he have killed Boyd? Boyd could do no wrong as far as he was concerned."

Austin heaved a deep sigh. "Damn. Wish I knew who killed him. I don't like having this guilty verdict hanging over my head."

"Doesn't seem to bother Loree."

"Loree looks at the world differently than most people. Someone murdered her family, but she somehow managed to hold onto a portion of her innocence. I'm afraid if we stay here . . . if she hears too many people whispering about me, speculating on who I might murder next . . . that she'll lose that little bit of innocence."

"You thinking of leaving?"

Austin shrugged. "I don't know where we'd go or what I'd do so probably not, but I think about it sometimes. Houston told me once that when a man loves a woman, he does what's best for her, no matter what the cost to himself. I'd pay any price to see Loree happy."

"She seems happy enough."

"I think I can make her happier. I know I can. Houston told me that he thought he might have fallen in love with Amelia the minute he saw her. I didn't feel that way with Loree, but when she stepped out of that house, I felt as though . . . I'd come home."

"Do you think Dallas fell in love with Dee when he first laid eyes on her?"

Austin shook his head, joyful memories surging through his mind like a kaleidoscope of forgotten images. "Nope. He probably fell in love with her when he discovered she had a nose. Do you remember the look on his face when he lifted her veil and saw her face for the first time?" Austin chuckled.

Cameron started laughing. "His face? You should have seen *your* face!"

"Mine? What about yours?"

Their laughter grew louder, mingling with the dawn.

LOREE SLIPPED HER fingers between the kitchen curtains and peered through the tiny opening. Austin laughed so hard that he very nearly doubled over, his chin almost hitting his drawn up knees.

"Oh my God!" Becky whispered behind her. "Tell me that's Austin and Cameron laughing."

Loree stepped back, surprised to see tears brimming in Becky's eyes as she peeked through the curtain.

"I could not have asked for a better Christmas present." Becky squeezed her eyes shut and released a quick breath. "It almost killed Cameron to lose Austin's friendship." She opened her eyes and grabbed Loree's hand. "Come on. Let's go sit with them."

"I'm not sure we should—"

"Oh, I am. I know it'll never be like it was . . . but this is sure close." Becky opened the door. "What are you two laughing about?" she demanded of the men sitting on the porch.

Holding her breath, Loree peered around Becky who stood with her hands planted on her hips, her legs akimbo. She saw Austin's smile increase, his eyes grow warm as he held out his hand. She wanted to crawl back into the house and die until she realized that his gaze was latched onto her.

"Come here, Sugar," he said in a slow drawl that sent her heart to racing.

She skirted around Becky and slipped her hand into his, thinking his had never felt so warm or comforting, so right as his fingers wrapped around her hand and he pulled her down to his lap. He opened his jacket and tucked her inside like she was a piece of fine jewelry to be protected between velvet. He held her close with one arm and enveloped her bare feet with his other hand. She was eye-level with him and from the intensity of his blue gaze, she would have thought he were only aware of the two of them sitting on this porch in the cold dawn.

"What were you laughing about?" Becky repeated as she plopped onto Cameron's lap and nearly sent him sprawling backward over the porch.

"We were remembering the day that Dallas married Dee," Cameron said, straightening himself and putting his arms around Becky.

"What was so funny about that?" Becky asked.

"Cameron had told me that Indians cut off Dee's nose," Austin said, his gaze never leaving Loree. She grew warmer, but she thought it had little to do with the heat of his body burning through her clothing. "I told Dallas. It came as a surprise to him to discover his wife had a nose."

"I remember now. Everyone's mouth dropped open when he lifted her veil, but I never knew why," Becky said. She wrinkled her brow. "He married her, thinking she didn't have a nose?"

"He was a desperate man," Austin said quietly. "Desperate men don't always think things through."

Loree wanted to tell him that desperate women didn't think things through either. She had been desperate once, so incredibly desperate that she had done something she never would have believed herself capable of doing. At unexpected times the memory would strike like a rattlesnake . . . only a rattlesnake gave warning. Her memory from hell wasn't as kind.

She heard the tread of heavy feet and twisted slightly. Dallas rounded the corner, burlap sacks bunched in his hand.

"What in the hell are you doing lollygagging back here?" he demanded without breaking his stride. He tossed the burlap sacks onto the porch. "Get this hay picked up."

Reaching behind him, Austin grabbed the sacks and handed a couple to Cameron. "Guess we'd better get to it."

Loree slid off his lap and tightened her wrap around herself. "I need to get dressed."

Austin's hand clamped onto her waist, preventing her from slipping back into the house.

"Me, too," Becky said. "I'll see you in a little bit, Cameron."

"Be sure and get the hay off the balcony in Rawley's room."

She smiled. "Guess he forgot we were going to sleep in his room last night." She disappeared into the house.

Austin shifted his gaze from Loree to Cameron. "Why don't you go on? I'll catch up."

"Sure thing." Cameron hopped off the porch and headed toward a distant scattering of hay.

Austin returned his gaze to her, his fingers tightening their hold.

"Is everything all right?" she asked.

She watched his Adam's apple slowly slide up and down. His blue eyes smoldered like flames on the verge of coming back to life. "Everything is just fine. As a matter of fact, I think it's been fine for a while and I just didn't notice." He cradled her cheek. "I love you, Loree."

Her heart slammed against her ribs. "You don't have to say that just because I did—"

"That's not why I'm saying it." He dipped his head slightly. "I'm saying it because it's true."

He closed the distance between their mouths, their hearts, with a kiss that made her body feel like a melted pool of wax, warm and molten, easily shaped to fit his desires. And more to fit her desires, desires that spiraled through her. She slipped her hands beneath the shoulders of his sheepskin jacket and felt the comforting heat of his body. He brought his coat around her. Her toes crept over his boots. And the baby rolled between them.

Austin drew away and glanced down at the small mound. Then he lifted his gaze. "Figure we'll spend the day here, pack up our stuff, go to that Christmas ball that Dee is giving in town . . . then head home."

She gave him a quick nod.

"Don't remind me of any promises I've made in the past when we get home."

Her voice caught in her throat, forcing her to push out the words. "I won't."

A slow lazy smile spread across his face and in it, she read a new promise, a promise she dearly wanted him to keep.

WITH LONG STRIDES, Austin carried the box of presents to the wagon. He and Loree had been blessed last night with an assortment of gifts that ranged from useable items for the baby to a picture from Faith that he suspected was a horse only because it had been scribbled in brown.

After setting the box in the back of the wagon, he dug through the contents until he found one of the music sheets Loree had given him. He opened it and again studied the black ovals with the strange sticks and flags. He supposed it wouldn't hurt to let Loree explain them to him. If they made sense to her, maybe they could make sense to him.

"Austin?"

Becky's serene voice came from behind him. He

stuffed the sheet into the box, spun around, and realized that he'd lied to Loree.

He'd told her once that a man couldn't tell if a woman had been made love to, but standing here, staring at the warm glow on Becky's cheeks, he had no doubt that she had just been well and thoroughly loved.

"I just wanted to thank you," she said softly.

"For what?"

"For whatever it was that you said to Cameron that made him stop doubting my love."

"I just told him the truth." He turned and shoved the box farther back into the wagon.

Becky came up alongside him. "I did love you, you know," she said quietly.

He met her gaze. "I know."

"What we had was so incredibly sweet . . . and young." She furrowed her brow. "I don't know if that makes sense."

"It does."

"If we had gotten married five years ago— even without you going to prison—I don't know if our love would have survived the passing years. I think we would have been content, but never truly happy."

Words backed up in his throat and he could do little more than give her an understanding nod.

"I know it's been hard on you since you got back. Cameron and I just finished talking about some things that we hadn't really discussed before. I'm willing to make a public announcement saying I was with you the night Boyd was killed."

Austin felt as though the air had been pulled

from his lungs. Emotions clogged his throat. He knew that announcement would cost Becky more than her reputation. It would cost Cameron his pride.

"I appreciate that, Becky. More than you'll ever know, but I think it would cause more harm than good. That's the reason I told you not to say anything five years ago. Most people would think you were lying to protect me, but your words would still plant the seeds of doubt about your reputation in everyone's mind. It's not worth taking the chance of hurting not only you and Cameron, but Drew as well."

He watched as relief washed over her face. "Just so you know we're willing."

He gave her a brisk nod. "Better get back to your husband. Wouldn't want to make him jealous."

"A part of me will always love you, Austin." She leaned over and brushed a kiss over his cheek. His heart tightened.

"Same here," he said hoarsely.

He watched her stroll back toward the house, her hips swaying gently from side to side. Within his heart, he bid the love of his youth a silent farewell.

Chapter Fifteen

*T*he Grand Ballroom of the Grand Hotel had changed over the years—like everything else in Austin's life. If windows didn't grace the wall, then floor-to-ceiling gilded mirrors did. The room seemed larger than it was as Austin stood beside his brothers, Loree at his side.

While Amelia and Dee rushed around the room making certain everything was in order, the children sat in chairs along the wall, like stair steps, from oldest to youngest, with the very youngest nestled in Houston's arms. The girls swung their feet, their heels hitting the underside of their chair. Rawley slumped forward, looking bored as hell. Austin understood that feeling.

Dallas's cook strode in, his legs bowed out like a man who still had a horse sitting beneath him, his fiddle tucked beneath his arm. He wore a fancy black suit that Austin had never expected the man to own.

"The fiddle player's here," Maggie announced. "You're gonna have to dance with me, Rawley."

Horror swept over Rawley's face. "Don't neither."

"Do to." Maggie tipped up her nose. "Uncle Dallas, doesn't Rawley have to dance with me?"

Absently, Dallas waved his hand in the air, his attention focused on his wife. "Can't see that it'd do any harm, Rawley. Probably be good practice."

Groaning, Rawley glowered at Maggie, who wore a smile of triumph. Faith slid out of her chair, tiptoed across the floor, and climbed onto Rawley's lap.

"Dance wiv me, too, Wawley."

He held up a finger. "One dance." He glared at Maggie. "One dance." Holding Faith in place with one arm, he leaned forward and glared at each of his cousins in turn, his finger pointing to the ceiling. "One dance each and that's it."

He slumped back against the wall, reached into his shirt pocket, and removed a sarsaparilla stick.

"Gimme some," Faith ordered.

"It's my last piece," Rawley said, even as he proceeded to break it into six pieces and distribute it to the girls, popping the last and smallest piece into his mouth.

He met Austin's gaze over the top of Faith's head. "I sure hope your baby is a boy."

"Reckon we need to even things out a little, don't we?"

Rawley gave him a brusque nod. "We men folk are sorely outnumbered."

Austin laughed, remembering a time when that was exactly what Dallas had wanted: more women out in West Texas.

Breathless, Amelia rushed over and took Gracie from Houston. "I think we just about have everything ready to go."

"Who's gonna watch the young 'uns while you and me dance?" Houston asked.

"I'll be happy to watch the girls," Loree said, her fingers tightening around Austin's. "I can't imagine I'll be doing any dancing tonight. In this red dress, I look like an apple that's been turned upside down."

Austin gave her a long slow perusal, then leaned over, and whispered in her ear, "I've always liked nibbling on apples."

Her face burned a deep crimson, and he wished he could find some dark secluded corner where he could taste her fully. His only fear was that once he got started, he'd be unable to stop. He couldn't remember ever wanting anything as much as he wanted Loree at this moment.

People began to arrive. The night they'd gone to the theater, Austin had only seen Leighton's successful citizens. They were here tonight, but so were the cowboys, the wranglers, the stonemasons, and the carpenters. The ladies who worked in Dee's hotel and restaurant glided into the room in their fancy gowns and were swept onto the floor to dance before the music began to play.

When the first strains from Cookie's fiddle filled the air, a roar went up and people began to dance in earnest.

"We're gonna take you up on that offer to watch the girls if you're sure you don't mind," Houston said.

"I don't mind," Loree assured him as she released Austin's hand and took Gracie into her arms.

"We'll just dance one dance," Amelia said.

"Dance as many as you like."

"I'm going to make my wife stop working and do some dancing," Dallas said before walking off.

With a huff, Rawley shifted Faith off his lap, stood, and held his hand out to Maggie. "Come on, Brat. You asked first."

Maggie hopped out of her chair and followed him onto the dance floor.

Austin helped Loree sit in the chair Maggie had vacated, then he sat beside her, easing Faith onto his lap. She reached up and planted a sticky sarsaparilla scented kiss on his cheek. "Love ya."

"I love you, too," Austin said quietly.

He glanced over at Loree. "And you."

She pressed her cheek against his shoulder.

"We won't stay long," he promised. He looked toward the waltzing couples.

"They all look so happy," Loree said quietly.

Cameron and Becky passed quickly in front of them before disappearing in the crowd. "Yeah, they do," Austin said.

When the music stilled momentarily, Amelia came over and took Gracie from Loree. "Come on, girls. Let's go get some punch."

Houston scooped A. J. into his arms before holding a hand toward Faith. "You thirsty?"

She nodded and slid off Austin's lap. Austin watched his nieces, all in identical red dresses, traipse toward the table like performers in a circus parade. He glanced at Loree, her hands folded over her apple red stomach. He leaned toward her. "Do you dance?"

She wrinkled her nose. "I went to a couple of balls in Austin, but that was a long time back."

He pulled gently on a curl dangling near her temple. "Is that where you met Jake?"

"I told you there was no Jake."

"Who did you dance with?"

Sighing, she narrowed her eyes. "I danced with somebody named John and . . . Michael."

"That's it?"

"I wasn't exactly the belle of the ball."

"What do city boys know?" he asked.

"A good-looking woman when they see one."

"Not on your life." He stood, held out his hand, and helped her to her feet.

"Thought I spotted you over here," Cameron said, diverting Austin's attention away from Loree. "Would you mind if I danced with your wife?"

Austin caught the look of surprise in Loree's eyes, and suddenly, he wanted every man in this room to dance with her. "No, I don't mind."

"You don't mind do you?" Cameron asked Becky. "I'll be leaving you in good company."

Becky smiled. "Go on."

Cameron held his hand toward Loree. She hesitated before slipping her hand into his. "I'm not very balanced these days."

Cameron grinned. "That's all right. Neither am I."

Austin watched Cameron lead Loree onto the dance floor. Their steps were awkward, mismatched. Cameron chuckled, and even with the din of the other dancers, Austin heard Loree's gentle laughter.

"You and I never got to dance," Becky said quietly.

Austin slid his gaze to her. The royal blue of her dress enhanced the shade of her eyes. "No, we didn't."

She licked her lips. "We're not going to dance tonight, are we?"

"No, we're not."

She shifted her gaze to the dancers. "Cameron wouldn't mind."

"But it might hurt Loree."

She peered at him. "Do you love her?"

"Yeah, I do."

"Then she's a very lucky woman."

"She hasn't been up until now, but I aim to change that." He tilted his head as the music drifted into silence. "If you'll excuse me, I think I'll dance with my wife now."

He glanced toward the dance floor, reining in his impatience as Cameron escorted Loree back to him. Her cheeks were flushed, her eyes sparkling. He would have grabbed her and hauled her back onto the dance floor right then and there, but he had something special in mind.

"Didn't topple over, huh?" he asked as they neared. He laughed when Loree stuck her tongue out at him.

"Come on, Sugar, sit down," he ordered.

Loree plopped into the chair, grateful to be off her feet. "Thank you, Cameron," she called out.

Cameron glanced over his shoulder and winked

at her before he led Becky back toward the dance area. Loree released a deep sigh. "I didn't want to but I think I like Cameron. He's nice."

"Of course, he's nice. You think I'd have mean friends?" Austin asked as he knelt in front of her and lifted her foot.

She leaned forward. "What are you doing?"

"Taking off your shoes."

She jerked her foot back. "Austin, not here," she whispered hoarsely.

He looked at her with blue eyes that reflected the innocence of a child. "Why?"

She stared at him, trying to think of an acceptable reason. "It's not proper. A woman doesn't show her ankles in public."

"Your skirt is long enough that your ankles won't show. Besides, your toes have gotta be hurtin'. I've seen Cameron dance before. He may be nice but he doesn't know his right foot from his left."

She slapped a hand over her mouth to stop herself from laughing out loud. Her toes were hurting. He patted his thigh. "Come on, Sugar."

She gnawed on her lower lip. She supposed if she just sat here . . .

"Oh, all right, but don't let anyone see what you're doing," she whispered as she placed her foot on his thigh.

She loved to watch his long fingers nimbly work to unbutton her shoes. She wanted to see his fingers gliding along the strings on his mother's violin. She knew he had been touched by the case she had given him for Christmas, but she'd been disappointed that he hadn't shown more of an interest in the music sheets she'd given him.

He slipped her shoe under the chair, and when she would have brought her foot to the floor, he held it in place on his thigh, rubbing his thumbs in a circle over the balls of her foot. "Oh, Lord, that feels good," she said. "You have such nice hands."

"Wait until you see how nice they're gonna be later on."

She didn't know if the gleam in his eyes spoke of teasing or seriousness, and she wasn't certain she wanted to know. He placed her foot on the floor, brought her other foot up, and removed her shoe. He rubbed her foot until every little pain vanished.

"How does that feel?" he asked.

"Wonderful."

"Good." He stood and held out his hand. "Will you honor me with this dance?"

Loree widened her eyes. "I don't have shoes on."

He smiled warmly. "I know that, Sugar. I just took 'em off."

"I can't dance without shoes."

"Sure you can."

She thought of being held within his arms, her stockinged feet gliding over the smooth hardwood floor. . . .

"Cameron said that you never learned how to dance."

"He doesn't know everything."

The music stilled. "So you have danced before."

"Once . . . with Amelia."

She scooted up in the chair, hope flaring within her. "Only with Amelia?"

"Only with Amelia. I was sharing her with a dozen cowboys at the time, and all we knew how to do was swing her around, stomp our feet, and clap our hands."

"Have you ever waltzed with anyone?"

"Never."

Slowly, she rose to her feet. "What else have you never done?"

She knew from the darkening of his eyes that he understood what she was asking.

"Never danced with a woman I love."

Jealousy was a petty thing, but she'd never known such gladness. She smiled warmly. "I wouldn't want to miss this opportunity to be your first."

"Sugar, it's more important that I intend for you to be my last."

Before she had the chance to respond, he'd placed his hand on her waist and swept her onto the dance floor. The room contained two hearths, but neither fire burned as brightly as his eyes. Her stockinged feet glided over the floor and she wondered why women bothered to wear shoes at all.

When the music drifted into silence, she slipped her arm through his and allowed him to lead her from the dance floor.

Cameron and Becky caught up with them. "I've never seen you dance before," Cameron said. "Didn't know you could."

Austin shrugged. "Now, you know."

"I guess it's because you were always playing the music."

Austin started to walk away, but Loree stood fast, staring at Cameron, her heart thundering in her ears. "What . . . what do you mean he played the music?"

"Austin plays the violin and whenever we had occasion to dance, he provided the music." He glanced at Austin. "I figured you'd be playing tonight."

"I don't play anymore."

"I'm sorry to hear that," Cameron said. "No one played music the way you did. You should have heard it, Loree. It was beautiful."

She felt Austin's gaze boring into her. She slipped her arm from beneath his. "Yes, I should have heard it."

The strains of the waltz floated around the room. She began to tremble from her head to her toes. "I'm not feeling well. Will you excuse me?"

She didn't wait for his answer. She didn't bother to gather up her shoes or her coat. She simply ran. Shouldering her way through the crowd like a mad woman, her heart breaking.

She finally managed to burst through to the lobby. She hurried to the front, shoved open the door, and stumbled into the cold night. Tears stung her eyes. She had told him that she loved him.

And she realized now that she didn't know anything about him.

THE RIDE HOME was quiet. Too quiet.

Austin had given their excuses and apologies

for having to leave early. Naturally, everyone had wanted to check on Loree and make certain the baby wasn't planning to come early.

The one time she had met his gaze, he'd seen nothing but hurt in her eyes. He drew the wagon to a halt. Loree shifted on the seat.

"Loree, wait for me to get over there."

He leapt off the wagon and raced around to the other side. She'd already reached the ground.

"You're gonna hurt yourself with your stubbornness," he chastised.

"And you hurt me with your lies."

"I never lied."

"You never told me the truth, either."

She spun on her heel and headed into the house. Austin grabbed their box of presents from the back of the wagon and traipsed in after her. Shafts of moonlight pierced the darkness.

"Will you start a fire in the hearth?" she asked. "I'm cold."

He set the box on the table, walked to the hearth, and hunkered down. He struck a match to the kindling and watched the flames flare to life. He heard a scrape and bang. He twisted around and watched Loree remove something from the box.

"Your music box is on the bottom," he told her.

"I'm not looking for the music box."

Slowly, he unfolded his body. "Loree—"

She spun around, marched to the hearth, and threw something at it.

The sheets of music.

He dropped to his knees, grabbed them from the fire, and beat out the flames that were already greedily devouring the pages. He glared up at Loree. "What did you do that for?"

"You already know how to play the violin. All these months, you let me make a fool out of myself—"

"No, I never meant that."

"Why didn't you tell me? When I asked you—begged you—to let me teach you, why didn't you say, 'I already know how to play, Loree.'"

He saw the tears glistening within her eyes. "Loree—"

"You told me that you love me. Do you think love is supposed to hurt? It's not. Whatever Becky taught you about love is wrong. It's supposed to heal. It's supposed to make you feel glad that you're alive. It's supposed to help you live with the past.

"You can't love me if you won't let me inside your heart. Either open your heart and invite me in or take me back home. But don't tell me you love me when you don't know what it is to love."

She spun on her heel, walked into their bedroom, and slammed the door.

Austin bit back the agonizing wail that would have been her name. What did she know about the things in his heart? What did she know about love? Love looked deeply within a person. Hadn't Amelia looked beyond Houston's scars to his soul? Love understood what others couldn't begin to fathom. Hadn't Dee understood Dallas's hard nature when no one else had?

Loree was the one who knew nothing about love. He stalked to the bedroom door, put his hand on the knob, and heard her wrenching sobs. He pressed his forehead to the door.

Christ, how many times had he made her cry? How often had he hurt her?

She was right. He should take her back home. She had his name. That was all she needed.

He stormed across the room, opened the front door, rushed through it, and slammed it in his wake. The last thing he needed her to hear was his heart breaking.

LOREE AWOKE TO the sound of a child crying. She rubbed the salt of her dried tears from the corners of her eyes and squinted through the darkness. Shafts of moonlight sliced through the window, forming the silhouette of a man, standing, his head bowed, his arm pushing and pulling, pushing and pulling the bow slowly across the taut strings of a violin.

The resonant chords deepened and an immense lonesomeness filled the room. Loree sat up in bed, sniffing through her stuffed nose. She clutched her handkerchief as the wailing continued. She wanted to slip out of bed and wrap her arms around someone, ease the pain she heard in the echoing strains of the violin. The poignant melody released fresh tears and caused her heart to tighten. In all her life, she'd never had a song reach out to capture her soul.

The melody drifted into an aching silence. Austin lifted his head, and she saw his tears, trailing along his cheeks, glistening in the moonlight.

She slipped from beneath the blankets, her

bare feet hitting the cold floor. "What were you playing?" she asked reverently, not wanting to disturb the ambiance that remained in the room.

"That was my heart breaking," he said, his voice ragged.

She felt as though her own heart might shatter as she took a step toward him. "Austin—"

"Don't stop loving me, Loree. You want me to learn what those little black bugs on those pieces of paper mean, I'll learn. You want me to play the violin from dawn until dusk, hell, I'll play till midnight, just don't stop loving me."

She flung her arms around his neck and felt his arms come around her back, the violin tapping against her backside. "Oh, Austin, I couldn't stop loving you if I wanted."

"I do know how to love, Loree. I just don't know how to keep a woman loving me."

"I'll always love you, Austin," she said trailing kisses over his face. "Always."

She felt a slight movement away from her as he set the violin aside, and then his arms came around her, tighter than before. "Let me love you, Loree. I need to love you."

His mouth swooped down, capturing hers, desperation evident as his tongue delved swiftly, deeply. And then, as though, sensing her surrender, his exploration gentled. His hands came around, bracing either side of her hips, hips that had widened as she carried his child.

His hands traveled upward, until her breasts filled his palms. His long fingers shaped and molded what nature had already altered, preparing for the day when she would nourish their child.

He cradled her cheek, deepening the kiss, as his other hand worked the buttons of her nightgown free. He slipped his hand through the parted material, his roughened palm cupping her smooth breast. She felt his fingers tremble as his thumb circled her nipple, causing it to harden and strain for his touch.

His breathing harsh, he trailed his mouth along the column of her throat. He dipped his tongue into the hollow at the base of her throat.

"I'm only thinking of you, Loree," he rasped.

She dropped her head back. "I know." And she did know, deep within her soul, where his music had dared to travel only moments before, she did know that he was thinking of her. The tears he had shed had been for her. The music he had played had been for her.

His kiss, his gentle touch—they belonged to her now, just as he did.

His mouth skimmed along her flesh, between the valley of her breasts, his breath warm like a summer breeze. He trailed his mouth over the curve of her breast. His tongue circled her nipple before he closed his mouth around the taut tip and suckled.

Like a match struck to kindling, her body responded, heat flaming to life. Her knees buckled and he caught her against him, steadying her. Slowly, he unfolded his body and within the faint moonbeams, she saw the deep blue of his smoldering gaze.

He slipped his hands between the parted material of her gown, spreading it over her shoulders until it was free to slide down her body and pool at her feet. She heard him swallow.

"God, you're beautiful."

His voice sounded as thick as molasses, and his gaze spoke more eloquently than his words. Her fingers trembled as she ran her hands over his wide shoulders and along his broad chest, knowing that she was on the verge of sealing forever the vault that held old promises. One movement, one touch, one word . . . and they could never return to what had been.

"Tell me again," she whispered.

"I'm only thinking of you, Loree," he said, his voice ragged, his breathing uneven.

She smiled warmly into the face of the man she loved. "No, tell me you love me."

"I love you."

She wrapped her hand around his, took a step back toward the bed, and watched his lips spread into a slow, seductive smile. Another step back and she sank onto the bed.

Austin tore his shirt over his head and dropped his britches to the floor. She watched the moonlight play over the hard muscles of his body before he stretched out beside her on the bed.

"Now, you gotta tell me," he said as he nipped on her earlobe and swirled his tongue around the shell of her ear.

"I love you," she whispered as her body curled.

"Ah, Sugar, I'm gonna make you damn glad that you do."

His promise carried assurances that she didn't doubt. "I'm already glad."

He rose up on his elbow. "Everything is gonna be better, Loree. Everything."

He lowered his mouth to hers with a renewed urgency. She touched her hand to his chest and felt the hard steady pounding of his heart. Where once he might have lain over her, now he only pressed his body against her side, his warm hand gliding over her stomach to the juncture between her thighs.

She moaned as his fingers imitated the action of his tongue, sweeping, plunging, warming, heating. She ran her hand down his side, dug her fingers into his lean hip, and rolled to her side, needing him close, knowing a moment of regret with the realization that her swollen stomach would never allow him to be as close as she needed.

Need spiraled through her, desire flamed. She trailed kisses over his face, his dew-covered throat and chest, wanting him as she'd never wanted anything. He fell onto his back and tugged on her hand. "Come here, Loree."

His shoulders rolled off the bed as he leaned up slightly and put his large hands on either side of her hips, guiding her until she straddled him. She watched the shadows and moonlight caress his magnificent body as she wanted to and knew a moment of doubt. Keeping one hand planted on her hip, he cradled her cheek with the other and held her gaze. "Stop me if I hurt you."

She trailed her gaze along the length of his body to the place where her body met his. She wrapped her fingers around him. He groaned and she felt a tremor wrack his body. Cradling her hips, he lifted her and eased her down as easily as the dawn met the day until they were one.

He released a long deep sigh. "Oh, Sugar, you feel so good."

She rolled her shoulders forward. "So do you."

Chuckling low, he threaded his fingers through her hair, bracketing her face between his palms. "I don't want to hurt you, so I need you . . . to do the ridin'."

She wished she could double over and kiss the furrows between his brow. He looked as though he were afraid he might have disappointed her. But how could he disappoint her when he loved her?

She ran her hands over his chest, along his side, leaned forward slightly, circled her hips, and relished the sound of his sharp intake of breath. He had given her so much: the power to love him, the power to satisfy him.

Keeping her eyes trained on his, she began to rock her hips. His hands glided to her breasts, the long fingers that she loved taunting and teasing, and she realized he had not relinquished all power.

Unbridled sensations ripped through her, and she felt as though he played her as easily as he played his violin. The sensations rose until her body went taut, and she uttered a cry of ecstasy.

She heard Austin's guttural groan as he shuddered beneath her, and into the stillness that followed, she heard their harsh breathing. Supporting her shoulders, he gently rolled them to their sides, his body never leaving hers. He threaded his fingers through her hair, his palm resting heavily upon her cheek as though all strength had been drained from him. Beneath her hand, his heart thudded.

Her lips spread into a contented smile and she sighed. Then her smile disappeared and her brow furrowed. "Austin?"

"Mmm?"

"What little black bugs?"

"What?" he asked sleepily.

She lifted her head, trying to make out his features in the shadows. "Earlier you said something about bugs on paper—"

"Oh, that. I was talking about those sheets of music you gave me for Christmas. I'll let you teach me how to read them."

She came up on her elbow. "Don't you know how to read music?"

"Nope."

"But that song you played—"

"Told you . . . it was my heart breaking. And I hope I never hear it again."

She sat up completely, drawing the blankets around her bare shoulders to ward off the chill of the room. "Austin, I don't understand."

"I don't know if I can explain it."

"Try."

He placed his hand on the back of her head. "Cuddle up against me first."

She nestled her cheek against the crook of his shoulder as his arm came around her, his hand trailing from her shoulder to her elbow. She spread her hand over his chest, her fingers toying with the light dusting of hair that sometimes tickled her nose.

"Don't know where to start," he finally said into the silence.

"At the beginning would be nice."

"Explaining things with words has never come easy for me. I don't know if what I say will make sense."

"I'm a patient listener."

"You are that, Sugar. All right. I'll try." He cleared his throat. "I reckon I was about seven the first time. We were herding cattle north along the Shawnee Trail."

"You were herding cattle when you were only seven?"

"Mostly I followed Dallas and picked up cow chips for the campfires at night. Anyway one night I'd been sleeping under the chuckwagon. I heard this noise. It sounded like the wind, but there was no breeze that night. It was still as death, like something was waiting. So I got up. Cookie—that's the man that played the fiddle tonight—was fixin' food for the men about to come off the two o'clock watch. I asked him if he'd heard anything. He wanted to know what it sounded like. I couldn't describe it. He always kept his fiddle nearby so I picked it up . . . and played what I heard."

"Just like that?" she asked in awe.

"Just like that."

She lifted her head. "How could you do that?"

"All I can figure is that all those nights I watched my ma when I was a boy stuck with me."

She'd never heard of anything like it, but she couldn't discount the fact that the song he had played earlier had been flawless.

"Cookie taught me a few notes, a couple of songs, but he doesn't have your patience. Then one Christmas, Dallas and Houston gave me a violin, but I was sixteen before I found out it had been my ma's."

"But you told me you couldn't play. Why did you lie—"

He rolled her over, rising above her, cupping her cheek. "I wasn't lying, Loree. I've always heard the music in my heart . . . but I lost the ability to do that when I went to prison. It was like the music just shriveled up and died. I thought I'd never hear it again. How could I play the violin if I couldn't hear the music? Then lately, I started going crazy because I'd hear snatches of music—when you'd look at me or smile at me. But I couldn't grab onto it, I couldn't hold it. Then last night, you told me that you loved me and I heard the music, so sweet, so soft. It scared me to hear it so clearly after I hadn't for so long.

"Tonight, I hurt you—again. I was going to let you go, Loree. I was gonna take you back to Austin. But I heard my heart break . . . and I knew that's all I'd hear for the rest of my life. Don't leave me, Sugar."

Joy filled her and she brushed the locks of hair back off his brow. "I won't."

She saw his broad smile in the moonlight.

"You should hear the music filling my heart right now," he said quietly.

"Will you play it for me?" she asked.

"Sure will, Sugar, but not with my violin."

His mouth descended to cover hers, and his hands began to play a song of love over her body.

Chapter Sixteen

The January winds blew cold and bitter as Loree scooted across the bench seat of the wagon and snuggled against Austin.

"Stubborn woman," he mumbled as he slipped his arm around her. "You could be at home sitting in front of a nice warm fire."

"I'd rather be sitting beside you."

He leaned toward her and brushed a quick kiss over her lips. "I'm glad."

She tucked her shawl beneath her chin, bringing it in closer around her ears. The winds howled across the plains like a woman mourning a lost love. She imagined Austin would play the tune for her when they got home.

The town came into view. Her stomach always knotted at the memory it brought to mind. She brought the chilled air deep into her lungs, blowing it out in a smoky breath.

"Looks like Santa brought Cameron a new sign," Austin said.

Loree looked toward the general store, her breath hitching.

McQueen's General Store.

Her fingers tightened on Austin's arm. "I thought their name was Oliver."

"No, that was Becky's pa." He glanced sideways at her, an incredulous expression on his face. "All this time you thought their name was Oliver?"

She nodded, fear clogging her throat. "So Dee is a McQueen, too?"

"No, she's a Leigh. Used to be a McQueen."

"Do they have other family?"

"They have a brother, Duncan."

"And that's all?"

"As far as I know."

He drew the wagon to a halt in front of the store, clambered down, and held his arms up to her. She scooted across the bench and he helped her down to the ground, his arms coming around her.

"Good God, Loree, you're shaking like a leaf in the wind."

"I'm just cold," she lied.

"Let's get you inside."

He headed for the store—the last place she wanted to go. He shoved open the door and hustled her inside. The bells above the door clanged and nearly made her jump out of her skin.

Cameron walked out from the back, drying his hands on a towel. "You picked a bad day to come into town."

"Wasn't this cold when we left," Austin said as he led Loree to the black potbellied stove. "Sit here, Loree."

She did as he instructed and gave him the freedom to remove her gloves.

"There, just rub your hands in front of the stove."

"I'll be all right," she assured him.

He smiled and leaned low. "I'll warm you up all over when we get home. How's that for a promise?"

She returned his smile. "I'll make you keep it."

He touched his finger to her nose before turning to Cameron. "You still carry violin strings?"

Cameron's face split into a wide grin. "You playing again?"

Austin shrugged. "A little. Now and then. When the music comes over me."

Loree listened with half an ear as their conversation continued. She had once known a man named McQueen, but Cameron didn't favor him in the least, not in looks or temperament. Maybe they were cousins or distant relatives or had nothing more in common than the same name.

She rubbed her hands together and almost imagined she saw the blood—bright red, glistening in the moonlight. "Austin, could I please have my gloves back?"

"Sure."

He handed the thick gloves back to her, and she slipped her hands inside. She always felt safer when her hands were covered.

"Did you want to get that rattle you were telling me about?" he asked.

She nodded and forced herself to stand on trembling legs. She glanced at Cameron. He gave her a warm smile that calmed her fears.

No one as nice as he was could be related to the devil who had murdered her family.

"OH, COME ON, Loree. Please!"

Loree pursed her lips, crossed her arms over her stomach, and fought hard to resist the plea in those mesmerizing blue eyes. He'd replaced the string he'd broken two days before, and no longer had an excuse not to practice. "No. Not until you've mastered this."

Austin slumped back in the chair like a petulant child and started to randomly pluck the strings on his violin. "It's such a boring song. Just the same sounds over and over and over. No wonder Rawley hated his piano lessons."

"You can't play the complicated songs until you've learned the easy ones."

He sprung forward. "Take pity on me, and just let me try. If you're right . . . I'll go back to 'Mary Had a Little Lamb' . . . unless I kill the lamb first."

Loree couldn't stop her laughter from bubbling up. How could she expect a man who played from his heart to be content with other people's music? For the first time, she was catching true glimpses of the young man he had been before he went to prison.

When he awoke at dawn, he still carried his coffee out to the porch and sat on the top step, but instead of staring into the distance, he'd tuck his violin beneath his chin, and Loree would hear the sunrise as well as see it.

She knew the sound of twilight and midnight . . . and her husband's easy laughter. The ranch chores that had once exhausted him no longer fazed him. He came home, anxious for her kiss and her arms around his neck. Through his gift, he would give her an accounting of his day until she could hear the bawling of the cattle he'd branded or the snap of the barbed wire he'd mended. He might not be a man who could explain things with words, but with his music, he had the ability to create worlds.

Against her better judgment, she unfolded a more complicated piece of music and slapped it down in front of him. "There. Play that."

Eagerly, he scooted up and studied the sheet of music. Then he took a deep breath, lifted his violin, and without shifting his gaze from the notes, he began to play—the most beautiful melody she'd ever heard.

She sat in awe, watching his fingers coax the notes from the strings, following the path of the bow as he stroked it—slow and long—over and over. It was little wonder that the man was skilled at stroking her.

She lifted her gaze to his only to find his eyes closed, his expression serene. He stilled the bow, opened his eyes, and met her gaze.

"You were right," he said quietly. With a sigh, he tossed the sheet of music aside and turned his attention back to the tune he'd been playing earlier.

"I was wrong," she said as she pulled the sheet away from him. "What were you playing?"

"Did you like it?"

"I thought it was beautiful."

"How beautiful?"

"How much praise do you want?"

"A lot. How beautiful was it?"

She sat back in the chair, narrowing her eyes, wondering if the truth would go to his head, but how could she lie? "I thought it was the most beautiful song I've ever heard."

A slow warm smile spread over his face. "I call it 'Loree.' It's what I hear in my heart whenever I look at you."

"Either you or your heart needs spectacles."

He set the violin aside, came out of his chair, and knelt beside her, wrapping his hands around her arms. "Why can't you believe that you're beautiful?"

She had become angry at him for not telling her that he played the violin. How would he feel if she revealed the truth about herself now? She had just gained his love. With a few well-chosen words, she knew she could lose it . . . and never regain it.

He leaned forward, latching his mouth onto hers, sweeping the past and the doubts away. Her bones turned to mush, her thoughts scattered like autumn leaves before the winter winds. She dug her fingers into his shoulders.

"You are beautiful, Loree," he rasped as he trailed his mouth along her throat. "God, I want you."

She loved those words, whispered from his lips. "I know, but the doctor says we have to practice abstinence now."

With a heavy sigh, he rocked back on his heels.

"That's worse than practicing 'Mary had a Little Lamb.'"

"It won't be for much longer."

Reaching behind him, he grabbed the violin and tapped the bow against her protruding stomach. "Listen up, young fella."

Open-mouthed, Loree stared at him as he slipped the violin between his chin and shoulder. "You said it was foolish to talk to a child before it was born."

"It is foolish to talk to it," he said, grinning. "But I'm going to play for him. That ain't foolish at all."

"What are you going to play?"

"Something fast and spirited to take my mind off the long slow kiss that I want to play against his mother's lips."

SIPPING ON HIS coffee, Austin sat on the porch in the predawn darkness. His coat warded off the chill in the late winter air. Spring would arrive soon. Last year it had heralded his release from prison. This year he would celebrate the coming of spring with a wife and a child.

And an uncertain future.

Fewer people stared at him than before. He no longer heard whispers behind his back. But the fact remained that in the eyes of the law he was a murderer.

That fact had reached out to touch Loree.

He feared it would touch their child.

He understood ranching, but Dallas was the only rancher he knew who would hire on a family man. He hated ranching, but it was the only skill he possessed. He wanted to give Loree the world, but he couldn't see that ever happening.

He heard his wife's gentle footsteps. Smiling, he twisted around. The fear on her face sent panic surging through him. He came to his feet. "Loree, what's wrong?"

"I felt a pull in my stomach and heard a loud pop. When I slipped out of bed, water ran down the inside of my legs. There was a little blood."

"You think maybe the baby's coming?"

Her eyes grew wide and she gripped the doorjamb. Austin rushed to her side, holding her while she breathed heavily. Finally her breathing eased and she looked up at him. "I think the baby's coming."

"All right. Don't panic."

"I'm not," she assured him.

He scooped her into his arms and started down the steps.

"Where are we going?" she asked.

"I'm gonna take you to the doctor."

"What if there's not time? I don't want to be out on the prairie—"

"You're right. You're right. We'll just—" He turned and headed into the house. "We'll just put you back into bed . . ." Gingerly he laid her on the mattress. He wrapped his hand around hers and pressed his forehead against her temple. "Sugar, I don't know what to do."

"Go get Amelia and send Houston for the doctor."

Relief coursed through him, and he wondered where the hell his common sense had gone. He lifted his head and brushed the hair from her brow. "I can do that."

Her hand tightened around his, and she began to breathe harshly again, her face a grimace of pain. What in the hell had possessed Houston to put his wife through this five times? Austin planned to practice abstinence for the remainder of his life.

Her hold on him loosened, and the fear reflected in her eyes was deeper than before. "I don't think the pains are supposed to come this fast, this soon."

"Sure they are," he lied. "I remember when Amelia had Maggie, it all happened so fast that we barely had time to catch our breaths."

"I want a girl," she said breathlessly.

"Then that's what we'll have."

"Or a boy."

He chuckled low. "It'll be one of the two, Sugar. That I can promise you."

"I DON'T UNDERSTAND why we have to be out here while she's in there," Austin said as he wore down the weeds in front of his porch with his constant pacing. Two-bits shadowed his every step as though he, too, realized there was cause for concern. Twilight was settling in. What was taking so damn long?

"That's just the way it's done," Houston said.

"I think it's a dumb way to do it," Austin said.

"I agree," Dallas said. "I think if you want to be in there watching her suffer, you ought to be in there."

Austin staggered to a stop. "How much do you think she's suffering?"

Dallas shrugged. "Well, she's not screaming . . ."

"That don't mean anything. Amelia never screams and she suffers plenty," Houston said.

"Then why do we do this to them?" Austin asked.

His brothers stared at him as though he'd just eaten loco weed.

"Why does it take so long?" he asked.

"That's just the way it is," Houston said.

He glared at his brother. "Think you could come up with some better answers?"

"Nope. I ask these same questions every time."

"I'm never touching her again," Austin swore.

"You'll touch her," his brothers said in unison.

And damn it, he knew he would, first chance he got. He leapt onto the porch, stormed into the house, and threw open the door to his bedroom—and wished to God he hadn't.

Loree's face was contorted with pain as she strained and pushed, grunted and groaned. Then she dropped back on the bed, breathing heavily. Austin heard a tiny indignant wail, and Loree's lovely face filled with wonder and love.

"It's a boy," Dr. Freeman announced.

Austin watched the physician place the child in the crook of Loree's arm. Loree smiled softly, then she looked at Austin, her eyes brimming with tears through which the gold glistened like treasure.

But the treasure was nestled within her arms.

"It's a boy," she said breathlessly. "I knew it would be."

Smiling, Austin walked toward the bed like a man ensconced in a dream. He had a wife. He had a son. The responsibility should have weighed heavy on him, but he thought he might actually float to the clouds.

He knelt beside the bed. She touched the child's head. "Look, he has black hair just like you." Her smile was radiant as she proceeded to stroke the baby's hand. "And your long fingers."

She snapped her gaze to Austin. "I'm so glad he has your hands and not mine."

He cradled her cheek. "He's beautiful, Loree. Just like his mother." He brushed his lips over hers. "God, I love you."

"Do you want to hold him?"

He jerked his gaze to his son. "Hold him?"

"Uh-huh." She moved the child closer to him. "Surely you want to hold him."

"What if I drop him?"

"Did you ever drop your nieces?"

"I never held them while they were this tiny. I waited until they were big enough to latch onto me."

"He doesn't have teeth yet, so he won't bite," she assured him.

He swallowed hard and gave her a nod, not wanting to disappoint her after she'd worked so hard. He slid his hands beneath hers.

"His head is kinda wobbly so be sure you hold it."

"Won't fall off or nothing, will it?" he asked.

She laughed with joy. "No."

He brought the boy into the crook of his arm. "Hello there, young fella."

The babe blinked his blue eyes.

"He's looking at me, Loree. Look at that." He tilted the baby toward her. "He's looking at me. You think he knows who I am?"

"I'm sure he does."

"Can I show him to Houston and Dallas?" he asked, feeling like a child with a new toy.

"I don't see why not."

With the greatest of care, he stood and turned toward the door. His brothers were already standing there, grinning almost as much as he was. "I've got a son. Can you believe that? A son."

He looked over his shoulder at Loree. "What are we gonna name him?"

She licked her lips. "I'd like to name him after my family—Grant."

"Grant," Austin repeated. "I like it."

That night after everyone left, while Loree listened with tears in her eyes, Austin played his violin, lulling his son to sleep with a song that bore his name.

Chapter Seventeen

*T*he cool breeze blew over the front porch as Loree rocked, her son cradled within her arms. Three weeks had passed since his birth, and she didn't think she'd ever anticipated the coming of spring more.

She heard the rumble of carriage wheels and glanced up from her sleeping son's face. She smiled and waved as Becky brought the horses to a halt.

Loree sent the spark of jealousy she usually felt when she first saw Becky to oblivion. She had given Austin the one thing Becky never had: a son.

Becky bounced up the steps and leaned over, slipping the baby shawl away from Grant's cheek. "Isn't he precious?" Becky whispered. Smiling broadly she met Loree's gaze. "I think he looks like Austin."

"He has his eyes," Loree admitted. "When they're open."

Becky straightened and leaned against the porch railing. "I always thought Austin had the prettiest eyes—too pretty for a man really." She sighed as though blowing away a memory.

"Would you like something to drink?" Loree offered as she started to rise.

Becky placed her hand on her shoulder and guided her back down. "Don't get up. I just brought you a few things. I wanted to come sooner but Drew got the chicken pox. Then Cameron got them. I've never seen anyone as sick as he was. I wanted to wait until I was certain I wouldn't bring them out here, but it was hard not to come."

"I appreciate your coming out."

Becky smiled. "I can't tell you how happy I am for Austin." Her smile grew. "You should have seen him, strutting through the town, passing out cigars. I've never seen him so proud and it's been a long time since I've seen him so happy. It did my heart good to see that."

She gazed off into the distance. "I always felt so guilty."

"For marrying Cameron?"

Becky shifted her gaze back to Loree. "No. For not telling people that Austin was with me the night Boyd McQueen was murdered."

Loree felt her heart slam against her ribs, and the blood drain from her face. Becky's eyes widened.

"Oh my goodness. Didn't he tell you? I was certain he would have, you being his wife and all. I'm so sorry. I should have kept my mouth shut. Let me get the items I brought out of the buggy."

Loree surged to her feet and dug her fingers

into Becky's arm to halt her leaving. "Why . . . why would people care that he was with you the night Boyd McQueen died?"

"If they knew he was with me, then they might have believed that he hadn't killed Boyd."

Loree released her hold on Becky and sank into the rocker. "Boyd McQueen? He went to prison for killing Boyd McQueen?"

"Surely you knew that," Becky said.

Loree shook her head. "I knew he'd gone to prison for murder. He never told me the name of the man he was supposed to have murdered. I never thought to ask."

"Well, let me tell you right here and now that he did not murder Boyd McQueen."

Loree lifted her gaze to Becky. "I know that. With all my heart I know that."

AUSTIN SAUNTERED INTO the house, the first flowers of spring clutched in his hand. He spotted Loree sitting in a rocker before the empty hearth, rocking back and forth.

He knelt beside her, the sadness in her eyes causing a knot to form in his chest. "Where's Grant?"

"Sleeping in his cradle."

He extended his gift toward her. "I brought you some flowers."

She shifted her vacant gaze to his hand. "You were innocent."

Reaching across, he grabbed the arm of the rocker and turned the chair so he could see her more clearly. "Pardon me?"

She lifted dull eyes to his. "Becky came by today."

"Did she say something to upset you?"

She shook her head slightly, tears brimming within her eyes, and she touched her trembling fingers to his shadowed cheek. "You went to prison for killing Boyd McQueen. I didn't know. All these years, I didn't know."

"All these years? Sugar, you've known me less than a year. If I never mentioned his name, it was because I didn't figure it would mean anything to you."

"I didn't know you were innocent."

"I told you I wasn't a murderer."

"I thought you meant you hadn't killed anyone in cold blood. I thought it had been self-defense."

"And you married me anyway, thinking I'd killed someone?"

"It was your eyes, your dang blue eyes. They weren't the eyes of a killer."

He smiled warmly. "There, see. You did know. You just didn't listen to your heart. I was doing the same thing with my music. Not listening."

"They beat you in prison, didn't they?"

"Loree, that's all in the past. It doesn't matter anymore. I've got you and Grant—"

"Who gave you that cut on your back? The one I tended."

He gave a deep sigh wondering why she was hanging onto this discovery like a starving dog with a bone. "Duncan McQueen. Boyd's brother. We got into a fight right after I got out of prison. Seems he thinks I should have hanged."

"Is he the one who attacked you the night of the play?"

"I don't know who attacked me that night. It was dark."

"But it could have been him—"

"What does it matter—"

She shot out of the rocker like a bullet fired from a gun and turned on him. "It matters. God, you don't know how much it matters and you'd hate me if you did."

She ran into the bedroom and slammed the door. He heard his son give a pitiful wail. Silence quickly followed, and he knew instinctively that Loree had carried his son to her breast.

Right now he wouldn't mind being held to Loree's breast, comforted, and loved.

He looked at the sagging flowers in his hand and somehow felt as though they reflected his life.

AUSTIN KNOCKED ON the door and waited an eternity for Becky to open it. "What exactly did you tell Loree?"

Becky grimaced and groaned. "I told her we were together the night Boyd was killed."

Austin cursed harshly and jerked his hat from his head.

"I thought she knew!"

"Thought who knew what?" Cameron said as he came to stand in the doorway.

Austin watched the blood drain from Becky's face.

"I thought Loree knew that Austin was with me the night Boyd died."

Cameron's cheeks flamed red and he averted his gaze. "Oh."

"I don't want to cause you any embarrassment, Becky, but is that all you said?"

"That's all I said."

"You didn't say anything specific, anything that might have . . . hurt her?"

"Nothing. I am so sorry."

Austin settled his hat onto his head. "It's not your fault. For some reason, this damn thing won't go away."

"You and Loree break a fence?" Houston asked.

Austin glanced toward the front porch of Houston's house where his wife sat in the rocker. He couldn't tell if she was talking to Amelia. Damn he wished she'd talk to someone.

He hefted the board for Houston's new corral and held it in place while Houston hammered one end to the post and Dallas hammered into the other end. "I don't know what happened. It makes no sense to me. She married me, thinking I'd killed someone. She found out I didn't and now she won't talk to me. I can't figure it out."

"That's 'cuz she's a woman," Dallas said around the nail protruding from his mouth. He removed it from between his teeth and pointed it at Austin's nose. "You can't figure women out so don't even try. I was married to Dee for weeks before I realized when she said something was fine—it wasn't fine at all."

"But wouldn't you be happy if you discovered

that you weren't married to a murderer?" Austin insisted.

"It's the baby," Houston said.

Austin jerked his head around and glared at Houston. "What's Grant got to do with it?"

Houston gave the nail a final whack and stepped back to inspect his work before waving the hammer at Austin. "Whenever Amelia has a baby, she gets . . ." He scraped his thumb over the scars on the left side of his face, just below the leather eye patch. "She gets . . . difficult. Yep, that's the best way to describe it."

"Can't imagine Amelia being difficult," Dallas said. "She wasn't when I was married to her."

"She didn't give you any young 'uns either. Trust me. She gets difficult."

"In what way?" Austin asked, thinking maybe Houston had hit upon his problem.

"Well, as you know Gracie was born in November. About a week after she was born, Amelia hollers for me. Almost broke my neck gettin' to her, and you know what she wanted?"

Austin glanced at Dallas who was shaking his head.

"She wanted me to sit down right then and there and order Christmas presents from the Montgomery Ward catalog. Got it into her head that we had to order them that day or they wouldn't get here in time. Had to take the blasted order into the post office in Leighton—that day mind you. It didn't matter that I had horses to work—"

"You coulda just told her no," Dallas said.

Houston looked at Dallas as though the man had gone loco. "I suppose you tell Dee no all the time."

"Never tell her no, but we're not talking about me. We're talking about you—"

"Actually, we're talking about me," Austin reminded his brothers with disgust.

They both snapped their attention to him. Houston rubbed the side of his nose. "That's right." He squinted. "How'd she find out she was wrong about you after all this time?"

Austin dropped his gaze and kicked the toe of his boot into the dirt. "Becky. She visited Loree and somehow it came up in conversation that she and I were together that night."

"She's probably just feeling slighted then," Dallas said.

"Why would she feel slighted? That was six years ago—"

"Like I said earlier, you can't figure women out. They make no sense."

"Then what do I do about it?"

"Talk to Dee."

"Talk to Amelia."

His brothers offered their advice at the same time, and he wondered why they hadn't just told him that to begin with.

"You're both useless, you know that?" he said.

"Well, this might cheer you up," Dallas said. "I got a telegram from Wylan. He was playing in a private poker game and Boyd's name came up. Something about cheating someone out of some land. So he's gonna see what else he can find."

Austin shook his head. "I'm sure he's a good man, but after this long, he's not gonna find anything. Whatever trails were left behind are nothing more than dust in the wind now."

"I DON'T WANT to go," Loree insisted.

Austin sighed heavily. "Dee says you need to get out of the house—"

"I got out of the house last Sunday when you went to help Houston with his corral," she pointed out.

She watched him work his jaw back and forth. She knew what she needed to do. She needed to tell him the truth and ask him for forgiveness. But what if he were unable to forgive her?

He held the tickets toward her. "This is a special performance. They're only going to be in the theater tonight. Amelia offered to watch Grant—"

"And what if someone attacks you—"

Sympathy filled his eyes and he cradled her face. "Is that what's worrying you? Now that you understand why I was attacked, you're afraid I'll get hurt?"

She nodded briskly. "Let's just stay here, Austin."

"Sugar, don't you see? If we hide out here, then whoever attacked me has won. Whoever killed Boyd has won. And I'm not gonna let either of those bastards run my life."

She turned away, wrapping her arms around herself. "I can't go."

She expected further protests, but instead she only heard the echo of his boot heels as he left the room. She could stop people from staring at him.

She could stop people from whispering about him. She could stop people from attacking him. But she couldn't give him back the five years she had unknowingly stolen from him. And without that, what good were the others?

She heard the sharp brief whine of the violin and spun around. Austin stood in the doorway, instrument in hand.

"Please?" He gave three quick strokes to the strings. "Please? Please? Please?"

She bit back her smile. "No."

Three more quick strokes as he stepped into the room. "I'll have to play something sad." A forlorn sound filled the room. "And I'd rather play something happy." He played a quick fast tune. "Give me a reason to play something happy."

For him, she forced herself to set her fears aside. "All right."

He whooped, tossed the violin onto the bed, clamped his hands on her waist, and lifted her toward the ceiling. "You'll be glad, Sugar."

She looked into his beloved face, his shining blue eyes, and wished to God that she'd never fallen in love with him.

THE LOBBY WAS nearly empty when they arrived, and Loree couldn't have been more grateful as Austin took her hand and rushed up the sweeping staircase to the balcony level.

He drew back the drapes and she stepped into the dark alcove. She barely made out Dee's silhouette as the woman turned, smiled, and motioned them over. Loree eased down to the chair beside Dee.

Dee squeezed her hand. "I'm so glad you could come. This is a special performance."

Austin leaned forward. "What play is it anyway?"

Dee's smile grew. "It's not a play."

The stage curtains parted to reveal a group of people sitting in a half circle, instruments poised. Loree's breath caught as Austin wrapped his hand around hers and shifted up in his chair.

A man walked onto the stage, bowed sharply from the waist, then stepped onto a box. He lifted a long thin stick, swept it through the air, and music reached up to the rafters.

Austin's hand closed more tightly around hers, and she knew he had spoken the truth. She was glad that she came, glad that she'd given him the opportunity to hear a symphony. She eased up in the chair, tears stinging her eyes at the sight of awe and wonder revealed on his face.

"Look at all those violins," he whispered. "They're all moving the same, like a herd of cattle heading to pasture."

"They're following the same music."

"Reading those little black bugs. How long do you think it took them to learn to play together like that?"

"Years."

"It's mighty fine sounding, ain't it?" he asked.

She brushed her fingers through his hair and pressed her cheek to his shoulder. "Mighty fine."

THEY ARRIVED HOME with no mishaps. Loree wished she could believe that Austin was safe. It had been a year since his release, six months since someone had slammed him into a building. If only she knew for certain that no harm would come to him, she could keep her secret buried deep within her soul.

Grant released a tiny mewling sound. She sat on the bed, unbuttoned her bodice, and smiled as he rooted at her nipple, his mouth working feverishly. "Got hungry, did you?" she asked as she brushed her fingers over his black hair.

"When you get bigger, you can help your pa put the horses away after we go to town." Leaning down, she pressed a kiss to his forehead. "I'm gonna get better, Grant. I'm gonna stop worrying. I can't change the past, but I can be a good wife and make everything up to your pa that way. I realized that watching him tonight. Oh, you should have seen his face—"

She heard the front door close and shifted Grant within her arms. Austin walked into the room, dropped onto the bed, and tossed the sheets of music toward her hips.

"Teach me, Loree."

She blinked her eyes. "What?"

"Teach me. I won't complain. I'll play the same song over and over and over—just like you wanted me to. I'll do whatever it takes."

"It takes time—"

"Which is the one thing I haven't got so just for tonight, teach me one song, one fancy song."

She shifted Grant to her shoulder and began to rub his back. "You want me to teach you tonight?"

He rolled off the bed and began to pace. "All

my life, Loree, I've been searching for something, wondering where I belonged. Dallas always knew that he belonged with cattle and Houston . . . hell, he practically becomes a horse when he's working with them. But I never knew what I should do. Not until tonight.

"There was a time when I thought if I could make a violin I could find a way to live on forever. It never occurred to me that I could stand on a stage and fill people's hearts with music."

He dropped to his knees by the bed and wrapped his arm around her waist. "I want to go see Mr. Cowan—the conductor—tomorrow. I wanna play for him. I wanna ask him to take me with him, to let me be part of his orchestra."

"What about us?"

"You and Grant will come with me. We might have to leave Two-bits with Rawley, but the boy loves him. He'll give him a good home. And I'll show *you* the world."

The world. She would miss Two-bits, but she saw Austin's dream reflected so clearly in his eyes of blue—burning brighter and hotter than any flame in the center of a fire, and she knew deep within her heart that every dream he had ever lost had been because of her.

This one last dream he had found was hers to give.

She laid Grant, asleep, on the bed beside her and combed her fingers through Austin's dark, curling locks. "No," she said quietly.

"No?" Confusion mired his eyes.

"No, I won't teach you to play a song. If you're

going to impress Mr. Cowan, you're going to have to play from your heart, and you'll only be able to do that if you play the songs that are within you."

She watched him swallow. "What if he doesn't like what I play?"

"How can he not like it? You have a rare gift. Your heart isn't in any of the songs I gave you for Christmas. You need to play one of your songs."

"Which one?"

"The one that means the most to you."

He gave a slow hesitant nod. "How can I convince him that I'll be able to play with the others?"

"You just play for him, and he'll find a way to make it work."

"Will you iron my Sunday-go-to-meetin' shirt?"

She smiled. "And I'll cut your hair and trim your nails."

He chuckled. "You probably ought to shave me, too." He lifted his hands. "Look at how much I'm shaking."

She wrapped her hands around his. "Just play from your heart."

"I want this, Loree, like I've never wanted anything."

SHE SAW HIM off at dawn, his violin safely housed in the wooden case she'd given him for Christmas, tucked beneath his arm. Then she sat on the top step, Grant in her arms, and waited.

She gauged the distance into town, the time it would take him to play, and figured he'd ride home at a gallop. It was late morning before he returned, and she'd never been so glad to see anyone.

He dismounted, set the violin case on the porch, and sat beside her.

"Brought these for you," he said, holding out a handful of red and yellow flowers.

"They're beautiful," she said as she took them.

"I couldn't find you any that were blue."

"That's all right. I like these."

He touched Grant's tiny fist. The boy's fingers unfurled and wrapped around the larger finger that was waiting for him.

"He's got a strong grip," Austin said quietly. "It won't be much longer, and he'll be able to hold a bow."

"I didn't think it'd take you this long," Loree said, anxious to know all that had transpired. "I guess you had a lot of details to work out, traveling to arrange—"

"He can't use me, Loree."

She couldn't have been more shocked if he'd told her the sun was going to start setting in the east. "Is he deaf?"

He gave her a sad smile. "No."

"Why didn't he want you?"

She watched his Adam's apple bob. "He didn't think the people in his company would be comfortable traveling with a murderer."

"But you're not a murderer!"

"The law says I am and that's all that matters." He unfolded his body. "I need to change clothes and repair some fence for Dallas on the east side."

She watched him disappear into the house, and even without the aid of his violin, she heard his heart breaking.

LOREE DREW THE wagon to a halt and studied her husband, standing with one leg straight, one leg bent, his elbow resting on the gnarled and crooked fence post, the barbed wire curling on the ground like a ribbon recently removed from a girl's hair.

His hat shadowed his face, but she knew he was staring in the distance, toward the railroad tracks that he couldn't see, but knew existed. She heard the lonesome train whistle rent the afternoon air.

Austin stepped back, turned, slid his hat up off his brow with his thumb, and gave her a warm lazy smile. "Hey, Sugar, wasn't expecting to see you out here."

He ambled to the wagon and Loree's throat grew tight. "I brought you some lunch."

"I sure could use some."

He put his hands on her waist and lifted her off the bench seat. "Could use a little sugar, too," he said, his gaze holding hers.

She raised up on her toes and wrapped her arms around his neck, kissing him as she hadn't in weeks.

"Mmm, I've missed that." Reaching around her, he grabbed the picnic basket while she picked up Grant.

She sat on the quilt Austin had spread over the ground and laid Grant near her hip. Austin stretched out beside her.

"You caught me daydreaming," he said, his voice low.

"What were you dreaming?"

"Different things. I ran into Houston on my

way back from town this morning, and we got to talking."

"About what?" she asked, handing him a hunk of cheese. She'd thrown the picnic together as hastily as they'd thrown their marriage together.

He set the cheese aside as though it really held no interest for him. "He's gaining a widespread reputation for having the best horse flesh this side of the Rio Grande. He's needing some help so I offered to start working for him on my off-day. I thought we could set the money aside until we have enough to go somewhere on a little trip."

"Where would we go?"

"Wherever you want." He leaned toward her and cupped her chin. "I'm gonna give you a good life, Loree. You'll see. It might never be filled with any of the things you dreamed of, but it'll be good."

"If they found the person who killed Boyd McQueen—everything would change for you, wouldn't it?"

"Damn sure would. But that's not gonna happen, Loree. It's been six years. The fact of the matter is that man got lucky, and I didn't."

Chapter Eighteen

Austin sat on the porch, staring at the moonless sky, knowing sleep would be as elusive as his dreams.

He heard the door open, but he didn't bother to turn around. Dallas had once told him that a man had to learn from the mistakes he made. Austin had never expected the lessons to be so damn hard.

He caught a glimpse of bare toes as Loree sat beside him. He felt a ghost of a smile touch his lips. He turned slightly and brought her feet to his lap, rubbing his thumb over her sole.

"Daydreaming again?" she asked.

"You can't daydream at night," he said quietly. "But I was thinking—there's no reason I couldn't play in Dee's theater." He leaned toward her and smiled. "A special performance."

"Would that make you happy?"

He moved his thumb in an ever widening circle. "You make me happy."

She jerked her feet off his lap. Even in the shadows, he could make out tears glistening within her eyes. "I told you that I'll make everything all right."

"It'll never be all right. Oh, God, Austin. I didn't know, and now I'm so afraid, more afraid than I was then because I have so much more to lose."

"Loree, you're not making any sense."

She scooted across the porch until their thighs touched and took his hand in hers, holding his open, rubbing her fingers over it again and again, as though she wanted to memorize every line and callus.

"My mother hated West Texas."

His gut clenched, and he wished he'd kept his dream of playing for the orchestra to himself. He'd given her hope of leaving only to disappoint her with mistakes from his past. "We'll travel, Loree."

She shook her head. "Let me say everything before you say anything."

"All right."

She cleared her throat. "My father bought some land after the war. He got it cheap, and it wasn't a lot of land. So he extended his boundaries and posted a notice in a newspaper."

"Your father was a land grabber?"

She nodded. The practice had been widely used following the war, saving men considerable time and effort in filing deeds. Dallas had always cautioned his brothers that the practice would bring trouble. He'd filed legal claims for every inch of land he owned.

"My father used to say that land grabbing was like gambling—sometimes you won, sometimes you didn't. He was a good man, but gambling was his weakness.

"When my mother refused to move out here, he put his deed and his dream of ranching away. He used to take them out on my birthday, show me the land on the map, and tell me that I could be a rancher.

"One night he got involved in a private high stakes poker game in Austin. He ended up owing one of the players a great deal of money . . . money he didn't have. So he handed over the deed to the land, claiming the boundaries went farther than his original entitlement.

"The land was so vast. Many successful ranchers had extended their boundaries through land grabbing so my father felt confident that Boyd McQueen would be satisfied with the bargain they'd struck."

Austin's stomach clenched. "Boyd McQueen got his land from your father?"

"A little west of here. My father didn't know that someone had a legal claim to a good portion of the land, the best part where the river flowed. I don't know why it took McQueen so long to exact his revenge once he realized my father had deceived him. He didn't strike me as a man of patience—"

"He's the one who killed your family?"

"And I killed him."

She spoke the words with no emotion: no hatred, no anger, no fear.

Austin stared at her, and then he burst out laughing. "God, Loree, you scared me to death there for a minute. You were so serious." He took a deep breath. "I appreciate that you're willing to lie and take the blame for Boyd's murder so I can—"

"I'm not lying. It took me three months to get strong enough to travel after he shot me, another month to track him down."

He jerked his hand from hers and surged to his feet. "You're telling me that you honest to God shot Boyd?"

"Shot and killed. Dewayne was with me."

He trembled so hard that he thought the ground might shake. His wife was a murderer. His *wife* was a murderer!

No matter how he repeated it in his mind, no matter how he thought of it, he couldn't see Loree murdering anyone. He began pacing. The music thundering through his soul was hideous. He wanted to cover his ears to block it out. He had wanted to find the person who had killed Boyd so he could clear his name.

Not only had he found the person, he'd married her and fallen in love with her. He brought his pacing to an abrupt halt and glared at his wife. "Forgive me for doubting your word, Loree, but you are the sweetest—"

She surged to her feet. "I was seventeen, trussed up like a pig for slaughter, along with my ma and pa. He took my brother outside and God only knows what he did to him. All we heard were his screams. Then he brought him back in and hanged him. He was fourteen, Austin. Look at Rawley and imagine what McQueen might have done to him."

Austin didn't have to imagine. He knew exactly

what Boyd had done to him, something no man should ever do to a boy.

"Do you know how long it takes for a person to die when they're hanged?" she asked. "My brother didn't deserve to die that way. My pa didn't deserve to watch his son suffer like that."

She dropped onto the porch, wrapped her arms around herself, and began to rock back and forth. "I know I should have gone to the authorities, but . . . I didn't want my father's name dragged through the mud. And I didn't want people to know what McQueen had done to my brother. There were no witnesses. It was just my word against his. I didn't come here with the intent to murder him. I wanted a fair fight. But then he started to laugh . . ."

Crouched in the dimming twilight, she and Dewayne waited. When Boyd McQueen slipped from the house, mounted his horse, and rode north, they followed until the ranch was no longer in sight and Loree had gathered her courage. Then she spurred her horse into a gallop, Dewayne following in her wake.

She yelled his name. McQueen circled about and brought his horse to a halt. Loree drew her gun. "Get off your horse."

He did as she instructed, and Loree dismounted as well.

"You're Grant's daughter. I thought I'd killed you."

"You thought wrong," she replied with false bravado.

Her heart was pounding, and her hands shaking. She'd practiced drawing her gun from the holster, but she feared when it came right down to it, she wouldn't be able to do it. "I'm gonna give you what you didn't give my family. A chance."

He flashed a sardonic smile that didn't reach up to touch his eyes. "Oh? Like a duel? I draw, you draw, and the one left standing is the winner? And what about your friend here, do I get to kill him, too?" He snorted derisively. "You haven't got the guts to kill. Want to know what I did to your brother when I took him out-side? I enjoyed hearing him scream." He started to laugh. "Your brother wanted me to stop"—his laughter grew harsher—"begged me to stop—"

Loree didn't realize she'd pulled the trigger until she heard the explosion and watched McQueen's arms flail out as he staggered backward to the ground.

"Oh, God," she cried as she dropped beside him, jerked free the linen sticking out of his pocket, and pressed it to the dark stain spreading over his white shirt. He groaned.

Dewayne knelt beside her. "You gut shot him, Loree. He's as good as dead. We gotta get out of here."

"Help me stop—"

Then McQueen released a deep roar and grabbed her wrist. The blood coating her hands made it easy to slip free. She stumbled back.

"You bitch! I'll drag you into hell with me." He started to laugh. "Mark my words! I'll drag you into hell with me!"

"And he did. He did drag me into hell. I lived alone, afraid that if I had a family, what I'd done would reach out to hurt them. I didn't know I'd al-ready hurt you." Tears streaming along her cheeks, Loree doubled over and pressed her face to her knees.

"You thought you could outdraw him?" Austin asked stunned.

"Blame it on my youth, my grief, or my shame. I just didn't want anyone to know everything that led to that night, all that happened that night. And I couldn't *not* do anything."

"So once you shot him, you left?"

Wiping at her tears, she nodded. "He was fumbling to get his gun out of his holster so we mounted up and rode out. We came to a river. I couldn't get his blood off my hands. I tried and tried, but I couldn't." She started wiping her hands on her gown. "Sometimes, I feel like his blood is still there."

Austin had listened with increasing horror and dread . . . and more, with the realization that she spoke the truth. She was tied to the land . . . the missing link the detective had uncovered. He dropped beside her and took her ice cold, trembling hands into his. "Loree, listen to me." He shook her until her head snapped back and the vacant gaze left her eyes to be replaced by tears.

"I'm so sorry, Austin. I never knew anyone went to prison for killing McQueen. I thought we were safe. I would have come back and confessed if I'd known—"

"It doesn't matter, but I gotta talk to Dallas right now. I want you to go into the house and take care of Grant. Can you do that for me? Trust me to take care of everything. All right?"

"You'll tell the sheriff, won't you? We'll clear your name—"

He pressed his finger to her lips. "I need to talk to Dallas tonight. Then we'll decide tomorrow what we're gonna do." He put his arm around her and helped her stand. She was trembling as badly as he was. He escorted her into the house, eased her into bed, and brought the blankets around her, tucking them below her chin.

"Don't hate me, Austin," she said quietly.

"I don't hate you, Loree. You take care of Grant if he wakes up. Remember months back, before he was born, when we said he has to come first? That still holds true. Nothing's changed that."

She gave him a weak nod. Lord, he didn't want to leave her, but he knew it was imperative that he talk to Dallas as soon as he could. "I won't be long," he promised.

He hurried from the house, saddled Black Thunder, mounted up, and rode through the night like a man hounded by demons.

DALLAS LOVED THOSE first few moments when he crawled into bed and his wife cuddled up against him. She purred like a contented kitten, and he hadn't even gotten around to ensuring her contentment yet.

He covered her mouth with his, drinking deeply of the glory she offered.

The bedroom door banged against the wall, and he shot out of bed, naked as the day he was born. He jerked a blanket off the bed to cover himself and glared at his baby brother. "What in the hell do you think you're doing?"

"I need to talk to you," Austin said, his breathing labored. His worried gaze shifted to Dee. "You, too."

"Do you mind if we get dressed?" Dallas barked.

Austin looked him over as though just noticing his lack of apparel. He gave a brusque nod. "That'd be fine." He disappeared down the hallway.

Dallas looked at Dee. "The last time one of my brothers burst into my bedroom like that, I lost a wife."

Smiling, she slipped out of bed and reached for her wrapper. "Well, you don't have to worry about that happening this time."

He pulled on his trousers before following her to his study. Like a caged animal, Austin paced back and forth in front of the window that ran the length of the wall. He pointed to the desk without breaking his stride. "Why don't you sit down?"

Dallas dropped into the leather chair behind his desk, propped his elbow on the armrest, and rubbed his thumb and forefinger over his mustache while Dee sat in her chair beside the desk and drew her legs up beneath her. Austin continued his pacing.

"You had something you had to tell us at this ungodly hour?"

"I don't rightly know how to say it."

"Straight out is usually best."

Austin nodded and came to an abrupt halt. "I killed Boyd."

Dallas grew as still as death and stared at his brother. "I beg your pardon?"

"I killed Boyd."

Dallas planted his hands on his desk and slowly brought himself to his feet. "Let me make sure I understand everything you just said. For six years, you claimed to be innocent, you allowed your family to stand by you and proclaim your innocence, and I have been paying a man to find proof of your innocence. And now you're telling me that you're guilty of murder?"

He watched the blood drain from Austin's face before he gave a brusque nod. "That's right."

"But you were with Becky that night," Dee reminded him.

"Afterward. I killed him and then I fetched Becky, planning to use her as my alibi, but I couldn't bring myself to do it. I know I've destroyed your trust in me, and I can never regain that. Tomorrow, I'll pack up my family and we'll leave—"

"Let's not do anything rash," Dallas ordered. "We'll just sleep on it. Things will look clearer in the morning."

"In the morning, I want you to telegraph Wylan and tell him to stop his search for the murderer."

Dallas narrowed his eyes and gave his brother a long slow measuring nod. Austin took a step toward the desk. "Give me your word that you'll send that telegram first thing in the morning."

"Give you my word."

He watched relief course down his brother's face like water rushing over rocky falls. Austin turned to Dee. "I know I owe you the most, Dee, Boyd being your brother and all. I don't know how, but I'll find a way to pay back all I owe."

"You don't owe me anything, Austin," she assured him.

"I need to tell Houston and Amelia. I'll do that tomorrow. And Cameron." He jerked his gaze to Dallas. "I could take out an announcement in the newspaper, couldn't I?"

"Like I said, let's not do anything without thinking it through."

Austin slipped a hand into his hind pocket and took a step backward. "I need to get home to Loree."

"I'll come by in the morning and we'll work this out."

Austin nodded. "I'm really sorry."

"So am I," Dallas said quietly. He watched his brother high-tail it from the room. He walked to the window and caught sight of Austin galloping into the night. "So who the hell do you think he's protecting now?"

"If he's following in the footsteps of his older brothers, it would have to be the woman he loves," Dee said softly as she came up behind him and wrapped her arms around his chest.

"Christ, I hope you're wrong."

LOREE HEARD THE footsteps on the porch and slowly brought herself out of the rocking chair. The door opened quietly, and Austin slipped inside. He hung his hat on the peg by the door and stood staring at his boots. He looked like a man who had just taken the weight of the world on his shoulders.

"Austin?"

He snapped his head around and gave her a weak smile. "Thought you'd be asleep. Must be near midnight."

"Almost. What did Dallas say?"

"That we'll take care of it."

She furrowed her brow. "What does that mean?"

He crossed the short expanse separating them. "It means we'll take care of it. I don't want you to ever tell anyone what you told me tonight."

"How will that clear your name?"

"Don't you be worrying about my name. You worry about that little boy that's sleeping in the cradle in our room."

"You didn't tell Dallas, did you?"

He dropped his head back and plowed his hands through his hair. "He'd hired the detective I told you about. Recently he notified Dallas that he thought he'd discovered a link to the land. I don't know why it took him so long—"

"Because my father bought the land under a false name. So many men used different names after the war, especially if they had something to hide. He'd deserted. He was afraid they wouldn't sell him the land if they knew the truth . . ." She looked at him imploringly. "Honestly my father wasn't a bad man—"

"He just lied and cheated."

Tears burned her eyes. "I never wanted anyone to know—"

"No one will know. I told Dallas to send a telegram to the detective and tell him his services were no longer needed."

"And he agreed to do that . . . on your say-so?"

"He's my brother. He trusts me." He hunkered down before the hearth. "I'll bank the fire. You go on to bed. I'll be there directly."

She padded into their bedroom and clambered onto the bed, drawing the blankets over her. Relief swamped her when she heard his footsteps and saw his silhouette in the doorway. As though she'd never see it again, she watched the way he held onto the doorjamb while slipping the heel of his boot into the bootjack and jerking his boot off. She listened to the thud of one, then the other, and the soft tread of his stockinged feet as he walked to the bed, yanking his shirt over his head as he went. She watched his shadow as he dropped his britches onto the floor. In the morning, she'd gladly pick up all his clothes and check them for tears and missing buttons before she laundered them.

The bed sank beneath his weight as he stretched out beside her, folded his arms beneath his head, and stared at the ceiling.

"Why did they think you killed McQueen?" she finally dredged up the courage to ask.

She heard him swallow in the silence that followed her question.

"Lots of reasons."

"You said you'd made some mistakes—"

"Yep."

"What did you do?"

He sighed deeply. "The land your father claimed was his belonged to Dallas. Boyd and Dallas fought over it. Dallas made a pact with the devil. He'd marry his sister and when she gave him a son, he'd deed the land over to Boyd. I told you what happened behind the hotel.

"We didn't know it was Boyd at the time. Dee had heard a child cry out—Rawley. Boyd had hurt him in ways a boy should never be hurt. When Rawley confided in me, I went into the saloon—like a big man—fired my gun right over Boyd's head and told him that I'd like nothing better than to rid the ground of his shadow.

"There were plenty of witnesses. So when he showed up dead, they figured I'd carried out my threat."

"But Becky knew differently," she said softly, understanding the full extent of his love for Becky. He had to have known what their silence might cost him.

"I didn't think they'd find me guilty so I told her not to say anything."

"But after they found you guilty—"

"Didn't see that it would have made any difference. Boyd wrote 'Austin' in the dirt before he died."

"I wonder why he didn't write my name."

"My guess is that he planned to but he died before he got around to it. Writing your name wouldn't have helped if no one knew where to find you so he wrote that first."

Her heart slammed against her ribs with the realization of what had brought him to Austin. "The man you were looking for in Austin—"

He rolled over and cradled her cheek. "Seems he wasn't a man at all."

She squeezed her eyes shut. "How you must hate me."

His thumb circled her cheek in a gentle caress. "Loree, make no mistake. I would have killed him that night but Becky sidetracked me. Boyd had paid some men to kill Dallas, and they'd lashed him to within an inch of his life. We couldn't prove anything because he'd murdered them in their sleep. He was spawned by the devil, and I'm damned tired of him reaching out from hell and touching our lives. We're gonna put this behind us. I'm not saying it'll be easy, but by God, I'm not going to let him steal something else away from me." He dropped his hand down to her shoulder and squeezed gently. "Come here."

She scooted over until she was nestled in his embrace.

"Tomorrow, we'll decide what we're gonna do," he told her. "But right now I gotta get some sleep." She heard his deep yawn. "Last night, I didn't sleep at all, worrying about this morning."

This morning. How long ago it seemed since he had set out in search of his dream. Every dream he had ever dreamed, she had stolen from him.

His hold on her loosened, his fingers unfurling from around her shoulder. She heard his breathing deepen and slow. She was amazed he slept after all that she'd told him, and thought how much easier it would have been if he'd ranted and raved and told her that he hated her.

She could only surmise that the full implications of her confession hadn't hit him yet. Sooner or later, he would look across the room and realize all that she had cost him.

She heard the small cry, tempered by the night. She slipped from beneath the weight of Austin's arm and walked the familiar path in the darkness, lifting her son into her arms and settling into the rocker near the window. She held him to her breast. His tiny fist pressed against her flesh as he suckled greedily.

She loved the child as much as she loved the father. Her gaze traveled across the room until she saw the dark shadow of her husband, asleep. She wondered what he would dream tonight.

She wondered how long before his love turned to hate. How long before he ticked off and counted all the things she'd stolen from him.

Five years of his life spent in prison, and she could only imagine what horrors he'd experienced there—a man with a heart that heard music as beautiful as his did. Little wonder the music had died within him.

She couldn't give him back those years. She couldn't remove the scars from his back . . . or return to him the woman he had once loved—a woman he would be married to today if only Loree had known they had arrested someone for killing Boyd McQueen. She would have turned herself in six years ago, confessed then had she known.

She couldn't give Austin back anything she'd unknowingly taken from him, but she could return what she'd recently taken. With his innocence proven, he would be truly free of the walls that still held him. He could pursue his dream and there would be nothing to stop him from reaching it.

She glanced down at the bundle of joy in her arms. How could she leave him? If she turned herself in, she had little doubt she would leave her son. She would go to prison just as Austin had. To give Austin his dream, she had to give up hers. Her heart shattered with the thought of never holding this child again, of not watching him grow, of not watching him take his first step. But each day she waited, the debt she owed for killing McQueen increased.

And she could no longer tolerate the thought of Austin continually paying for her actions. Tears streamed along her cheeks. How was she to have known that Fate was more cruel than Boyd McQueen?

AUSTIN AWOKE TO a strangeness that he couldn't identify. He heard birds chirping outside the window. He heard his son gurgling in the cradle nearby. But he couldn't hear Loree.

He threw back the blankets and swung his legs off the bed. His gaze landed on his son, his blue eyes wide, his fists and feet swinging at the air. "Hey there, young fella. Where's your ma?"

Grant cooed and his feet kicked excitedly. Austin yanked on his trousers before lifting his son into his arms. "Well, you're dry and you ain't hollering so she must have fed you." With his thumb, he wiped the drool from his son's mouth.

"We got a lot of things to work out—your ma and me—but I don't want you to worry none. I'm doing enough worrying for all of us."

He padded into the front room. Morning light slanted through the windows. A chill swept through him that was as cold as the stove. He headed for the door. Something on the table caught his eye. He ambled back and picked up the paper. With uneven lines as though she'd been trembling at the time, she'd scribbled, "Forgive me."

Dread shot through his vitals like the well aimed bullet of a Winchester rifle. He tore through the front door and stumbled onto the porch. "Loree!"

Holding his son close, trying not to jar the boy, Austin rushed to the corral as though going nearer would change what he was already seeing. Her horse was gone. He slammed his palm against the post and screamed her name, knowing even as he did so that it was pointless. She couldn't hear him.

Grant started to fuss. Austin jostled him slightly. "It's all right. I'm sure your ma just went for an early morning ride." Dear God, he hoped that was all she'd done.

He walked back into the house and stared at every inch of it as though just seeing it for the first time. "Reckon we missed the sunrise. I don't hardly know how to start the day without seeing the sunrise, but I still need my morning coffee."

He set Grant down on a pile of quilts, but the boy started hollering like his heart would break. Big fat tears rolled down his cheeks.

"All right, all right," Austin said as he tucked his son into the crook of his arm. The tears and hollering stopped as quickly as they'd begun. "I'll wait until your ma gets home to have my coffee." He plowed a hand through his hair. "She can't be much longer."

He heard a horse whinny and relief surged through him. He rushed outside and stumbled to a stop at the sight of Dallas sitting astride his horse.

"Did you send that telegram to Wylan?"

Dallas swept his hat from his head and draped his forearm over the saddle arm. "Sure did. First thing this morning, just like I promised."

"Good."

"Ran into Sheriff Larkin while I was in town. Seems your wife paid him a visit bright and early this morning."

Austin felt all the blood drain from his face, his knees went weak, and his heart was pounding like stampeding cattle.

"She told Sheriff Larkin that *she* killed Boyd McQueen."

TAKING A DEEP breath, Austin swung open the door to the jail and stepped into the front office. The cells were kept in the back behind another door, which Austin knew from experience Larkin kept ajar. Sweat popped out on Austin's brow and he trembled as though he were the one to be locked up.

He had no fond memories of jail. His trial had been held in the saloon. The judge presided from a stool behind the bar. Austin sat at a table, humiliation wrapping itself around him because Larkin wouldn't unshackle his hands. He rubbed his wrists now as though the cold metal still bit into his skin.

Larkin was sprawled in his chair, his feet on his desk, his belly lapping over his belt. Austin knew that somewhere behind that insolent gaze the man had some redeeming qualities or his brother never would have hired him.

Austin swallowed hard. "Heard my wife came in this morning with some tale about killing Boyd McQueen."

Larkin removed the match from between his teeth. "Yep."

"She lied."

Larkin raised a graying brow. "Do tell."

Austin felt a spark of hope ignite within him and he stepped nearer. "I wanted to leave town with that orchestra that was here a few days back, but they didn't want a man who'd been convicted of murder traveling with them. Loree, bless her sweet heart, thought if she said she'd killed Boyd, they'd let me go with them." He scoffed and shook his head. "Women. They don't understand the intricacies of the law."

Larkin pointed the match at him. "So you're telling me you killed Boyd?"

"That's right. When you arrested me six years ago, you sure knew what you were doing. I resented like the devil that you figured out it was me—but I had to admire you as well."

Larkin dropped his feet to the floor. "Well, I'll

be damned. Your wife sure did tell a convincing story."

"I'll bet she did."

Larkin stood and picked his ring of keys off his desk. He ambled toward the back door like a man in no hurry. Then he stopped, turned, and rubbed his ear. "Suppose you told her where you hid the gun."

Austin felt as though Larkin had just gut-punched him. "What?"

"The gun you used to kill Boyd. Your wife knew exactly where it had been all these years. Reckon you must have told her."

"Yeah, I did."

"And where was it?"

Austin slammed his eyes closed. Hell, he didn't even know where Boyd had died. "I buried it under some sagebrush—" He opened his eyes and breathed a sigh of relief as Larkin slowly nodded.

"And you'd wrapped something around the gun before you buried it. Want to tell me what that was?"

"A strip of blanket."

He knew from the hard look in the sheriff's eyes that he'd given the wrong answer. "A linen handkerchief that had Boyd's initials sewn into it and his blood soaked through it," Larkin said.

"Larkin, let her go."

"Can't do that. My job is to see that justice is served, and six years ago an injustice was done that I can't overlook." He jerked his head to the side. "You want to talk to her?"

"No, I don't by God want to talk to her." He

spun on his heel, stalked through the office, and slammed the door in his wake.

If he saw her, he was afraid he would tell her that by turning herself in, she had taken from him the most precious dream he'd ever held.

And what good would that knowledge do either of them?

AUSTIN LAID HIS sleeping son in the cradle. Three days had passed—three days without Loree—and every minute had been hell. He wanted to see her like he'd never wanted anything in his life, but he was afraid looking at her behind bars, caged like an animal, would bring him to his knees.

As quiet as a mouse, he tiptoed from the room.

"You look like hell."

His head came up, and he glared at Houston, standing in the front doorway. "I feel like hell. You want some coffee?"

"Nope." Houston stepped inside, his hat in his hand. "Just thought you'd want to know that the circuit judge arrived. Loree's trial will be tomorrow."

Austin's stomach clenched. "Considering the fact that McQueen killed her family, maybe they'll let her go," he said hopefully.

"If you'd been meeting with her lawyer like the rest of the family, you'd know Boyd ain't the one on trial here."

He didn't like the censure he heard in his brother's voice. "What do you want me to do, Houston? My responsibilities didn't go away just because my wife decided to clear her conscience.

I've got chores to take care of along with a baby. Takes me hours to get any milk into him. Every time I go to change him, he pisses on me—"

"I knew he was smart."

"What does that mean?"

"You told me once that if a woman loved you as much as Amelia loved me, you'd crawl through hell for her."

"I've crawled through hell. I don't recommend the journey." The fury that had been building inside him burst through unexpectedly like a raging river. He planted his hands beneath the table and sent it crashing to its side. "And now Loree's gonna crawl through hell. I told her I'd take care of everything." He spun around, the anguish nearly doubling him over. "Why did she have to confess?"

He heard Grant's startled cry and felt as though the roof would cave in on him at any moment.

"Let me get him," Houston offered, crossing into the bedroom without waiting for an answer. Austin heard the blissful silence and wondered how long it would last. Houston came out of the bedroom, holding Grant in his arms. "Why don't I take him home? Amelia can feed him—"

"I don't know what I'm gonna do, Houston. I can't stand the thought of her going to prison."

"See if you like this thought better. Duncan has petitioned for her to hang."

Chapter Nineteen

Austin stood inside the doorway, staring along the length of iron bars that made up the jail cells. He saw Loree in the cell at the far end, the cell in which he'd once slept, ate, and worried while awaiting his trial. He hadn't meant to abandon her, but he realized now with startling clarity that he had.

She stood on her cot beside the brick wall, stretched up on her bare toes, hanging on to the bars of the window, and looking into the night.

"What are you doing?" he asked as he ambled toward the last cell.

She spun around and nearly toppled off the cot before catching her balance. Her eyes wide, her hand pressed just below her throat, she grabbed onto one of the iron bars and stepped off the cot onto what he knew was a cold stone floor. "I was looking for a falling star so I could make a wish."

"What'd you wish?"

She angled her head slightly and gave him a quivering smile. "If I tell you, it won't come true.

But then it probably won't come true anyway. I was wishing you'd forgive me."

She looked so damn tiny standing in that cell in her yellow dress and bare feet. He furrowed his brow. "That a new dress?"

She nodded quickly. "Dee brought it over. She made Larkin take me over to the hotel so I could have a bath. He didn't want to, but when she started shouting, he jumped. I wish I had her courage."

He smiled slightly at a distant memory. "You should have seen her when she first married Dallas. She hid under his desk on their wedding night."

Her eyes widened. "I can't imagine that."

"That's the way it was."

She gnawed on her lower lip. "How's Grant?"

"Missing his ma."

Tears brimmed in her eyes.

"He wouldn't eat much so Houston took him to Amelia so she could nurse him."

"I wouldn't be able to do him any good anymore. My milk dried up . . . on account of the worry I guess."

Against his will, his gaze dropped to her breasts . . . and her tiny waist . . . and her rounded hips. How would she survive the harshness of prison?

"Why did you have to come here and confess? I told you I'd take care of it."

"By admitting that you'd killed McQueen. Isn't that how you took care of it? Isn't that what you told Dallas to make him send the telegram to the detective?" Wrapping her arms around herself as though she were in pain, she spun around.

He saw her narrow shoulders shaking. Even if he reached through the bars, he'd be unable to touch her.

"Loree?" he rasped.

She turned slowly, tears spilling onto her cheeks. She walked toward him, and her hands clasped the bars until her knuckles turned white. "Austin, don't you see? You lost five years of your life because of me. If it weren't for me, you never would have lost the music to begin with, you could have your dream of playing your violin with an orchestra. If it weren't for me, you would be married to the woman you love."

Tears clogged his throat and burned his eyes. Reaching through the bars, he cupped her cheek. "Loree, I *am* married to the woman I love. Have I been so poor at showing you?"

A ragged sob broke through from her chest. Austin pulled her close and felt her arms go around his back.

"Larkin!"

The sheriff ambled over and leaned against the doorway.

"Unlock the cell so I can go in."

Larkin removed the match from between his teeth and shook his head. "Can't do it."

"She's not going to escape. Just let me go inside."

"Every time some member of your family walks in here, I'm having to bend the rules. Not this time." He walked away.

Loree sniffed. "It's all right, Austin."

"No, it ain't."

He released his hold on her, walked to the wall, and slid down it until his backside hit the floor. Loree strolled over and did the same. He slipped his hand through the bars and wrapped it around hers.

"You scared?" he asked quietly.

"Terrified."

A suffocating silence began to spread between them.

"Will you do me a favor?" Loree asked.

"Anything."

"Will you think of something nice to tell Grant about me when he's growing up? I think that's gonna be the hardest part, having to miss watching him grow up . . . and watching you grow old."

He couldn't argue with that. He thought of all he'd missed out on—how quickly his nieces and nephew had grown and changed and become people he'd barely recognized. "I'll tell him how much you like sugar and how sweet it made you."

A corner of her mouth lifted momentarily, then dipped lower than before. "I want you to divorce me."

"What?"

Her fingers tightened around his. "My lawyer thinks I'll get at least five years, maybe more. I've already told him to draw up the papers so we can sign them before I go. I want you to marry someone who'll be a good mother for Grant."

He shifted onto one hip so he faced her squarely. "No. I'm gonna wait for you, Loree. The day you get out of prison, I'll be standing at the gate with Grant beside me."

She shook her head vigorously. "We both know

how easy that promise is to make and how hard to keep."

"Ten years, twenty, twenty-five. It won't matter, Loree. I'll wait."

He reached through the bars, drawing her as closely as he could with the damn iron separating them, wishing he had the power to hold back the dawn.

DAWN ARRIVED, SHAFTS of sunlight piercing the gloom of the jail. Austin had brought Loree a meal from the hotel and watched as she nibbled on the toast he'd coated with butter, sugar, and cinnamon. He'd poured so much sugar into her coffee that the bottom of the cup felt like the silt of a river when he'd tried to stir it.

Now they stood, toe to toe, fingers intertwined, words insignificant as they waited for Sheriff Larkin. The only thing Austin found to be grateful for was the fact that Leighton now had a town hall and her trial wouldn't be held in the saloon.

"Aunt Loree?"

Austin jerked his head around at Rawley's hesitant voice. He felt Loree's fingers tighten around his, and he knew she wished the boy hadn't seen her here. "Hey, Rawley, shouldn't you be in school?" Austin asked kindly.

Rawley took a step toward him. "Ain't no school today on account of the trial."

Loree looked at him as though she wished she were anywhere but where she was.

"Aunt Loree, they're saying you killed Boyd McQueen. Did you?"

"Rawley—" Austin began, but Loree pressed her finger to his lips.

She angled her head, tears glistening within the golden depths of her eyes. "Yes, Rawley, I did."

He removed his dusty black Stetson as though he'd just walked into church. "Then I'm obliged to you."

Loree jerked her baffled gaze to Austin, then looked back at Rawley. "Rawley, I'm not proud of what I did."

"Didn't figure you were. Once Mr. D told me that there's a difference between being good and doing bad things. Sometimes, a person does something because he don't have a choice. He might not like what he did . . . but it don't make him bad. I reckon that's the situation you're in, and I've been there myself." He settled his hat into place. "I aim to take good care of Two-bits for you till you get home so you don't have to fret over that."

"I appreciate it," Loree said softly, giving him a warm smile.

He gave her a brusque nod before walking out.

She squeezed her eyes shut. "At least McQueen will never touch our son."

Heavy footsteps echoed outside the hallway. Larkin strolled in, twirling the key ring around his finger. "Well, it's time."

Austin stepped aside and Larkin jammed the key into the lock. He grated and ground it until an audible click echoed between the cells. He swung the squeaking door open. "Step out."

Loree walked hesitantly out of the cell. Austin

drew her into his arms, ignoring the scowl Larkin threw his way.

"It's gonna be all right, Sugar."

She nodded against his chest.

"Remember that I'll wait, no matter how long."

She lifted her face away from him, tears brimming in her eyes. "I wish you wouldn't."

He gave her a warm smile and wiped a tear from the corner of her eye. "You were right, Sugar. If you tell me what your wish is, it won't come true."

He heard the clanging of chains and looked over Loree's shoulder to see Larkin unlocking the shackles.

"Jesus, Larkin, don't put those on her."

"I've got no choice. It's the rule."

"Whose goddamn rule?" Austin demanded. "She turned herself in, for Christ's sake. Show her some respect for doing that."

Larkin rolled the match from one side of his mouth to the other. "All right," he said reluctantly. He jerked his head to the side. "Let's go."

Loree took a step forward, halted, and glanced over her shoulder. Austin shook his head. "I can't go, Loree."

She gave him a smile filled with sympathy and understanding. "I know."

She angled her chin proudly, squared her shoulders, and followed Larkin down the hallway and into the front office. He waited until he heard the front door close before he gave into the pain. His agonizing wail echoed between the empty cells. He pounded on the brick wall until his knuckles were scraped raw and bleeding.

Somehow, in spite of all she had endured, Loree had managed to maintain an aura of innocence and sweetness. Prison would do what Boyd McQueen had been unable to do: It would kill her spirit and rip every shred of kindness from her.

He slammed his palm flat against the wall and pain ricocheted up his arm. Even knowing the hell that waited, he'd gladly go to prison in her place.

LOREE DECIDED IT wasn't a trial, but more of a hearing. People got to hear her say how she'd killed Boyd McQueen. They got to hear Duncan demand that she hang for killing his brother. And they got to hear her lawyer ask for leniency because she'd confessed.

And now Judge Wisser was pondering her fate, although it looked to her like he'd fallen asleep, his hands crossed over his stomach, his lips pursed, his eyes closed. Only the flies in the crowded room dared to make a sound.

She was glad that Austin hadn't come with her. She thought she could accept hearing her sentence with dignity as long as she didn't have to see how much her going to prison would hurt him.

Judge Wisser popped his eyes open and leaned forward. "Loree Leigh, it is the decision of this court that you are indeed guilty. Do you have anything to say on your behalf before I pronounce your sentence?"

Loree's mouth went as dry as the parched earth, and her heart was pounding so hard against her ribs that she was certain they would crack. She could do little more than shake her head.

"Very well, then. In light of the circumstances—"

"I've got something to say."

Loree twisted around. Austin walked down the aisle between the bench seats, a purpose to his stride, while people craned their necks to see around each other, whispering and muttering.

"Six years ago you sent me to prison for a murder I didn't commit."

"An injustice I intend to set right today . . ."

"You can't set it right," Austin told him. "No matter what you do, you can't undo what you've already done. I lived in hell for five years, not because of Loree, but because of Boyd McQueen. He was a mean-spirited man who hurt children for the pleasure of it. She listened to the screams of her fourteen-year-old brother while McQueen tortured him. Then she had to watch while he hanged him. McQueen shot her, her mother, and her father. He paid a man to kill my brother, slit the throats of three men on the prairie—"

"You can't prove that!" Duncan roared.

Austin spun around. "Then who did it, Duncan? You? Cooper told Dee that her brother paid him to kill Dallas. If it wasn't Boyd, then it had to be you because I damn sure know it wasn't Cameron."

Duncan paled and dropped back into his chair. "It wasn't me."

Austin turned back to the judge. "I know we can't take the law into our own hands. I'm not saying Loree should have gone after Boyd, but I know the man isn't worth all our worry. An injustice was carried out here six years ago. Don't worsen it today by seeking justice for a man who didn't know the meaning of the word.

"I gave up five years of my life for his murder. Let those years serve as Loree's and if that's not enough then send me back to prison—"

Loree jumped to her feet. "No!"

"Duncan wants somebody to hang, then hang me—"

"No!" Loree cried.

"Because by God if you take her from me now I'm gonna die anyway—and where's the justice in that?"

Loree had never been so terrified in her whole life because it looked to her as though the judge was seriously contemplating what Austin had just said.

Judge Wisser sliced his gaze over to her. "Loree Leigh, I sentence you to life . . ."

Austin slammed his eyes closed, bowed his head, and clenched his fists.

"With this man."

Austin jerked his head up.

"May God have mercy on your soul." Judge Wisser slammed his gavel down. "This court is adjourned."

The courtroom erupted with shouts and cheers. Loree looked at her lawyer. He smiled and nudged her arm. "Go on. You're free."

She turned and found Austin waiting for her. He spread his arms wide and she fell against him, entwining her arms around his neck. He enfolded her in his embrace.

"Ah, Loree," he whispered near her ear. "You should hear the music."

EXHAUSTED, LOREE SANK into the steaming hot water. The day had been spent enjoying her freedom: feeling the breeze blow over her face, listening to each of the children tell her how much they'd missed her, holding Grant close, enjoying the warmth of Austin's hand wrapped around hers.

And now they were home, and he was rubbing the soap-filled cloth over her limp arm.

"You don't have to wash me," she said softly although she wasn't certain she had the strength to do it herself. She hadn't slept at all after she'd turned herself into Sheriff Larkin.

"I want to."

He stroked the cloth slowly over the curve of her breasts.

"Dr. Freeman said if I let Grant suckle, my milk might come back." Her eyes drifted closed. "I'd like that."

"Then I hope it happens."

"You . . . don't . . . have to wash me."

"So you said," he reminded her and she heard the smile in his voice. "I don't *have* to love you either, but I do."

She forced her eyes open. "How can you love me when I took so much from you?"

"How can I not love you when you gave me so much back?"

Tears welled in her eyes. "It would have killed me if they'd hanged you."

"Well they didn't. Cameron and Dee had a long talk with Duncan after the trial. Think he just couldn't accept the kind of man his brother was."

"So he'll leave you alone?"

He combed her hair back from her face. "He'll leave us alone."

"What about your dream?"

"I'm gonna finish washing her up and put her to bed."

She smiled tiredly. "I meant your music."

"I'll play for you. I'll play for Grant. I'll play for my family."

She wondered if he would be forever content with that, knew that if she asked him, he would tell her yes whether it was the truth or not. She held her doubts and worries to herself, and relished the attention he paid her as he washed her, dried her, and carried her to bed.

He tucked the blankets around her, and as she drifted off to sleep, she heard him stroking the bow over the violin creating music that sounded very much like contentment.

"IT WAS THE most beautiful song I'd ever heard," Mr. Cowan said as he reached for another cookie. "Couldn't get it out of my mind."

Bouncing Grant on her lap, Loree smiled. "Austin has a way of playing music that comes from his heart. I think it makes it unforgettable."

"And if the music is unforgettable, so shall he be, my dear." He leaned forward and winked. "And me, right along with him."

Loree heard the footsteps on the porch and

rose from the chair as Austin stepped through the doorway. She smiled brightly. "Austin, look who's here."

Austin removed his hat and studied Mr. Cowan skeptically. "What brings you out here?"

"You do, my dear boy. As I was telling your lovely wife here, your song has been haunting me ever since I heard it. I want you to come play for me."

Austin hung his hat on the peg. "Appreciate it, Mr. Cowan, but I'm not interested."

Mr. Cowan looked taken aback. Loree simply stared at her husband. "What do you mean you're not interested?"

"I wasn't good enough before. Nothing's changed that."

"Everything—"

"No, Loree. This isn't what I want."

With pleading eyes, Loree looked at Mr. Cowan. "Let me speak to him privately about this opportunity—"

"I'm not going to change my mind," Austin insisted.

At that moment she wished she had a skillet in her hand so she could bang it against his hard head. She knew pride was making him cast his dream before the wind.

Mr. Cowan brought himself to his feet. "I know this isn't a decision to be made lightly. It'll affect your family for many years. I'm staying at The Grand Hotel in Leighton—finest hotel this side of the Mississippi—and I have to confess it was part of the reason I didn't mind traveling back to this area. But I must catch the train in the morning so I'll leave a list of my destinations with Mrs. Curtiss at the front desk. If at anytime you change your mind, you just send me a telegram." He held up a finger. "But you'll need to decide before next spring because we'll be leaving for Europe then and it'll be harder for me to make the arrangements."

He lifted his bowler hat from the table. "Mrs. Leigh, it was a pleasure to spend the afternoon in your company."

He strode out of the house like a man without a care in the world.

"You shouldn't have sent him a telegram without discussing it with me first," Austin said.

"I didn't send him a telegram."

"You didn't tell him that I was innocent?"

"No."

Austin rushed outside, Loree in his wake. Mr. Cowan was climbing into the buggy.

"Mr. Cowan, how did you hear about my innocence?"

Mr. Cowan pulled his foot out of the buggy and straightened. "Didn't hear about it until this very second. But that's excellent news."

"You came here still thinking I was guilty of murder?"

"That's right."

"I don't understand. A week ago—"

"A week ago your song hadn't kept me awake with regret every night."

Austin glanced over at Loree and slipped his hand around hers before looking back at Mr.

Cowan. "I don't know how to read music. Loree's been teaching me, but I'm not a very dedicated student."

Mr. Cowan shrugged. "Doesn't matter, dear boy. You won't be playing with the orchestra."

Austin furrowed his brow. "You've lost me again. Why are you here—"

"Because I want you to be my soloist. It's your songs I want. Your gift."

"What about my family?"

"They'll come with you, of course."

Austin gave him a nod. "Let me talk it over with my wife this evening, and I'll let you know in the morning."

"Good enough."

THE NIGHT WAS pleasant as Austin drew their horses to a halt. They had left Grant with Amelia so Loree and Austin could have some time to sort things out. She had allowed him to lead the way in silence because she sensed that something was bothering him.

After all that had transpired in the past few days, she would not blame him for seeking a divorce.

She heard water rushing over rocks. Through the darkness, she saw a series of waterfalls in the moonlight. Austin helped her dismount, then he guided her onto the quilt he'd spread near the falls. He dropped down beside her.

"This is beautiful," she whispered in awe.

"Houston married Amelia here. I didn't even know the place existed until that day."

A moment of silence echoed between them before he said quietly, "This is where I was the night Boyd died."

Her heart slammed against her ribs. "Austin—"

"I want to tell you about that night—"

"You don't have to. Becky did—"

He cradled her cheek. "Loree, I *need* to tell you about that night."

She dropped her gaze to her lap and nodded. "All right."

"Dallas had always been there for me—so strong. I began to think of him as invincible. Rawley's father had taken a whip to Dallas's back until it looked like raw meat. Dee managed to get Dallas home, but he was fighting a fever. He'd lost a lot of blood. I was terrified that he'd die . . . and then who would we turn to? We knew Boyd was behind it and I planned to confront him. But I stopped to see Becky first and we came out here."

He tilted her face until their gazes met. Holding his gaze was the hardest thing she'd ever done.

"I want you to understand that I was twenty-one and scared. I loved Becky as much as a twenty-one-year-old man who knows little of life can love. When she offered comfort, I gladly took it."

She heard him swallow.

"Whores had never appealed to me . . . until that night, I'd never . . ." His voice trailed off.

"You don't have to tell me."

"I'd never been with a woman until that night—not in that way. And I never touched another woman until you."

He released his hold on her and reached for

his violin. "Listen to this," he ordered. He began
to play a soothing melody, over and over. "That's
Becky's song."

She licked her lips. "It was lovely."

"But it never changes. It stays the same. It
doesn't grow. It doesn't deepen. It doesn't challenge. It never did." He placed his violin on his
shoulder. "I want you to hear the song I played for
Mr. Cowan, the song he couldn't forget."

She drew her legs up to her chest and wrapped
her arms around her knees. The music began
softly, gently, and she imagined a child discovering the wonders of a dandelion, blowing the petals, and watching them float upon the breeze. As
smoothly as the dawn pushed back the night, the
song grew deeper, stronger. The chords echoed
around them, thundering against the falls, filling the night until chills swept through her and
her heart felt immense gladness. The song rang of
destiny and glory and splendor.

She marveled that the melody came from
within the man she loved, and she knew that
she would forever remember it even as the final
chords vibrated into silence.

She knew no words worthy of his efforts, no
praise adequate enough for what he had just
shared with her, so she said inanely, "That was
beautiful."

"I call it 'My Loree.' That's what I hear in my
heart when I look at you, when I hold you, when I
love you." He set the violin aside and scooted up
until they were connected hip to hip. He framed
her face with his hands. "Becky was a part of my

youth and I'll always love her—just as I'll always love my mother. That doesn't mean that I love you any less. She was the first woman I ever made love to, and that memory will never leave me. But everything about her pales in comparison to all that I hold dear regarding you. I loved her as much as a boy can love." He trailed his thumb along her cheek. "I love you as much as a man can love."

He settled his mouth over hers with a tenderness that mirrored his words. He removed her clothes in the same manner that dawn removed the darkness, calmly, quietly, with reverence and tranquillity. Then he tore off his own clothes and gently eased her down to the quilt.

The night air carried a hint of spring, and she knew she should feel cold, but all she felt was the glorious warmth of his body covering hers. She touched her fingers to the old scar on his shoulder. "You never told me who shot you."

He pressed a kiss to the puckered flesh on her shoulder. "The same man who shot you."

"He was so intricately woven through our lives—"

"Through our pasts, Loree. He'll never touch us again."

She was weary of the past having a tight hold on her present. She wanted a future rich with the love this man could give her. "Love me, Austin."

He gave her a warm lazy smile. "Oh, I do, Sugar. With all my heart."

He lowered his mouth to hers, and their tongues waltzed to the music created by their hearts. She threaded her fingers through his thick hair, holding him near. He nipped at her chin, before trailing his mouth along the column of her throat.

"So sweet," he rasped.

And she felt sweet. For the first time in over five years, she truly felt sweet and untainted by the past. He knew her ugly secrets, her foolish mistakes, accepted them and loved her in spite of them. For both of them, she knew the innocence was forever lost, but together they could regain the laughter, the joy, and the promise of tomorrow.

And the music. Although he wasn't playing his violin, she almost imagined that she heard the chords thrumming through her heart as he brushed his lips over the curve of her breast. His tongue swirled around her nipple, taunting, teasing. She rubbed her hands along the corded muscles of his shoulders, shoulders that had tried to carry her burden.

"Hear the music, Loree," he whispered before returning his mouth to hers, hot and devouring, his fingers stroking, bringing to the surface the symphony housed within her soul.

Then he eased his body into hers and the crescendo reached new heights, thundering around her, with the force of his love. Each thrust carried her higher, farther, until she reached the tallest pinnacle. As he rose above her, she held his startling blue gaze and felt the heat of the hottest flames as he carried her over the edge into fulfillment.

Her body arched as his did, both quivering like the taut strings of a violin, masterfully played. With his final thrust, he cried out her name.

It echoed over the falls and through her heart in such a way that even when it fell into silence . . . it remained.

Epilogue

April 1898

$\mathcal{B}$limey! What's that!"

Austin's fingers tightened around Loree's hand, and she knew he was cringing at his eight-year-old son's choice of words. He leaned forward slightly to look out the window of the passenger car as the train rumbled over the tracks.

"A cow," he told Zane.

"But it's got such long 'orns."

"That's why we call it a Longhorn. If we could see its backside, we'd know from its brand who it belongs to."

"I'll wager it belongs to Uncle Dallas," Grant said. At ten, he was the authority on all things.

"Father, can I ride one of Uncle 'Ouston's 'orses?" six-year-old Matt asked.

"Sure can. I wouldn't be surprised if he gives you one."

"To keep?" Matt asked, his eyes wide with disbelief.

"To keep."

"I'm going to name 'im 'Is 'Ighness," Matt said, his blue eyes gleaming.

Austin leaned toward Loree. "Please tell me that somewhere in all our luggage you packed their H's."

Laughing, she squeezed his hand to offer reassurance. "I'm sure they'll show up once our sons have spent some time with their cousins."

"We shouldn't have stayed in London as long as we did."

"Does that mean we'll never go back?"

"Sugar, if you want to back, we'll go back. I'll give you whatever you want. You know that."

Yes, she knew that. In the passing years, he had given her the world—Rome, Paris, London, among others—his hand within hers more often than not, and five sons.

Joseph slipped out of his seat, crossed the short expanse, and placed his small hands on Austin's knee. Unlike his brothers who had inherited Austin's long slender fingers, Joseph had Loree's short stubby fingers. "Can I be a cowboy?" he whispered.

Austin lifted him onto his lap. "You can be anything you want to be."

"I don't play music so good," he said as though sharing a secret.

"You play better than I did when I was four."

Joseph's golden eyes widened as the sun glinted off his blond hair. "Truly?"

"Give you my word."

Loree flashed her husband an appreciative smile. At four, Austin had never played the violin, but she knew he would never mention that fact to Joseph. He loved Joseph because the boy favored Loree. He loved all his other sons because they resembled him in looks, temperament, and talent.

The train whistle pierced the air.

"I see the town!" Zane cried, and the boys scrambled to the window and pressed their noses against the glass.

Austin took Mark from Loree's lap and held him up so he could see over his brothers' heads.

"Is that big building Aunt Dee's theater?" Zane asked.

"Yep."

"Are we going to perform there?" Grant asked.

"We might. We'll have to discuss it with your Aunt Dee."

"I'll wager that she'll let us," Grant assured him.

The train lurched to a stop. Giving the other passengers time to disembark, Loree gathered up the boys while Austin reached for his violin case. Along with the instrument nestled within it, it had gained a few scars to remind them of its journeys over the years.

With two-year-old Mark firmly placed on her hip, she allowed Austin to herd the boys onto the wooden platform. He reached for her hand.

"Not nervous, are you?" she asked.

"It's been a long time."

"Uncle Austin?"

Austin turned at the deep slow drawl. Loree watched recognition and surprise dawn in his eyes as he stared at the tall, lanky man dressed as though he'd just come in off the range.

"Good God! Rawley?"

The man smiled and extended a hand. "Yes, sir."

Austin jerked him into his embrace. "Good Lord, boy. You grew up."

Rawley stepped back. "Yes, sir, I reckon I did." He removed his hat and gave Loree a warm smile. "Aunt Loree."

Austin took Mark from her. She stood on the tips of her toes and wrapped her arms around Rawley. "It's so good to see you."

He hugged her close. "You're a sight for sore eyes, that's for sure."

He released his hold on her. "Ma said the platform would break beneath the weight of the whole family so everyone else is waiting in the ballroom at the hotel."

"Blimey! Are you a cowboy?" Zane asked.

A slow smile tugged at the corner of Rawley's mouth. "I reckon I am."

"Have you got a gun?"

"Yep, but I can't wear it into town on account of the city ordinance that prohibits guns."

"And a 'orse?"

"Yep." Rawley reached for the violin case. "I'll carry that for you."

"Thanks," Austin said as he handed it over.

Rawley jerked his thumb back. "We'd best head to the hotel before Ma sends the posse out lookin' for us."

"You ever seen a posse?" Zane asked as he hurried to keep pace with Rawley's long strides.

"Once I rode with one. Some men held up the bank here in town, and that didn't sit well with us."

"Did you catch them?" Zane asked.

"Nope. Last I heard they were hiding out in some hole in the wall." Rawley stepped off the platform and hit his thigh. "Two-bits!"

The dog eased out from beneath the shade and trotted to his side. Loree knelt in the dirt, laughing with delight as the dog licked her face.

"You 'ave a dog?" Zane asked as the boys began petting Two-bits.

"Nah, he's your ma's dog. I've just been taking care of him."

"Does that mean 'e gets to live with us?" Matt asked.

"Reckon it does," Rawley said.

Loree rose to her feet. "Won't you miss him?"

Rawley glanced over his shoulder. "We really need to get to the hotel."

"Is Two-bits going to live with us, Mother?" Zane asked.

"I don't think so. I think he'd miss Rawley too much." Rawley turned his head, and she saw the relief in his eyes. "But I'm sure we can find another dog somewhere."

"That's if we decide to stay," Austin reminded her and the boys.

"I want to stay," Zane said, "if it means we can have a dog."

"And a 'orse," Matt chimed in.

Austin slipped his hand around Loree's. "Come on."

The town had grown, and Austin couldn't help

but feel that his brother had done himself proud. And any man would have busted his buttons to have fathered the young man who patiently answered the boys' questions as they entered the hotel.

Rawley threw open the door to the ballroom. Tightening his hand around Loree's, Austin took a deep breath and stepped beneath the archway. Screams and cheers resounded around him. Tiny bits of paper and ribbon flew in front of his face.

More than his family welcomed him home. It looked as though most of the damn town had crowded into the room.

"Uncle Austin!"

Turning, Austin felt as though he'd been thrown back in time—over twenty years—looking at Amelia again, smiling and radiant . . . only he had never been Amelia's uncle. "Maggie May?"

She nodded briskly and threw her arms around his neck. "I missed you so much," she cried.

"I missed you, too," Austin said hoarsely.

Rawley leaned close. "Watch what you say to her. She thinks she's smarter than all of us now that she's going to that university in Austin."

"You could go, too, Rawley," Maggie said, a daring glint in her green eyes.

"Not on your life, Brat. I got cows to watch."

"You and your cows." She looked at Austin's sons. "Are you boys gonna help Rawley take care of his cattle?"

All his sons bobbed their heads excitedly.

"Good God, don't you know how to make girls?" Houston asked.

Austin smiled at his brother. "You don't look like you've changed at all."

"It's just not as noticeable when a face is as unattractive as mine."

Austin saw tears spill from the eyes of the woman standing beside Houston. Her hair wasn't as blond as it had once been, but he thought it still looked as though it had been woven from moonbeams. He held out his arms. "Amelia."

She hugged him closely.

"You started all this you know," he whispered. "You were the first, the one who taught us that we didn't have to be so strong."

She patted his back. "I wouldn't have missed it for the world."

"I need a hug."

Austin looked over Amelia's head and smiled at Dee. "Who would have thought you'd turn out to be so bossy?"

Her arms came around him in a fierce hug. "You haven't seen me be bossy yet. I have you scheduled for three performances at my theater."

"Dee—"

She wagged her finger at him. "I am not going to have a world-famous violinist in our town and not have him play in my theater."

"I don't know how world famous I am—"

"Loree sent us all your newspaper clippings—"

He glanced at his wife, who simply smiled at him.

"Of course, we can't read most of them what with their being written in a foreign language and all—"

"I can read the ones from France now," Maggie said.

Rawley rolled his eyes. "See, I told you she thinks she's smarter than us—"

"Not smarter, just more educated," she said.

"Experience is the best educator," Rawley said. "Dallas taught me that."

"And here I didn't think you were paying attention."

Austin turned at his oldest brother's booming voice. The years had turned Dallas's hair silver and shadowed his mustache with varying shades of gray. The creases had deepened around his eyes and mouth. Dallas's gaze slowly roamed over Austin, and he hoped with all his heart that his brother didn't find him wanting.

A slow smile eased onto Dallas's face. "I always knew your dreams would take you away from us. Just didn't expect them to keep you away so long."

"Well, we're home now." He hadn't known the words were true until he embraced his brother. He had given Loree the world . . . and now he wanted to give her and their boys a home.

RAWLEY STEPPED OUT of the ballroom onto the veranda. "Faith, Uncle Austin and Aunt Loree are here. Aren't you gonna come in and welcome them home?"

She spun around, tears brimming in her eyes. "Oh, Rawley, I don't want him to see me like this, not after all these years."

He looked her up and down. He didn't understand ladies' fashions, but he thought she looked beautiful in the red gown. "Nothing wrong with the way you look."

"I've got no bosom."

His gaze fell to her chest, flat as a well-sanded plank of wood. Irritation surged through him because he'd looked. "Jesus, Faith, you're only thirteen. You're not supposed to have a bosom."

"I'm almost fourteen. A. J.'s only eleven and she has a bosom."

"I wouldn't call those two little bumps on her chest—"

"You noticed!"

He slammed his eyes closed. "You're gonna get me skinned alive." He opened his eyes. "It's not like I was lusting after her or anything. She's my cousin, for God's sake."

"But you noticed."

And who wouldn't? All of Uncle Houston's daughters had nice curves, but it didn't mean he had lascivious thoughts just because he'd noticed. He leaned against the wall, dug the heel of his boot between the bricks, and decided to hold his tongue because there was no way in hell he could win an argument with her. He pulled a sarsaparilla stick from his pocket.

"Gimme," she ordered holding out her hand.

"It's my last one," he said as he broke it in half and handed her a piece. "Want to tell me what's really bothering you?"

"I love John Byerly and he loves Samantha Curtiss. I know it's because she already has a bosom and I don't."

"What do you want with John anyway? He's a runt."

"All the boys are runts next to me."

He couldn't argue with that. She already came up to his shoulder, and he had a feeling she wasn't finished growing.

"No one is ever gonna love me, Rawley."

He shoved himself away from the wall and put his arm around her. "I love you, Faith."

"But you're my brother so that doesn't count."

He cupped her chin. "You don't want somebody that's just looking at the outside of you. You want somebody who cares enough to look inside because what's inside never grows old or wrinkled or gray."

She sniffed. "If no one asks me to dance, will you dance with me?"

"Why, Miss Leigh, I'd be honored."

He slipped her arm through his and led her into the Grand Ballroom. He had a feeling in future years, Faith was destined to break an abundance of hearts. His greatest fear was that one of them would be his.

WITH HIS BROTHERS flanking him on either side, Austin allowed his gaze to wander the room. Cookie played his fiddle and couples waltzed. Men still outnumbered women, but not by much. His nieces were growing into young ladies, his nephew a fine young man.

"Is this what you envisioned when you answered Amelia's ad all those years back?" he asked Dallas.

"Nope. I had no idea it would turn out this good," Dallas said.

"Even if you didn't end up with her?" Houston asked.

"Even though you stole her from me," Dallas emphasized.

"I always thought that worked out for the best," Austin said.

"It did," his brothers concurred at once.

Austin watched as Rawley sauntered over. "Dallas, I need to get back to the ranch and check on the herd."

Dallas gave him a long slow nod. "Whatever you think best."

Rawley held his hand out to Austin. "Uncle Austin, it's good to have you home. Reckon we'll see you up at the house later."

"Reckon so."

"Uncle Houston, I'd keep an eye on that fella dancing with Maggie."

"Him and the other three that followed her home from school. I told her she could miss school because this was a special occasion, but those fellas . . . not dedicated to their studies from what I can tell."

"They're dedicated to her." Laughing, Rawley patted Houston's shoulder before wandering out of the room.

"Still can't get him to call you 'Pa'?" Austin asked.

Dallas shook his head. "Nope, but it doesn't matter. He's my son and he damn well knows it."

Austin caught sight of his own son ambling toward him, a young girl in tow.

"Father, this is Mary McQueen," Grant said.

The girl had eyes the blue of a summer sky and hair that glinted red. Austin hunkered down. "Hello, Mary McQueen."

"Your boy talks funny."

"That's because he hasn't been in Texas very long."

"You aim to remedy that?"

At the sound of an old friend's voice, Austin slowly unfolded his body and held out his hand. "Cameron."

Cameron's handshake was firm. "Austin, you look like a man who has met with a great deal of success."

"I could say the same for you. How's the general store business?"

"Booming, although he's too modest to admit it," Becky said as she stood beside him. "He expanded the store to include the second floor and has all the merchandise divided into departments. We actually live in a house now." Her smile softened. "We've been so proud following you around the world. Dee has all your news written up in the newspaper."

"You look happy, Becky."

"I am." She turned slightly to the young boy standing beside her. "Do you remember Drew?"

"I sure do."

"And you've just met our Mary."

"I told Mary that you would play for her," Grant informed him.

Austin raised his brow at his firstborn. "Oh, you did, did you?"

His son nodded. "If you'll play for her, then I'll play for you because I know Mother wants to dance, and the gentleman who's playing hasn't quite got the knack of it."

"Don't tell him that."

"No, sir, I wouldn't want to hurt his feelings. So will you play for Mary?"

"I think that's a wonderful idea," Dee said as she slipped her arm through Dallas's. "You could play for all of us. I realize we're not royalty—"

"How can you say that, Dee, when you're married to the king of West Texas?"

Dallas snorted. "If you're gonna play, get to it. I've got a hankering to dance with my wife."

LOREE KNEW THE moment when the crowd hushed that Austin intended to play for them. The reverence he held for his gift was apparent as soon as he stepped on stage and lifted his violin to his shoulder.

The first strains of the sweet music filled the air, and Loree smiled. She knew the song. It always began the same, but the ending had changed over the years, growing deeper and stronger, a reflection of their love. She never tired of hearing it. Never tired of watching her husband coax the melody from the strings in the same way that he elicited passion: with care and devotion and attention paid to the tiniest of details.

His three oldest sons already exhibited a preference for music. Grant had, on occasion, joined

Austin on the stage and wooed audiences with his talent.

"He'll go farther than I ever dreamed," Austin had told her once. And she wondered if it was that revelation that had brought him back home, so he could give his sons roots as well as wings.

The music drifted away like dandelion petals on the wind. An awed silence permeated the air before someone dared disturb it by clapping. Austin smiled and bowed. The cry rose up for another song, and her husband simply shook his head.

"If you'll excuse me, I'd like to dance with my wife now." He handed his violin to Grant and whispered something into his ear before stepping down from the makeshift stage.

Loree's heart warmed as he approached, knelt in front of her, and slapped his thigh. "Come on, Sugar."

He removed one shoe, then the other before standing and signaling their son. The music floated toward them, and Austin swept her onto the dance floor. His blue gaze never strayed from hers, but grew warmer and held promises she knew he would keep.

She had toured the world. She had waltzed with royalty.

But she was happiest when Austin held her within the circle of his arms, and she was surrounded by the splendor of his love.

**Be sure to check out the rest of
Lorraine Heath's captivating
Texas Trilogy!**

TEXAS DESTINY

He's fallen for a woman . . .

Anxious to meet her soon-to-be-husband, Dallas Leigh, for the first time, mail-order bride Amelia Carson is en route to Fort Worth, Texas. When she steps off the train and locks eyes with her betrothed, she immediately feels drawn to him. But the cowboy standing before her isn't Dallas. Instead, Dallas' brother Houston has been sent to accompany her on the three-week journey to the ranch where she'll begin her new life.

Who belongs to another . . .

The war Houston Leigh fought has left him with visible scars, a daily reminder of his cowardice on the battlefield. Denying his intense attraction to Amelia, he is determined to deliver her untouched, as promised. But during their long, dangerous trip, he can't help but admire her inner strength and fearlessness. And when she looks at him—as if she can see beyond his scarred face and read his innermost thoughts—he loses his heart to her. Now as they near the ranch, Houston must choose to remain loyal to his brother—or find the courage to fight for the woman he's convinced is his destiny . . .

TEXAS GLORY

She never dreamed of the happiness . . .

Cordelia McQueen is little more than a prisoner in her father's house until he barters her off to a stranger in exchange for land and water rights. Now in a new place and married to a man as big and bold as untamed Texas, Cordelia prepares to live within her husband's shadow and help him achieve his goals.

Only he could promise her . . .

Dallas has one driving ambition: to put West Texas on the map. Convinced he's too harsh a man to be loved, he expects nothing except a son from his shy wife. But with each passing day, Dallas discovers a woman of immense hidden courage and fortitude. He is determined to give her his heart, even if it means letting her go to achieve her own dreams and find her own glory.